NATIONAL BESTSELLER

"Achingly lovely. . . . With her sophomore novel, Gyasi is narrowing her scope. *Transcendent Kingdom* is the story of one specific girl in one specific family: it is interior, psychological, and deeply focused on sifting through the layers of Gifty's mind as she studies and prays and experiments to try to find her way to what lies at the core of human beings."

—Vox

"Will stay with you long after you've finished it."

—*Real Simple*

"Elegant. . . . Burrows into the philosophical, exploring with complexity what it might mean for us to live without firm answers to the mysteries that wound us. . . . The measured restraint of Gyasi's prose makes the story's challenging questions all the more potent."

—*San Francisco Chronicle*

"A study of origin stories and the ways they can be wielded against people, particularly ones who grew up poor and Black. . . . Gyasi has returned to her roots, and they run deeper now."

—*The New Republic*

"Gyasi excels. . . . [*Transcendent Kingdom*] insightfully explores many pressing issues of our time, and in marrying science with faith, explores the limits and possibilities of both."

—*The Christian Science Monitor*

"An evocative portrayal of the immigrant experience and an astutely written character study of an individual reconciling with her past, along with her struggle with faith and science."

—*Chicago Review of Books*

"Haunting. . . . Astute and timely. . . . [A] meditation on life's big themes of love and loss, and one woman's quest to understand the human condition as she grapples with both." —*Women's Review of Books*

"Meticulous, psychologically complex. . . . At once a vivid evocation of the immigrant experience and a sharp delineation of an individual's inner struggle, the novel brilliantly succeeds on both counts."

—*Publishers Weekly* (starred review)

"Unforgettable. . . . *Transcendent Kingdom* has an expansive scope that ranges into fresh, relevant territories—much like the title, which suggests a better world beyond the life we inhabit." —*BookPage* (starred review)

"Gyasi's contemporary novel of a woman's struggle for connection in a place where science and faith are at odds is a piercingly beautiful tale of love and forgiveness."

—*Library Journal*

"Gyasi's wise second novel pivots toward intimacy. . . . [In] precise prose, Gyasi creates an ache of recognition, especially for readers knowledgeable about the wreckage of addiction. Still, she leavens this nonlinear novel with sly humor." —*Kirkus Reviews* (starred review)

YAA GYASI

Transcendent Kingdom

Yaa Gyasi was born in Ghana and raised in Huntsville, Alabama. Her debut novel, *Homegoing*, won her the National Book Critics Circle's John Leonard Prize for best first book, the PEN/Hemingway Award for a first book of fiction, the National Book Foundation's "5 Under 35" honors for 2016, and the American Book Award. She lives in Brooklyn.

Yaa Gyasi is available for select speaking engagements. To inquire about a possible speaking appearance, please contact Penguin Random House Speakers Bureau at speakers@penguinrandomhouse.com or visit www.prhspeakers.com.

ALSO BY YAA GYASI

Homegoing

Transcendent Kingdom

TRANSCENDENT KINGDOM

YAA GYASI

VINTAGE BOOKS

A Division of Penguin Random House LLC

New York

FIRST VINTAGE BOOKS EDITION, JULY 2021

The Library of Congress has cataloged the Knopf edition as follows:
Names: Gyasi, Yaa, author.
Title: Transcendent kingdom / Yaa Gyasi.
Description: First edition. | New York : Alfred A. Knopf, 2020.
Identifiers: LCCN 2019039844 (print) | LCCN 2019039845 (ebook)
Classification: LCC PS3607.Y37 T73 2020 (print) | LCC PS3607.Y37 (ebook) |
DDC 813/.6—dc23
LC record available at https://lccn.loc.gov/2019039844
LC ebook record available at https://lccn.loc.gov/2019039845

Vintage Books Trade Paperback ISBN: 978-1-9848-9976-7
eBook ISBN: 978-0-525-65819-1

Book design by Soonyoung Kwon

www.vintagebooks.com

Printed in the United States of America
10 9 8 7 6 5 4 3

For Tina

The world is charged with the grandeur of God.
It will flame out, like shining from shook foil.

GERARD MANLEY HOPKINS,
"God's Grandeur"

Nothing comes into the universe
and nothing leaves it.

SHARON OLDS,
"The Borders"

Transcendent Kingdom

I

Whenever I think of my mother, I picture a queen-sized bed with her lying in it, a practiced stillness filling the room. For months on end, she colonized that bed like a virus, the first time when I was a child and then again when I was a graduate student. The first time, I was sent to Ghana to wait her out. While there, I was walking through Kejetia Market with my aunt when she grabbed my arm and pointed. "Look, a crazy person," she said in Twi. "Do you see? A crazy person."

I was mortified. My aunt was speaking so loudly, and the man, tall with dust caked into his dreadlocks, was within earshot. "I see. I see," I answered in a low hiss. The man continued past us, mumbling to himself as he waved his hands about in gestures that only he could understand. My aunt nodded, satisfied, and we kept walking past the hordes of people gathered in that agoraphobia-inducing market until we reached the stall where we would spend the rest of the morning attempting to sell knockoff handbags. In my three months there, we sold only four bags.

Even now, I don't completely understand why my aunt singled the man out to me. Maybe she thought there were no crazy people in America, that I had never seen one before. Or maybe she was thinking about my mother, about the real reason I was stuck in Ghana that summer, sweating in a stall with an aunt I hardly knew while my mother healed at home in Alabama. I was eleven, and I could see that my mother wasn't sick, not in the ways that I was used to. I didn't understand what my mother needed healing from. I didn't understand, but I did. And my embarrassment at my aunt's loud gesture had as much to do with my understanding as it did with the man who had passed us by. My aunt was saying, "*That*. That is what crazy looks like." But instead what I heard was my mother's name. What I saw was my mother's face, still as lake water, the pastor's hand resting gently on her forehead, his prayer a light hum that made the room buzz. I'm not sure I know what crazy looks like, but even today when I hear the word I picture a split screen, the dreadlocked man in Kejetia on one side, my mother lying in bed on the other. I think about how no one at all reacted to that man in the market, not in fear or disgust, nothing, save my aunt, who wanted me to look. He was, it seemed to me, at perfect peace, even as he gesticulated wildly, even as he mumbled.

But my mother, in her bed, infinitely still, was wild inside.

2

The second time it happened, I got a phone call while I was working in my lab at Stanford. I'd had to separate two of my mice because they were ripping each other to bits in that shoebox of a home we kept them in. I found a piece of flesh in one corner of the box, but I couldn't tell which mouse it came from at first. Both were bleeding and frenzied, scurrying away from me when I tried to grab them even though there was nowhere to run.

"Look, Gifty, she hasn't been to church in nearly a month. I've been calling the house but she won't pick up. I go by sometimes and make sure she's got food and everything, but I think . . . I think it's happening again."

I didn't say anything. The mice had calmed down considerably, but I was still shaken by the sight of them and worried about my research. Worried about everything.

"Gifty?" Pastor John said.

"She should come stay with me."

I'm not sure how the pastor got my mother on the plane. When I picked her up at SFO she looked completely vacant, her body limp. I imagined Pastor John folding her up the way you would a jumpsuit, arms crossed about the chest in an X, legs pulled up to meet them, then tucking her safely into a suitcase complete with a HANDLE WITH CARE sticker before passing her off to the flight attendant.

I gave her a stiff hug and she shrank from my touch. I took a deep breath. "Did you check a bag?" I asked.

"*Daabi,*" she said.

"Okay, no bags. Great, we can go straight to the car." The saccharine cheeriness of my voice annoyed me so much I bit my tongue in an attempt to bite it back. I felt a prick of blood and sucked it away.

She followed me to my Prius. Under better circumstances she would have made fun of my car, an oddity to her after years of Alabama pickup trucks and SUVs. "Gifty, my bleeding heart," she sometimes called me. I don't know where she'd picked up the phrase, but I figured it was probably used derogatorily by Pastor John and the various TV preachers she liked to watch while she cooked to describe people who, like me, had defected from Alabama to live among the sinners of the world, presumably because the excessive bleeding of our hearts made us too weak to tough it out among the hardy, the chosen of Christ in the Bible Belt. She loved Billy Graham, who said things like "A real Christian is the one who can give his pet parrot to the town gossip."

Cruel, I thought when I was a child, to give away your pet parrot.

The funny thing about the phrases that my mom picked up is that she always got them a little wrong. I was *her* bleeding heart, not *a* bleeding heart. It's a *crime* shame, not a *crying* shame. She had a little southern accent that tinted her Ghanaian one. It made me think of my friend Anne, whose hair was brown, except on some days, when the sunlight touched her just so and, suddenly, you saw red.

In the car, my mother stared out of the passenger-side window, quiet as a church mouse. I tried to imagine the scenery the way she might be seeing it. When I'd first arrived in California, everything had looked so beautiful to me. Even the grass, yellowed, scorched from the sun and the seemingly endless drought, had looked otherworldly. *This must be Mars,* I thought, because how could this be America too? I pictured the drab green pastures of my childhood, the small hills we called mountains. The vastness of this western landscape overwhelmed me. I'd come to California because I wanted to get lost, to find. In college, I'd read *Walden* because a boy I found beautiful found the book beautiful. I understood nothing but highlighted everything, including this: *Not till we are lost, in other words, not till we have lost the world, do we begin to find ourselves, and realize where we are and the infinite extent of our relations.*

If my mother was moved by the landscape, too, I couldn't tell. We lurched forward in traffic and I caught the eye of the man in the car next to ours. He quickly looked away, then looked back, then away again. I wanted to make him uncomfortable, or maybe just to transfer my own discomfort to him, and so I kept staring. I could see in the way that he gripped the steering wheel that he was trying not to look at me again. His knuckles were pale, veiny, rimmed with red. He gave up, shot me an exasperated look, mouthed, "What?" I've always found that traffic on a bridge brings everyone closer to their own personal edge. Inside each car, a snapshot of a breaking point, drivers looking out toward the water and wondering *What if? Could there be another way out?* We scooted forward again. In the scrum of cars, the man seemed almost close enough to touch. What would he do if he could touch me? If he didn't have to contain all of that rage inside his Honda Accord, where would it go?

"Are you hungry?" I asked my mother, finally turning away.

She shrugged, still staring out of the window. The last time this happened she'd lost seventy pounds in two months. When I came back from my summer in Ghana, I had hardly recognized her, this woman who had always found skinny people offensive, as though a kind of laziness or failure of character kept them from appreciating the pure joy that is a good meal. Then she joined their ranks. Her cheeks sank; her stomach deflated. She hollowed, disappeared.

I was determined not to let that happen again. I'd bought a Ghanaian cookbook online to make up for the years I'd spent avoiding my mother's kitchen, and I'd practiced a few of the dishes in the days leading up to my mother's arrival, hoping to perfect them before I saw her. I'd bought a deep fryer, even though my grad student stipend left little room in my budget for extravagances like bofrot or plantains. Fried food was my mother's favorite. Her mother had made fried food from a cart on the side of the road in Kumasi. My grandmother was a Fante woman from Abandze, a sea town, and she was notorious for despising Asantes, so much so that she refused to speak Twi, even after twenty years of living in the Asante capital. If you bought her food, you had to listen to her language.

"We're here," I said, rushing to help my mother get out of the car. She walked a little ahead of me, even though she'd never been to this apartment before. She'd visited me in California only a couple of times.

"Sorry for the mess," I said, but there was no mess.

None that my eyes could see anyway, but my eyes were not hers. Every time she visited me over the years she'd sweep her finger along things it never occurred to me to clean, the backs of the blinds, the hinges of doors, then present the dusty, blackened finger to me in accusation, and I could do nothing but shrug.

"Cleanliness is godliness," she used to say.

"Cleanliness is *next to* godliness," I would correct, and she would scowl at me. What was the difference?

I pointed her toward the bedroom, and, silently, she crawled into bed and drifted off to sleep.

3

As soon as I heard the sound of soft snoring, I sneaked out of the apartment and went to check on my mice. Though I had separated them, the one with the largest wounds was hunched over from pain in the corner of the box. Watching him, I wasn't sure he would live much longer. It filled me with an inexplicable sorrow, and when my lab mate, Han, found me twenty minutes later, crying in the corner of the room, I knew I would be too mortified to admit that the thought of a mouse's death was the cause of my tears.

"Bad date," I told Han. A look of horror passed over his face as he mustered up a few pitiful words of comfort, and I could imagine what he was thinking: *I went into the hard sciences so that I wouldn't have to be around emotional women.* My crying turned to laughter, loud and phlegmy, and the look of horror on his face deepened until his ears flushed as red as a stop sign. I stopped laughing and rushed out of the lab and into the restroom, where I stared at myself in the mirror. My eyes were puffy and red; my nose looked bruised, the skin around the nostrils dry and scaly from the tissues.

"Get ahold of yourself," I said to the woman in the mirror, but doing so felt cliché, like I was reenacting a scene from a movie, and so I started to feel like I didn't have a self to get ahold of, or rather that I had a million selves, too many to gather. One was in the bathroom, playing a role; another, in the lab staring at my wounded mouse, an animal about whom I felt nothing at all, yet whose pain had reduced me somehow. Or multiplied me. Another self was still thinking about my mother.

The mouse fight had rattled me into checking on my mice more than I needed to, trying to keep ahead of the feeling. When I got to the lab the day of my mother's arrival, Han was already there, performing surgery on his mice. As was usually the case whenever Han arrived at the lab first, the thermostat was turned down low. I shivered, and he looked up from his work.

"Hey," he said.

"Hey."

Though we'd been sharing this space for months now, we hardly ever said more than this to each other, except for the day he'd found me crying. Han smiled at me more now, but his ears still burned bright red if I tried to push our conversation past that initial greeting.

I checked in on my mice and my experiments. No fights, no surprises.

I drove back to my apartment. In the bedroom, my mother still lay underneath a cloud of covers. A sound like a purr floated out from her lips. I'd been living alone for so long that even that soft noise, hardly more than a hum, unnerved me. I'd forgotten what it was like to live with my mother, to care for her. For a long time, most of my life, in fact, it had been just me and her, but this pairing was unnatural. She knew it and I knew it, and we both tried to ignore what we knew to be true—there used to be four of us, then three, two. When my mother goes, whether by choice or not, there will be only one.

4

Dear God,
I've been wondering where you are. I mean, I know you're
here, with me, but where are you exactly? In space?

Dear God,
The Black Mamba makes a lot of noise most of the time,
but when she's mad she moves really slowly and quietly and
then, all of a sudden, there she is. Buzz says it's because
she's an African warrior and so she's got to be stealthy.
    Buzz's impression is really funny. He sneaks around
and then, all of a sudden, he makes his body really big, and
picks something up off the floor and says, "What is this?"
He doesn't do impressions of the Chin Chin Man anymore.

Dear God,
If you're in space, how can you see me, and what do I
look like to you? And what do you look like, if you look
like anything at all? Buzz says he'd never want to be an
astronaut and I don't think I want to either, but I would
go to space if you were there.

5

When there were four of us, I was too young to appreciate it. My mother used to tell stories about my father. At six feet four inches, he was the tallest man she'd ever seen; she thought he was maybe even the tallest man in all of Kumasi. He used to hang around her mother's food stand, joking with my grandmother about her stubborn Fante, coaxing her into giving him a free baggie of achomo, which he called chin chin like the Nigerians in town did. My mother was thirty when they met, thirty-one when they married. She was already an old maid by Ghanaian standards, but she said God had told her to wait, and when she met my father, she knew what she'd been waiting for.

She called him the Chin Chin Man, like her mother called him. And when I was very little and wanted to hear stories about him, I'd tap my chin until my mother complied. "Tell me about Chin Chin," I'd say. I almost never thought of him as my father.

The Chin Chin Man was six years older than she was. Coddled by his own mother, he'd felt no need to marry. He had been raised Catholic, but once my mother got ahold of him, she dragged him to the Christ of her Pentecostal church. The same church where the two of them were married in the sweltering heat, with so many guests they'd stopped counting after two hundred.

They prayed for a baby, but month after month, year after year, no baby came. It was the first time my mother ever doubted God. *After I am worn out, and my lord is old, shall I have pleasure?*

"You can have a child with someone else," she offered, taking initiative in God's silence, but the Chin Chin Man laughed her away. My mother spent three days fasting and praying in the living room of my grandmother's house. She must have looked as frightful as a witch, smelled as horrid as a stray dog, but when she left her prayer room, she said to my father, "Now," and he went to her and they lay together. Nine months to the day later, my brother, Nana, my mother's Isaac, was born.

My mother used to say, "You should have seen the way the Chin Chin Man smiled at Nana." His entire face was in on it. His eyes brightened, his lips spread back until they were touching his ears, his ears lifted. Nana's face returned the compliment, smiling in kind. My father's heart was a lightbulb, dimming with age. Nana was pure light.

Nana could walk at seven months. That's how they knew he would be tall. He was the darling of their compound. Neighbors used to request him at parties. "Would you bring Nana by?" they'd say, wanting to fill their apartment with his smile, his bowlegged baby dancing.

Every street vendor had a gift for Nana. A bag of koko, an ear of corn, a tiny drum. "What couldn't he have?" my mother wondered. Why not the whole world? She knew the Chin Chin Man would agree. Nana, beloved and lov-

ing, deserved the best. But what was the best the world had
to offer? For the Chin Chin Man, it was my grandmother's
achomo, the bustle of Kejetia, the red clay, his mother's fufu
pounded just so. It was Kumasi, Ghana. My mother was less
certain of this. She had a cousin in America who sent money
and clothes back to the family somewhat regularly, which
surely meant there was money and clothes in abundance
across the Atlantic. With Nana's birth, Ghana had started to
feel too cramped. My mother wanted room for him to grow.

They argued and argued and argued, but the Chin Chin
Man's easygoing nature meant he let my mother go easy, and
so within a week she had applied for the green card lottery.
It was a time when not many Ghanaians were immigrat-
ing to America, which is to say you could enter the lottery
and win. My mother found out that she had been randomly
selected for permanent residency in America a few months
later. She packed what little she owned, bundled up baby
Nana, and moved to Alabama, a state she had never heard
of, but where she planned to stay with her cousin, who was
finishing up her PhD. The Chin Chin Man would follow
later, after they had saved up enough money for a second
plane ticket and a home of their own.

6

My mother slept all day and all night, every day, every night. She was immovable. Whenever I could, I would try to convince her to eat something. I'd taken to making koko, my favorite childhood meal. I'd had to go to three different stores to find the right kind of millet, the right kind of corn husks, the right peanuts to sprinkle on top. I hoped the porridge would go down thoughtlessly. I'd leave a bowl of it by her bedside in the morning before I went to work, and when I returned the top layer would be covered in film; the layer underneath that hardened so that when I scraped it into the sink I felt the effort of it.

My mother's back was always turned to me. It was like she had an internal sensor for when I'd be entering the room to deliver the koko. I could picture the movie montage of us, the days spelled out at the bottom of the screen, my outfits changing, our actions the same.

After about five days of this, I entered the room and my mother was awake and facing me.

"Gifty," she said as I set the bowl of koko down. "Do you still pray?"

It would have been kinder to lie, but I wasn't kind any-more. Maybe I never had been. I vaguely remembered a childhood kindness, but maybe I was conflating innocence and kindness. I felt so little continuity between who I was as a young child and who I was now that it seemed pointless to even consider showing my mother something like mercy. Would I have been merciful when I was a child?

"No," I answered.

When I was a child I prayed. I studied my Bible and kept a journal with letters to God. I was a paranoid journal keeper, so I made code names for all the people in my life whom I wanted God to punish.

Reading the journal makes it clear that I was a real "Sin-ners in the Hands of an Angry God" kind of Christian, and I believed in the redemptive power of punishment. *For it is said, that when that due Time, or appointed Time comes, their Foot shall slide. Then they shall be left to fall as they are inclined by their own Weight.*

The code name I gave my mother was the Black Mamba, because we'd just learned about the snakes in school. The movie the teacher showed us that day featured a seven-foot-long snake that looked like a slender woman in a skintight leather dress, slithering across the Sahara in pursuit of a bush squirrel.

In my journal, the night we learned about the snakes, I wrote:

Dear God,
The Black Mamba has been really mean to me lately.
Yesterday she told me that if I didn't clean my room no
one would want to marry me.

My brother, Nana, was code-named Buzz. I don't remember why now. In the first few years of my journal keeping, Buzz was my hero:

Dear God,
Buzz ran after the ice cream truck today. He bought a
firecracker popsicle for himself and a Flintstones pushpop
for me.

Or:

Dear God,
At the rec center today, none of the other kids wanted to
be my partner for the three-legged race because they said I
was too little, but then Buzz came over and he said that
he would do it! And guess what? We won and I got a
trophy.

Sometimes he annoyed me, but back then, his offenses were innocuous, trivial.

Dear God,
Buzz keeps coming into my room without knocking! I
can't stand him!

But after a few years my pleas for God's intervention became something else entirely.

Dear God,
When Buzz came home last night he started yelling at
TBM and I could hear her crying, so I went downstairs

to look even though I was supposed to be in bed. (I'm
sorry.) She told him to keep quiet or he would wake me,
but then he picked up the TV and smashed it on the floor
and punched a hole in the wall and his hand was bleeding
and TBM started crying and she looked up and saw
me and I ran back to my room while Buzz screamed get
the fuck out of here you nosy cunt. (What is a cunt?)

I was ten when I wrote that entry. I was smart enough
to use the code names and make note of new vocabulary
words but not smart enough to see that anyone who could
read could easily crack my code. I hid the journal under my
mattress, but because my mother is a person who thinks to
clean underneath a mattress, I'm sure she must have found
it at some point. If she did, she never mentioned it. After
the broken-television incident, my mother had run up to my
bedroom and locked the door while Nana raved downstairs.
She grabbed me close and pulled the both of us down onto
our knees behind the bed while she prayed in Twi.

Awurade, bɔ me ba barima ho ban. Awurade, bɔ me ba barima
ho ban. Lord, protect my son. Lord, protect my son.

"You should pray," my mother said then, reaching for
the koko. I watched her eat two spoonfuls before setting it
back down on the nightstand.

"Is it okay?" I asked.

She shrugged, turned her back to me once more.

I went to the lab. Han wasn't there, so the room was a livable
temperature. I set my jacket on the back of a chair, got myself
ready, then grabbed a couple of my mice to prep them for
surgery. I shaved the fur from the tops of their heads until

I saw their scalps. I carefully drilled into those, wiping the blood away, until I found the bright red of their brains, the chests of the anesthetized rodents expanding and deflating mechanically as they breathed their unconscious breaths.

Though I had done this millions of times, it still awed me to see a brain. To know that if I could only understand this little organ inside this one tiny mouse, that understanding still wouldn't speak to the full intricacy of the comparable organ inside my own head. And yet I had to try to understand, to extrapolate from that limited understanding in order to apply it to those of us who made up the species *Homo sapiens,* the most complex animal, the only animal who believed he had transcended his Kingdom, as one of my high school biology teachers used to say. That belief, that transcendence, was held within this organ itself. Infinite, unknowable, soulful, perhaps even magical. I had traded the Pentecostalism of my childhood for this new religion, this new quest, knowing that I would never fully know.

I was a sixth-year PhD candidate in neuroscience at the Stanford University School of Medicine. My research was on the neural circuits of reward-seeking behavior. Once, on a date during my first year of grad school, I had bored a guy stiff by trying to explain to him what I did all day. He'd taken me to Tofu House in Palo Alto, and as I watched him struggle with his chopsticks, losing several pieces of bulgogi to the napkin in his lap, I'd told him all about the medial prefrontal cortex, nucleus accumbens, 2-photon Ca^{2+} imaging.

"We know that the medial prefrontal cortex plays a critical role in suppressing reward-seeking behavior, it's just that the neural circuitry that allows it to do so is poorly understood."

I'd met him on OkCupid. He had straw-blond hair, skin

perpetually at the end phase of a sunburn. He looked like a SoCal surfer. The entire time we'd messaged back and forth I'd wondered if I was the first black girl he'd ever asked out, if he was checking some kind of box off his list of new and exotic things he'd like to try, like the Korean food in front of us, which he had already given up on.

"Huh," he said. "Sounds interesting."

Maybe he'd expected something different. There were only five women in my lab of twenty-eight, and I was one of three black PhD candidates in the entire med school. I had told SoCal Surfer that I was getting my doctorate, but I hadn't told him what I was getting it in because I didn't want to scare him away. Neuroscience may have screamed "smart," but it didn't really scream "sexy." Adding to that my blackness, maybe I was too much of an anomaly for him. He never called me back.

From then on, I told dates that my job was to get mice hooked on cocaine before taking it away from them.

Two in three asked the same question. "So do you just, like, have a ton of cocaine?" I never admitted that we'd switched from cocaine to Ensure. It was easier to get and sufficiently addictive for the mice. I relished the thrill of having something interesting and illicit to say to these men, most of whom I would sleep with once and then never see again. It made me feel powerful to see their names flash across my phone screen hours, days, weeks after they'd seen me naked, after they'd dug their fingernails into my back, sometimes drawing blood. Reading their texts, I liked to feel the marks they'd left. I felt like I could suspend them there, just names on my phone screen, but after a while, they stopped calling, moved on, and then I would feel powerful in their silence. At least for a little while. I wasn't accustomed to power in relationships, power in sexuality. I had never been asked on a date in high school. Not once. I wasn't cool enough, white enough, enough. In college, I had been shy and awkward, still molting the skin of a Christianity that insisted I save myself for marriage, that left me fearful of men and of my body. *Every other sin a person commits is outside the body, but the sexually immoral person sins against his own body.*

"I'm pretty, right?" I once asked my mother. We were standing in front of the mirror while she put her makeup on for work. I don't remember how old I was, only that I wasn't allowed to wear makeup yet. I had to sneak it when my mother wasn't around, but that wasn't too hard to do. My mother worked all the time. She was never around.

"What kind of question is that?" she asked. She grabbed my arm and jerked me toward the mirror. "Look," she said, and at first I thought she was angry at me. I tried to look away, but every time my eyes fell, my mother would jerk me to attention once more. She jerked me so many times I thought my arm would come loose from the socket.

"Look at what God made. Look at what I made," she said in Twi.

We stared at ourselves in the mirror for a long time. We stared until my mother's work alarm went off, the one that told her it was time to leave one job in order to get to the other. She finished putting her lipstick on, kissed her reflection in the mirror, and rushed off. I kept staring at myself after she left, kissing my own reflection back.

I watched my mice groggily spring back to life, recovering from the anesthesia and woozy from the painkillers I'd given them. I'd injected a virus into the nucleus accumbens and implanted a lens in their brains so that I could see their neurons firing as I ran my experiments. I sometimes wondered if they noticed the added weight they carried on their heads, but I tried not to think thoughts like that, tried not to humanize them, because I worried it would make it harder for me to do my work. I cleaned up my station and went to my office to try to do some writing. I was supposed to be working toward a paper, presumably my last before graduating. The hardest part, putting the figures together, usually only took me a few weeks or so, but I had been twiddling my thumbs, dragging things out. Running my experiments over and over again, until the idea of stopping, of writing, of graduating, seemed impossible. I'd put a little warning on the wall above my desk to whip myself into shape. TWENTY MINUTES OF WRITING A DAY OR ELSE. *Or else what?* I wondered. Anyone could see it was an empty threat. After twenty minutes of doodling, I pulled out the journal entry from years ago that I kept hidden in the bowels of my desk to read on those days when I was frustrated with my work, when I was feeling low and lonely and useless and hopeless. Or when I wished I had a job that paid me more than a seventeen-thousand-dollar stipend to stretch through a quarter in this expensive college town.

> *Dear God,*
> *Buzz is going to prom and he has a suit on! It's navy*
> *blue with a pink tie and a pink pocket square. TBM*
> *had to order the suit special cuz Buzz's so tall that they*
> *didn't have anything for him in the store. We spent*
> *all afternoon taking pictures of him, and we were all*
> *laughing and hugging and TBM was crying and saying,*

"You're so beautiful," over and over. *And the limo came to pick Buzz up so he could pick his date up and he stuck his head out of the sunroof and waved at us. He looked normal. Please, God, let him stay like this forever.*

My brother died of a heroin overdose three months later.

7

By the time I wanted to hear the complete story of why my parents immigrated to America, it was no longer a story my mother wanted to tell. The version I got—that my mother had wanted to give Nana the world, that the Chin Chin Man had reluctantly agreed—never felt sufficient to me. Like many Americans, I knew very little about the rest of the world. I had spent years spinning elaborate lies to classmates about how my grandfather was a warrior, a lion tamer, a high chief.

"I'm actually a princess," I said to Geoffrey, a fellow student in my kindergarten class whose nose was always running. Geoffrey and I sat at a table by ourselves in the very back of the classroom. I always suspected that my teacher had put me there as some kind of punishment, like she had seated me there so that I would have to look at the slug of snot on Geoffrey's philtrum and feel even more acutely that I didn't belong. I resented all of this, and I did my best to torture Geoffrey.

"No, you're not," Geoffrey said. "Black people can't be princesses."

I went home and asked my mother if this was true, and she told me to keep quiet and stop bothering her with questions. It's what she said anytime I asked her for stories, and, back then, all I ever did was ask her for stories. I wanted her stories about her life in Ghana with my father to be filled with all the kings and queens and curses that might explain why my father wasn't around in terms far grander and more elegant than the simple story I knew. And if our story couldn't be a fairy tale, then I was willing to accept a tale like the kind I saw on television, back when the only images I ever saw of Africa were those of people stricken by warfare and famine. But there was no war in my mother's stories, and if there was hunger, it was of a different kind, the simple hunger of those who had been fed one thing but wanted another. A simple hunger, impossible to satisfy. I had a hunger, too, and the stories my mother filled me with were never exotic enough, never desperate enough, never enough to provide me with the ammunition I felt I needed in order to battle Geoffrey, his slug of snot, my kindergarten teacher, and that seat in the very back.

My mother told me that the Chin Chin Man joined her and Nana in America a few months after they moved to Alabama. It was his first time on an airplane. He'd taken a tro-tro to Accra, carrying only one suitcase and a baggie of my grandmother's achomo. As he felt the bodies of the hundreds of other bus passengers press up against him, his legs tired and achy from standing for nearly three hours, he was thankful for his height, for the deep breaths of fresh air that floated above everyone else's heads.

At Kotoka, the gate agents had cheered him on and wished him well when they saw where he was headed.

"Send for me next, *chale*," they said. At JFK, Customs and Immigration took his baggie of chin chin away.

At the time, my mother was making ten thousand dollars a year, working as a home health aide for a man called Mr. Thomas.

"I can't believe my shithead kids stuck me with a nigger," he would often say. Mr. Thomas was an octogenarian with early-stage Parkinson's disease whose tremors had not deterred his foul mouth. My mother wiped his ass, fed him, watched *Jeopardy!* with him, smirking as he got nearly every answer wrong. Mr. Thomas's shithead kids had hired five other home health aides before my mother. They'd all quit.

"DO. YOU. SPEAK. ENGLISH?" Mr. Thomas yelled every time my mother brought him the heart-healthy meals his children paid for instead of the bacon he'd asked for. The home health service had been the only place to hire my mother. She left Nana with her cousin, or brought him to work with her, until Mr. Thomas started calling him "the little monkey." After that, more often than not, she left Nana alone while she worked her twelve-hour night shift, praying he'd sleep until morning.

The Chin Chin Man had a harder time finding a job. The home health service had hired him, but too many people complained once they saw him walk in the door.

"I think people were afraid of him," my mother once told me, but she wouldn't tell me why she'd come to that conclusion. She almost never admitted to racism. Even Mr. Thomas, who had never called my mother anything other than "that nigger," was, to her, just a confused old man. But walking around with my father, she'd seen how America changed around big black men. She saw him try to shrink to size, his long, proud back hunched as he walked with my mother through the Walmart, where he was accused of stealing three times in four months. Each time, they took him to a little room off the exit of the store. They leaned him against the wall and patted him down, their hands drifting up one pant leg and down the other. Homesick, humiliated, he stopped leaving the house.

This is when my mother found the First Assemblies of God Church on Bridge Avenue. Since her arrival in America, she had stopped going to church, opting instead to work every Sunday because Sunday was the day of the week most Alabamians wanted off for the two holy acts—going to church and watching football. American football meant nothing to my mother, but she missed having a place to worship. My father reminded her of all that she owed God, reminded her of the power held in her prayer. She wanted to summon him out of his funk, and to do so, she knew she needed to swim out of her own.

The First Assemblies of God Church was a little brick building, no bigger than a three-bedroom house. It had a large marquee out front that displayed cutesy messages meant to lure people in. Sometimes the messages were questions. *Have you met Him yet?* or *Got God?* or *Do you feel lost?* Sometimes, they were answers. *Jesus is the reason for the season!* I don't know if the marquee messages were what drew my mother in, but I do know that the church became her second home, her most intimate place of worship.

The day she walked in, music played over the loudspeakers in the sanctuary. As the singer's voice beckoned, my mother inched toward the altar. My mother obeyed. She knelt down before the Lord and prayed and prayed and prayed. When she lifted her head, her face wet with tears, she thought she might get used to living in America.

8

When I was a child I thought I would be a dancer or a worship leader at a Pentecostal church, a preacher's wife or a glamorous actress. In high school my grades were so good that the world seemed to whittle this decision down for me: doctor. An immigrant cliché, except I lacked the overbearing parents. My mother didn't care what I did and wouldn't have forced me into anything. I suspect she would be prouder today if I'd ended up behind the pulpit of the First Assemblies of God, meekly singing number 162 out of the hymnal while the congregation stuttered along. Everyone at that church had a horrible voice. When I was old enough to go to "big church," as the kids in the children's service called it, I dreaded hearing the worship leader's warbling soprano every Sunday morning. It scared me in a familiar way. Like when I was five and Nana was eleven, and we found a baby bird that had fallen out of its nest. Nana scooped it into his big palms, and the two of us ran home. The house was empty. The house was always empty, but we knew we needed to act fast, because if our mother came home to find the bird, she'd kill it outright or take it away and drop it in some small stretch of wilderness, leaving it to die. She'd tell us exactly what she'd done too. She was never the kind of parent who lied to make her children feel better. I'd spent my whole childhood slipping teeth under my pillow at night and finding teeth there in the morning. Nana left the bird with me while he poured a bowl of milk for it. When I held it in my hands, I felt its fear, the unending shiver of its little round body, and I started crying. Nana put its beak to the bowl and tried to urge it to drink, but it wouldn't, and the shiver that was in the bird moved in me. That's what the worship leader's voice sounded like to me—the shaky body of a bird in distress, a child who'd grown suddenly afraid. I checked that career off my list right away.

Preacher's wife was next on my list. Pastor John's wife didn't do much, as far as I could tell, but I decided to practice for the position by praying for all of my friends' pets. There was Katie's goldfish, for whom we held a toilet-bowl funeral. I said my prayer while we watched the flash of orange swirl down and disappear. There was Ashley's golden retriever, Buddy, a frantic, energetic dog. Buddy liked to knock over the trash bins the neighbors put out every Tuesday night. Come Wednesday morning our street would be littered with apple cores, beer bottles, cereal boxes. The trash collectors started to complain, but Buddy kept living out his truth, undeterred. Once, Mrs. Caldwell found a pair of panties near her bin that didn't belong to her, confirming a suspicion she'd had. She moved out the next week. The Tuesday night after she left, Mr. Caldwell sat outside next to his trash bin in a lawn chair, a rifle slung across his lap.

"Iffn that dog comes near my trash again, you'll be needin' a shovel."

Ashley, scared for Buddy's life, asked if I would pray for

him, as I had already made something of a name for myself on the pet funeral circuit.

She brought the dog by while my mother was at work and Nana was at basketball practice. I'd asked her to come over when no one was home, because I knew that what we were doing was in a gray area, sacrament-wise. I cleared a space in the living room, which I referred to as the sanctuary. Buddy figured out something was up as soon as we started to sing "Holy, Holy, Holy," and he wouldn't stay still. Ashley held him down while I placed my hand on his head, asking God to make him a dog of peace instead of one of destruction. I counted that prayer successful every time I saw Buddy out and about, alive, but I still wasn't sure if I was destined for the ministry.

It was my high school biology teacher who urged me toward science. I was fifteen, the same age that Nana was when we discovered he had a habit. My mother had been cleaning Nana's room when she noticed. She'd gotten a ladder from the garage so she could sweep out his light fixture, and when she put her hand in the glass bowl of the light, she found a few scattered pills. OxyContin. Gathered there, they'd looked like dead bugs, once drawn to the light. Years later, after all the funeral attendants had finally gone, leaving jollof and waakye and peanut butter soup in their wake, my mother would tell me that she blamed herself for not doing more the day she'd cleaned the light. I should have said something kind in return. I should have comforted her, told her it wasn't her fault, but somewhere, just below the surface of me, I blamed her. I blamed myself too. Guilt and doubt and fear had already settled into my young body like ghosts haunting a house. I trembled, and in the one second it took for the tremble to move through my body, I stopped believing in God. It happened that quickly, a tremble-length reckoning. One minute there was a God with the whole world in his hands; the next minute the world was plummeting, ceaselessly, toward an ever-shifting bottom.

Mrs. Pasternack, my biology teacher, was a Christian. Everyone I knew in Alabama was, but she said things like "I think we're made out of stardust, and God made the stars." Ridiculous to me then, weirdly comforting now. Then, my whole body felt raw, all of the time, like if you touched me the open wound of my flesh would throb. Now, I'm scabbed over, hardened. Mrs. Pasternack said something else that year that I never forgot. She said, "The truth is we don't know what we don't know. We don't even know the questions we need to ask in order to find out, but when we learn one tiny little thing, a dim light comes on in a dark hallway, and suddenly a new question appears. We spend decades, centuries, millennia, trying to answer that one question so that another dim light will come on. That's science, but that's also everything else, isn't it? Try. Experiment. Ask a ton of questions."

The first experiment I can remember performing was the Naked Egg experiment. It was for my middle school's physical science class, and I remember it, in part, because I'd had to ask my mother to put corn syrup on the grocery list, and she'd grumbled about it endlessly all week long. "Why doesn't your teacher buy you the corn syrup if she wants you to do this nonsense?" she said. I told my teacher that I didn't think my mother would buy the corn syrup, and, with a little wink, my teacher gifted me a bottle from the back of her storage closet. I thought this would please my mother. After all, it's what she had been asking for, but instead it only mortified her. "She'll think we can't afford corn syrup," she said. Those were the hardest years, the beginnings of the just-the-two-of-us years. We couldn't afford corn syrup. My teacher went to our church; she knew about Nana, about my father. She knew my mother worked twelve-hour shifts every day but Sunday.

We started the Naked Egg experiment at the beginning of the week by putting our eggs in vinegar. The vinegar dissolved the shell, slowly, so that by Wednesday's class we had a naked egg, urine-yellow and larger than a regular egg. We put the naked egg into a new glass and poured corn syrup over it. The egg we saw the next day was shriveled, flattened. We put the deflated egg in colored water and watched the blue expand, color pushing through the egg, making it larger and larger and larger.

The experiment was a way to teach us the principles of osmosis, but I was too distracted to appreciate the science behind it. As I watched the egg absorb that blue water, all I could think about was my mother shaking the bottle of corn syrup at me, her face almost purple with rage. "Take it back, take it back, TAKE IT BACK," she said, before flinging herself onto the ground and kicking her legs up and down in a tantrum.

The two of us back then, mother and daughter, we were ourselves an experiment. The question was, and has remained: Are we going to be okay?

Some days when I got home from the lab I would go into my room, my mother's room, and tell her all the things I'd done that day, except I wouldn't say them aloud, I'd just think them. *Today, I watched a mouse brain flash green,* I'd think, and if she stirred that meant she'd heard me. It made me feel like a silly child, but I did it all the same.

Han invited me to a party at his place, I thought toward my mother one night. *Move if you think I should go.* When her hand lifted to scratch her nose, I grabbed my jacket and left.

Han lived in one of those apartment complexes, uniform and labyrinthine, that feels like a prison or a military barracks in its sameness. I found myself going to 3H instead of 5H. Every turn led to another group of Spanish mission-style apartments with those signature clay tile roofs that were everywhere in the Southwest and California.

When I finally got to 5H, the door was ajar. Han welcomed me with an uncharacteristic hug. "Giftyyyyy," he said, lifting me up a little.

He was drunk, another rarity for him, and though I'd never noticed it before, I noticed it then—the tips of his ears were red, just like the day he'd found me crying in the lab.

"I don't think I've ever seen you in shorts before, Han," I said.

"Check out my bare feet too," he said, wiggling his toes. "Lab regulations have really deprived you from seeing me in all my natural beauty."

I laughed, and he flushed even deeper. "Make yourself at home," he said, waving me in.

I moved through the living room, chatting with my cohort. We ranged in age from twenty-two to forty-seven. Our backgrounds were similarly all over the place— robotics, molecular biology, music, psychology, literature. All roads had led to the brain.

I was bad at most parties but good at these. It's remarkable how cool you can seem when you are the only black person in a room, even when you've done nothing cool at all. I wasn't close to anyone at the party, certainly not close enough to tell them about my mother, but by the end of the night, the alcohol had loosened my lips and I started to get comfortable, to talk around the subject I most wanted to talk about.

"Do you think you'll ever go back to practicing psychiatry?" I asked Katherine. She was one of the more senior members of my lab, a postdoc who'd done her undergraduate studies at Oxford and a medical degree at UCSF before starting her PhD here. We had a tentative friendship, predicated mostly on the fact that we had both been raised in immigrant families and that we were two of the only women in the department. I always got the sense that Katherine wanted to get to know me better. She was friendly and open, too open for my comfort. Once, in the lounge, Katherine had confided in me that she had snooped through her husband's things and found little "o's" written in his calendar on the days when she was ovulating, and she thought that maybe he was trying to trick her into having a baby sooner than the time frame they'd planned on. She'd been so free with that information, like she was telling me about a cough she couldn't kick, but I was enraged, self-righteous. "Leave him," I said, but she didn't, and as I talked to her, Steve, her husband, was on the other side of Han's living room, sipping sangria, his head tilted back just slightly so that I could see his Adam's apple bob as the drink moved down. Knowing what I knew about Steve, I couldn't look at him, his Adam's apple, and not see a kind of menace, but there he was talking, drinking, ordinary.

"I think about going back to my practice all the time," Katherine said. "With medicine, I could see that I was helping people. A patient would come in, so wracked with anxiety that they were scratching their arms raw, and months later, no scratches. That's gratifying. But with research? Who knows."

My mother had hated therapy. She went in arms raw, came out arms raw. She was distrustful of psychiatrists and she didn't believe in mental illness. That's how she put it. "I don't believe in mental illness." She claimed that it, along with everything else she disapproved of, was an invention of the West. I told her about Ama Ata Aidoo's book *Changes,* in which the character Esi says, *"you cannot go around claiming that an idea or an item was imported into a given society unless you could also conclude that to the best of your knowledge, there is not, and never was any word or phrase in that society's indigenous language which describes that idea or item."*

Abodamfo. Bodam nii. That was the word for "crazy person," the word I'd heard my aunt use that day in Kejetia to describe the dreadlocked man. My mother refused this logic. After my brother died, she refused to name her illness depression. "Americans get depressed on TV and they cry," she said. My mother rarely cried. She fought the feeling for a while, but then one day, not long after the Naked Egg experiment, she got into her bed, got under the covers, and wouldn't get back up. I was eleven. I was shaking her arm as she lay there in bed, I was bringing her food before walking to school, I was cleaning the house so that when she finally woke up she wouldn't be upset with me for letting the place turn to filth. I was doing okay, I thought, so when I found her, sinking in the bathtub, the faucet running, the floor flooded, the first thing I felt was betrayed. We were doing okay.

I looked at Katherine's stomach. Still flat, all of these months later. Was Steve still making little "o's" in his calendar? Had she told him that she knew about his betrayal or did she keep it to herself, hold it in the clenched fist of her heart to open only when something between them was truly broken?

I had never been to therapy myself, and when the time came for me to choose what to study, I didn't choose psychology. I chose molecular biology. I think when people heard about my brother they assumed that I had gone into neuroscience out of a sense of duty to him, but the truth is I'd started this work not because I wanted to help people but because it seemed like the hardest thing you could do, and I wanted to do the hardest thing. I wanted to flay any mental weakness off my body like fascia from muscle. Throughout high school, I never touched a drop of alcohol because I lived in fear that addiction was like a man in a dark trench coat, stalking me, waiting for me to get off the well-lit sidewalk and step into an alley. I had seen the alley. I had watched Nana walk into the alley and I had watched my mother go in after him, and I was so angry at them for not being strong enough to stay in the light. And so I did the hard thing.

In undergrad, I used to poke fun at psychology—a soft science. It was about the brain and cognition, yes, but it was also about mood—feelings and emotions created by the human mind. Those feelings and emotions seemed useless to me if I couldn't locate them in data, if I couldn't see how the nervous system worked by taking it apart. I wanted to understand *why* the feelings and emotions came about, what part of the brain caused them, and, more important, what part of the brain could stop them. I was such a self-righteous child. First, in the days of my Christianity, when I said things like "I'll pray for you" to my classmates who were reading books about witches and wizards. Then, in those first few years of college, when I become dismissive of anyone who cried about breakups, who spent money frivolously, who complained about small things. By that time my mother had already "healed through prayer," as Pastor John put it. Healed, but in the way a broken bone that's healed still aches at the first signs of rain. There were always first signs of rain, atmospheric, quiet. She was always aching. She would come visit me when I was in undergrad at Harvard, bundled up against the winter, even if it was spring. I'd look at her coat, her head scarf wrapped tight, and wonder when I had stopped thinking of her as a strong woman. Surely, there's strength in being dressed for a storm, even when there's no storm in sight?

The party was winding down. Han's ears looked like they would be hot to the touch.

"You shouldn't play poker," I said to him. Almost everyone had gone at this point. I didn't want to go home. I hadn't been drunk in such a long time, and I wanted to linger in the warmth of it.

"Huh?" Han said.

"Your ears are a tell. They turn red when you're drunk and when you're embarrassed."

"So maybe I should only play poker when I'm drunk or embarrassed," he said, laughing.

When I finally got back to the apartment, there were signs that my mother had gotten up from the bed. A cabinet door in the kitchen was open, a glass in the sink. We were doing okay.

9

The Chin Chin Man got a job as a janitor at a day care center. He was paid under the table, seven dollars an hour, an hour a day, five days a week. After buying a monthly bus pass, he hardly broke even, but it was something to do. "It got him off the couch," my mother said.

The children liked him. They would climb up his tall body as though he were a tree, all limb-branches and torso-trunk. His accent delighted them. He told them stories, pretending he was one of two living-man trees from Kakum Forest. That he had started out as a small seed that rolled into the forest from bushland, that every day butterflies the size of dinner plates would flutter their wings over the earth where he was planted, trying to take root. The wind from the flapping wings would stir the ground, coaxing him to grow, grow, grow, and he did. Look how big he was. Look how strong. He'd toss one of the children in the air and catch them, tickling fiercely. The children couldn't get enough. Half of them were butterflies for Halloween that first year, though their parents didn't know why.

By that time Nana had started kindergarten, and every

day after the Chin Chin Man had finished cleaning the day care, he would take the bus to Nana's school and the two of them would walk home while Nana told him of every tiny, boring, magical thing they had done in school that day, and the Chin Chin Man would greet these things with an interest beyond my mother's comprehension.

When she got home from work, feet swollen, arms aching, ears stinging with Mr. Thomas's abuse, Nana would already be in bed. The Chin Chin Man would say things like, "You see? They put the string through the holes of the macaroni to form a necklace. Can you imagine this happening in Ghana? A necklace made out of food. Why don't they eat the macaroni instead and make necklaces out of something useful?"

My mother was jealous of how close Nana and the Chin Chin Man were. She never admitted this to me, but I could tell just by the way she delivered those stories to me over the years. She never kept a single thing that Nana or I made in school. Nana stopped giving her things, and he had never told her stories, preferring to save them for the Chin Chin Man instead. After Nana died, I think my mother wished she'd had something of his, something more than her memories, more than his basketball jersey, kept stinking in his closet, a story that was just hers to delight in.

When the Chin Chin Man put Nana to bed those nights, he would tell my brother the same story he told the day care children, that he was one of two living-man trees from Kakum Forest. Nana's the one who told the story to me.

"I believed it, Gifty," he said. I don't remember how old I was, just that I was young and in a phase where I never ate but was always hungry. "I actually believed the man was a tree."

"Who was the other living-man tree?" I asked.

"Huh?"

"He said he was one of two living-man trees. Who was the other one? Was it Ma?"

The look that came over Nana's face—darkly contemplative, deeply proud—surprised me. "Nah, couldn't have been Ma. If Pop was a tree, then Ma was a rock."

Han had left the thermostat turned low. I exhaled and thought I could see the wisp of my breath lingering in the air. I had a jacket I kept at the lab, and I slipped it on and sat down to work. My mice staggered around in their boxes like drunks in the tank. The analogy was apt, but it still made me sad to imagine them that way. I thought, for the millionth time, about the baby bird Nana and I had found. We never could get it to drink, and after about fifteen minutes of failure, we took it outside and tried to coax it to fly. It wouldn't do that either. Our mother came home to find us, shooing it away with our hands while it looked at us dumbly, stumbled, fell.

"It won't ever fly now," she said. "Its mother won't recognize it anymore because you touched it and it smells like you. It doesn't matter what you do now. It will die."

Nana cried. He loved animals. Even in his last months I could still hear him begging our mother for a dog. What would he have thought of me, this work I do?

I took one of the mice out. Its head was drooping slightly from the bar that I had attached to it. I put it under the microscope so I could better see my work. The virus I injected into its brain had allowed me to introduce foreign DNA into its neurons. This DNA contained opsins, proteins that made the neurons change their behaviors in response to light. When I pulsed light in the right area, the neurons spurred into action.

"It's kind of like an LED show for mice brains," I once explained to Raymond.

"Why do you do that?" he asked.

"Do what?"

"Diminish your work like that."

It was my first year of grad school and our third date. Raymond was a PhD candidate in Modern Thought and Literature who studied protest movements. He was also gorgeous, dark like dusk with a voice that made me tremble. I forgot myself when I was around him and none of my usual tactics of seduction—that is, diminishing my work—seemed to have any effect on him.

"It's just easier to explain it that way."

Raymond said, "Well, maybe you don't have to do easy with me. You picked a hard career. You're good at it too, right? Or else you wouldn't be here. Be proud of your career. Explain things the hard way."

He smiled at me, and I wanted to slap the smile off his face, but I wanted other things more.

When I first told my mother I was going to make a career out of science, she simply shrugged. "Okay, fine." It was a Saturday. I was visiting from Cambridge and had promised her I would go to church with her the next day. Maybe it was the promise, words I regretted as soon as they left my mouth, that had made me announce my career intentions to her the way I did—like I was hurling a ball after shouting "Think fast!" I thought she would object, say something like, God is the only science we need. I'd been finding creative ways to avoid church since Nana's funeral despite my mother's occasional pleading. At first, I'd simply made up excuses to get out of it—I'd gotten my period, I had a school project to complete, I needed to pray on my own. Finally, she took the hint and resorted to sending me long, disapproving glances before heading off in her Sunday best. But then, something about my going away to college changed her, softened her. I was already my mother's daughter by then, callous, too callous to understand that she was reckoning with the complex shades of loss—her son, an unexpected, physical loss; her daughter, something slower, more natural. Four weeks into my freshman year, she ended a phone call with "I love you," spoken in the reluctant mumble she reserved for English. I laughed so hard I started crying. An "I love you" from the woman who had once called the phrase *aburofo nkwaseasɛm,* white people foolishness. At first she chastised me for laughing, but before long she was laughing too, a big-bellied sound that flooded my dorm room. Later, when I told my roommate, Samantha, why I was laughing, she said, "It's, like, not funny? To love your family?" Samantha, rich, white, a local whose boyfriend would occasionally make the drive over from UMass, leaving me displaced in the common room, was herself the embodiment of *aburofo nkwaseasɛm.* I laughed all over again.

The first thing I noticed when I went back to the First Assemblies of God with my mother that day was how much it had grown since the time of my childhood. The church had taken over two stores in a strip mall and was waiting—impatiently, it seemed, given the number of prayers people made about it—for the mom-and-pop stationery store next door to give up and sell. I recognized a few people, but most of the faces were new to me. My mother and I stood out even more among all these new members—a church packed full of white, red-blooded southerners in their pastel polos and khakis, my mother brilliant in ankara.

The room hushed as Pastor John walked to the pulpit. He had grayed at the temples since the last time I saw him. He folded his hands, which had always looked to me to be two sizes too big, as though God had switched Pastor John's hands with another man's and, upon realizing his mistake, looked at himself in a mirror and shrugged. *"I am that I am."* I liked imagining another, larger man walking around with Pastor John's small hands. I liked to think that that man had also become a preacher with a congregation that could fit in his palm.

"Father God, we thank you for this day. We thank you for bringing our sons and daughters back to church after some time away, for leading them safely back to your feet after their stints away in college. God, we ask that you fill their heads with your Word, that you don't allow them to fall prey to the ways of the secular world, that you—"

I scowled at my mother as Pastor John continued to make vague references to me, but she looked straight ahead, unfazed. After the sermon, as he greeted us congregants on our way out, Pastor John squeezed my hand, a little harder than was welcome, and said, "Don't you worry none. Your mom's doing good. She's doing real good. God is faithful."

"You're doing real good," I said to the mouse as I put him down. Though I'd repeated this process dozens of times without fail, I still always said a little prayer, a small plea that it would work. The question I was trying to answer, to use Mrs. Pasternack's terms, was: Could optogenetics be used to identify the neural mechanisms involved in psychiatric illnesses where there are issues with reward seeking, like in depression, where there is too much restraint in seeking pleasure, or drug addiction, where there is not enough?

In other words, many, many years down the line, once we've figured out a way to identify and isolate the parts of the brain that are involved in these illnesses, once we've jumped all the necessary hurdles to making this research useful to animals other than mice, could this science work on the people who need it the most?

Could it get a brother to set down a needle? Could it get a mother out of bed?

10

My mother was surprised to find herself pregnant with me. She and the Chin Chin Man had stopped trying long before. America was so expensive, barrenness was its own kind of blessing. But then there was the morning sickness, the tender breasts, the ballooning of her bladder. She knew. She was forty years old, and she wasn't entirely happy with what everyone around her kept referring to as her "miracle."

"You weren't a very good baby," she told me all my life. "In my stomach, you were very unpleasant, but coming out you were a nightmare. Thirty-four hours of misery. I thought, Lord, what have I done to deserve this torment?"

Nana was the first miracle, the true miracle, and the glory of his birth cast a long shadow. I was born into the darkness that shadow left behind. I understood that, even as a child. My mother made certain of it. She was a matter-of-fact kind of woman, not a cruel woman, exactly, but something quite close to cruel. When I was young, I prided myself on being able to tell the difference. Nana was still around, and so I could stand being told I was a horrible baby. I could stand it because I understood the context; Nana was the context. When he died, every matter-of-fact thing became cruel.

When I was very little, my mother took to calling me asaa, the miracle berry that, when eaten first, turns sour things sweet. Asaa in context is a miracle berry. Without context, it is nothing, does nothing. The sour fruit remains.

In those early years of our family of four, sour fruit was everywhere, but I was asaa and Nana was context, and so we had sweetness in abundance. My mother still worked for Mr. Thomas then. Some of my earliest memories are of his endlessly trembling hands reaching for mine on the days my mother brought me to see him.

"Where's my little nugget?" he would stammer, the words fighting to push through the shaking door of his lips. Mr. Thomas loved my mother by then, perhaps more than he loved his own children, but his sharp tongue never dulled, and I never heard him say a kind word to her.

The Chin Chin Man had a steady job as the janitor for two of the middle schools. He was still beloved by the children, and he was a good, hard worker. My memories of him, though few, are mostly pleasant, but memories of people you hardly know are often permitted a kind of pleasantness in their absence. It's those who stay who are judged the harshest, simply by virtue of being around to be judged.

I'm told that as a baby I was loud and chatty, the exact opposite of the quiet, shy person I turned out to be. Verbal fluency in young children has long been used as a signifier of future intelligence, and while that holds true for me, it's the temperament change that I'm interested in. The fact that when I hear or see myself on tape from those early years of my life, I often feel as though I am witnessing an entirely different person. What happened to me? What kind of woman might I have become if all of that chattiness hadn't changed direction, moved inward?

There are recordings of me from back then, audiotape after audiotape of my fast talking, perfect Twi or, first, my nonsense babbling. In one of the tapes, Nana is trying to tell the Chin Chin Man a story.

"The crocodile tilts his head back and opens his large mouth and—"

A shriek from me.

"A fly lands on the crocodile's eye. He tries to—"

"Dada, dada, dada!" I shout.

If you listen to the tape closely, you can almost hear the Chin Chin Man's patience in the face of Nana's growing frustration and my unreasonable interruptions. He's trying to pay attention to us both, but, of course, neither of us gets what we really want: complete and utter attention, attention without compromise. I wasn't speaking real words yet, but still, there is an urgency to my nonsense babbling. I have something important to say. A disaster is on the horizon, and if no one listens to me the disaster will come to pass and my father and Nana will have no one to blame but themselves. The urgency in my voice is quite real. It's distressing to listen to, even all of these years later. I'm not pretending there is an impending disaster; I truly believe that there is one. At one point, I make a low, guttural, animal sound, a sound so clearly biological in its design to elicit attention and sympathy from my fellow animals, and yet my fellow animals—my father, my brother—do nothing but talk over me. They talk over me because we are safe, in a small, rented house in Alabama, not stranded in a dark and dangerous rain forest, not on a raft in the middle of the sea. So the sound is a nonsense sound, a misplaced sound, a lion's roar in the tundra. When I listen to the tape now, it seems to me that this itself was the disaster I foresaw, a common enough disaster for most infants these days: that I was a baby, born cute, loud, needy, wild, but the conditions of the wilderness have changed.

On the tape, Nana goes back to telling his story, but it's of no use. I grow increasingly desperate, not letting him get a word in edgewise. Finally, you can hear a little smack, Nana shouting "Shut up shut up SHUT UP."

"No hitting," the Chin Chin Man says, and then he begins to speak to Nana in low tones, too low to hear on the tape, but you can still sense the anger underneath those hushed sounds. The anger has notes of understanding in it. He's saying, *Yes, she's insufferable, but she's ours and so we must suffer her.*

My mother was eating again, though not in front of me. I came home from the lab a couple of times to find empty cans of Amy's Chunky Tomato Bisque in the trash, and so I started buying loads of them at the Safeway near campus.

I wasn't eating much myself in those days, the lean, unhealthy grad student days. My dinners all came in boxes or cans, announcing themselves by the microwave's ding. At first, I was embarrassed about my diet. It didn't help that the cashier I always seemed to get at my local Safeway was improbably beautiful. Dark olive skin with an undercut that I caught a glimpse of every time she tucked her hair behind her ear. Sabiha, her name tag, always crooked and fastened just above her left breast, announced. I couldn't bear it. I started to imagine her internal responses to the contents of my shopping cart. That "Sesame Chicken Lean Cuisine for dinner again, huh?" look I was certain she'd once flashed me. I decided to spread my shopping around to different grocery stores in the area. Now that my mother was staying with me, I felt less embarrassed about the soup cans overflowing in my cart. If anyone asked, I was armed with an excuse. "My mother, she's ill," I imagined myself saying to that beautiful cashier.

"Would you mind if I eat dinner with you?" I asked my mother. I brought two bowls of soup into her room, my room, and sat in a dining chair I'd dragged in. The room was so sparsely decorated that even the word "decorated" was too strong to describe it. There was a bed, a nightstand, now the chair. There was also a smell, that funk of depression, sturdy, reliable like a piece of furniture.

As was typically the case, my mother had her back to me, but I had decided to try to talk to her anyway. I set her bowl on the nightstand and waited for her to turn. I ate my soup loudly, slurping because I knew how much she hated eating noises and I wanted to get a rise out of her. Even anger would be better than this. She'd been living with me for a week and had spoken maybe five sentences.

I hadn't spoken much either. I didn't know what to talk about. What do you say to a woman's back, your mother's back? The curve of it, the sloping, sagging flesh of it, was more recognizable to me now than her face, which was once the one thing in this world that I sought out the most. Her face, which my face had come to look like, was the thing I'd studied on those evenings we'd spent in her bathroom, talking about our lives while she applied makeup, readying herself for work. In those just-the-two-of-us years after my return from Ghana, I had studied her face for any sign of collapse, trying to make myself an expert on the shades of sadness I recognized in her eyes. Was it lurking there again, the dark, deep sadness, or was it just the everyday kind, the kind we all have from time to time, the kind that comes and, more important, goes? It had been almost three days since I'd seen my mother's face, but I had studied her enough to know which kind of sadness I would find there.

In Edward Tronick's popular "Still Face Experiment" from the 1970s, babies and mothers sit facing each other. At first, they engage with each other readily and joyfully. The baby points and the mother's eyes follow her finger. The baby smiles and the mother smiles back. They laugh; they touch. Then, after a few minutes of this, the mother's face turns completely still. The baby tries all of the same moves that had elicited a response only moments before, but to no effect. The mother won't acknowledge her.

I first watched this experiment in my developmental psychology class in college, and it reminded me of the audio-tapes from my childhood, except the videos of this experiment were far more distressing. Unlike in my tape, there is no attempt at soothing the child's suffering, and the child is so clearly suffering. The look on her face is one of such pure betrayal, elementary, really, this betrayal. More treacherous still, perhaps, is the fact that it is the mother, of all people, who is ignoring the baby, not a sibling or a father. It is the one person who biologically, emotionally, unequivocally matters most at that stage of life. In class that day, watching the baby's wariness play out on the projector while my classmates and I took notes, we heard a sudden whimper. It wasn't the baby in the video. It was a fellow student, a girl whom I'd never really noticed, though she sat only a few chairs away from me. She left the room abruptly, knocking over my notebook as she did so, and I knew she knew what the baby knew. She'd been in the same wilderness.

My mother and I reenacted the Still Face Experiment, now repurposed as the Turned Back Experiment, except I was twenty-eight and she was only weeks away from sixty-nine. The harm done by her turned back would be minimal; I had already become the person I was going to become, a scientist who understood that what ailed my mother was in fact a disease, even if she refused to recognize it as such. Even if she refused doctors, medicine, her own daughter. She accepted prayer and only prayer.

"I still pray sometimes," I told my mother's back. It wasn't a lie, exactly, though it certainly wasn't the truth. The last time she'd spoken, she asked me about prayer, and so I was willing to forgo the whole truth if it meant she might speak again. Maybe religion was the only well that would draw water.

Rejoice always, pray without ceasing. I used to worry over that scripture when I was a child. "Is it possible?" I asked my mother. "To pray without ceasing?"

"Why don't you give it a try?"

So, I did. My first attempts involved getting down on my knees at the foot of the bed. I started by listing everything I was thankful for. My family, my friends, my blue bicycle, ice cream sandwiches, Buddy the dog. I looked up and not even a minute had passed. I kept listing, people I thought God should work on a little more, animals that I thought God had gotten right and a few that I thought he'd gotten wrong. Before long, I got distracted and my mind wandered so far off that I found that instead of praying, I was thinking about what had happened on my favorite television show the night before.

"I don't think it's possible," I reported back to my mother.

She was in the kitchen, straining used oil into an empty bottle. She had a habit of sticking her tongue out when she poured things. Years later, in the bathroom pouring soap into a dispenser, I'd caught myself in the mirror making that same face and it had startled me. The thing I feared, becoming my mother, was happening, physically, in spite of myself.

"With man this is impossible, but with God all things are possible," she said.

"Matthew 19:26."

My whole life, my mother had been quizzing me on Bible verses. Sometimes the verses were obscure, so obscure that I'm sure she looked them up moments before asking me, but I prided myself on getting them right. Now, from time to time, a verse will come to me at the oddest moments. I'll be at a gas pump or walking through the halls of a department store and a voice will say, *Oh, taste and see that the Lord is good! Blessed is the one who takes refuge in Him!* And I'll reply, *Psalms 34:8.*

"What is prayer?" my mother asked.

This question stumped me then, stumps me still. I stood there, staring at my mother, waiting for her to give me the answers. Back then, I approached my piety the same way I approached my studies: fastidiously. I spent the summer after my eighth birthday reading my Bible cover to cover, a feat that even my mother admitted she had never done. I wanted, above all else, to be good. And I wanted the path to that goodness to be clear. I suspect that this is why I excelled at math and science, where the rules are laid out step by step, where if you did something exactly the way it was supposed to be done, the result would be exactly as it was expected to be.

"If you are living a godly life, a moral life, then everything you do can be a prayer," my mother said. "Instead of trying to pray all day, live your life as prayer."

I was disappointed by her answer; she could see it in my face. She said, "If you find it difficult to pray, why don't you try writing to God instead? Remember, everything we do is prayer. God will read what you write, and he will answer your writing like prayers. From your pen to God's ear."

Later that night, I would write my first journal entry, and get hooked on how clearheaded I felt, how even just the act of writing to God made me feel like he was there, reading, listening. He was there in everything, so why couldn't prayer be a life lived? I watched my mother continue to pour used oil through the sieve. I watched the sieve catch the hardened, charred bits of food left over from the day's cooking. I watched my mother's tongue peek out from the corner of her lip, a snail slipping out of its shell. Was this pouring prayer?

I slurped the last sip of soup. My mother didn't stir; she didn't turn. I watched the slope of her back rise and fall, rise and fall. Was this prayer?

II

Dear God,
Buzz and I raced to the car after church today. He won,
but he said I'm getting faster. He better watch out. Next
time I'll beat him.

Dear God,
Please bless Buzz and TBM and please let Buzz get a
dog. Amen.

12

In deep brain stimulation, or DBS, the areas of the brain that control movement are stimulated with electrical signals. The surgery is sometimes performed on people with Parkinson's disease, and the goal is to improve their motor functions. I sat in on one of these surgeries during my first year of graduate school, because I was curious about how the procedure worked and whether or not it could be useful in my own research.

The patient that day was a sixty-seven-year-old man who had been diagnosed with Parkinson's six years earlier. He'd had a moderate response to medication, and the neurosurgeon, a colleague who'd spent a sabbatical year in my lab doing research, kept the patient awake while he carefully placed an electrode in the subthalamic nucleus and turned on the impulse generator battery. I watched as the patient's tremor, most pronounced in his left hand, stilled. It was amazing to see, as if the keys to a car had been lost while the engine was still on and thrumming, thrumming. And then, keys found, ignition turned off, thrumming stilled.

"How you doing, Mike?" the doctor asked.

"Pretty good," Mike said, and then, again incredulously, "Hey, I'm doing pretty good."

Seconds later, Mike was crying. Desperate, inconsolable crying, as though Pretty Good Mike had been nothing more than a figment of our imaginations. I got to see firsthand one of the problems with DBS and other methods like it, the fact that magnets and electrical signals cannot differentiate between individual neurons. The surgeon moved the electrode in Mike's brain one-tenth of a centimeter over to try to correct the wave of sadness that had suddenly gripped him. It worked, but what if it hadn't? One-tenth of a centimeter is all that stood between pretty good and unimaginable sorrow. One-tenth of a centimeter in an organ about which we know so very little, despite our constant attempts at understanding.

One of the exciting things about optogenetics is that it allows us to target particular neurons, allowing for a greater amount of specificity than DBS. Part of what interested me about Parkinson's disease studies was my research in optogenetics, but it was also my memories of Mr. Thomas. When I was three, the old man died. I wouldn't find out what Parkinson's was until many years later, in high school, when reading about the disease in my textbook conjured up an image of the man my mother used to work for.

There's a picture of my family at his funeral. We are standing near the casket. Nana looks like he is both bored and angry, the first signs of a look that my family will come to know well in his teenage years. The Chin Chin Man is holding me, taking care not to ruffle my black dress. My mother stands next to him. She doesn't look sad, exactly, but there's something there.

This is one of the only pictures of the four of us together.

I think that I remember that day, but I don't know if I've just turned my mother's stories about it into memories or if I've stared at that picture long enough that my own stories started to emerge.

What I think I remember: The Chin Chin Man and my mother fought that morning. He didn't want to go to the funeral, but she insisted. However horrible Mr. Thomas had been, he was still an elder and therefore deserving of respect. We'd all piled into our red minivan. My mother drove, which was rare when both of my parents were in the car together, and her hands gripped the steering wheel so hard I could see her veins pulsing.

Mr. Thomas's shithead kids were there, all three of them. The two sons, who were around the same age as my father, were crying, but his daughter is the one who stood out the most. She was stone-faced, staring at her father in his casket with an unmistakable look of contempt. She came up to my family as we took our turn viewing the body, and said to my mother, "He was a god-awful man, and I'm not sorry he's dead, but I am sorry you had to put up with him all these years, I guess."

She was the one who took our picture, though why anyone would want to commemorate that moment, I don't know. On the way home, my parents couldn't stop talking about what she'd said. It was a sin to speak ill of the dead like that; worse than a sin, it was a curse. As my parents discussed it, my mother got more and more agitated.

"Pull over," she said, for my father was driving this time. "Pull over."

The Chin Chin Man got onto the shoulder of the highway; he turned toward my mother, waiting.

"We have to pray."

"Can't this wait?" he said.

"Wait for what? For that man to jump out of his grave and come and find us? No, we must pray now."

Nana and I already knew the drill. We bowed our heads, and after a moment or so, the Chin Chin Man did too.

"Father God, we pray for that woman who spoke ill of her father. We pray that you do not punish her for saying those things and that you do not punish us for hearing them. Lord, we ask that you allow Mr. Thomas to be at peace. In Jesus's name, amen."

"In Jesus's name, amen," the most common ending to a prayer. So common, in fact, that when I was a child, I felt that no prayer was complete without those words. I would go to dinner at friends' houses, waiting for their fathers to say grace. If those four words were not spoken, I wouldn't lift my fork. I'd whisper them myself before eating.

We used those four words to end prayers at Nana's soccer games. In Jesus's name, we would ask that God allow our boys to defeat their opponents. Nana was five when he started playing the sport, and by the time I was born, he'd already made a name for himself on the field. He was fast, tall, agile, and he led his team, the Rockets, to state finals three years in a row.

The Chin Chin Man loved soccer. "Football," he said, "is the most graceful sport there is. It is performed with elegance and precision, like a dance." He'd pick me up, as he said this, and dance me around the bleachers behind the old high school where most of Nana's games were held. We went to every single one, me and the Chin Chin Man. My mother, usually working, would come when she could, the requisite cooler of grapes and Capri Suns in hand.

One of Nana's games stood out to me. He was about ten years old then, and he had already come into his growth like a weed in spring. Most of the boys I knew growing up were shorter than us girls until about fifteen or sixteen, when they rounded some invisible corner in the summertime and returned to school the next year twice our size, with voices that crackled like car radios being tuned, searching for the right, the clearest, sound. But not Nana. Nana was always taller than everyone else. To get him onto the soccer team that first year, my mother had had to produce his birth certificate to prove he wasn't older than the rest of the kids.

The day of this particular game had been hot and muggy, one of those quintessential Alabama summer days when the heat feels like a physical presence, a weight. Five minutes into the game and you could already see droplets of sweat flinging from the boys' hair every time they shook their heads. Southerners are, of course, accustomed to this kind of heat, but still it works on you, to carry that weight around. Sometimes, if you're not careful, it sinks you.

One of the boys on the other team slid in a careless effort to score a goal. It didn't work. He lay there on the ground for a second or so, as if stunned.

"Get up off the damn ground," a man shouted. There were only a few bleachers at the soccer field, because no one in Alabama really cared about soccer. It was a child's sport, something to put your kids in until they were ready to play football. The man was on the other side of the bleachers, but that was still quite close.

The game continued on. Nana was a forward, and a

good one. By halftime he had already scored two goals. The other team had one.

When the whistle blew, the boys came to join their coach on the bench, which was only a row in front of us. Nana grabbed a handful of grapes and carefully, methodically, started plucking them off the stem and popping them into his mouth while the coach talked.

On the other side, the man who'd shouted grabbed his son by the root of his sweat-soaked hair. "Don't you let them niggers win. Don't let them score another goal on you, you hear me?"

Everyone heard him. We'd only spent a little over half an hour in the company of this man, and yet it was already clear that he liked to be heard.

I was too young to understand the word the man had used, but I was old enough to understand the change in atmosphere. Nana didn't move, nor did the Chin Chin Man, but still everyone was staring at the three of us, the only black people on the field that day. Was "them niggers" simply a grammatical error, or was the plural supposed to include my father and me? What would we win? What was that man in danger of losing?

Nana's coach cleared his throat and muttered some half-hearted words of encouragement in an attempt to distract everyone. The whistle blew and the boys from both teams rushed back onto the field, but not Nana. He looked up toward the bleachers at the Chin Chin Man, who was sitting there with me on his lap. Nana's look was a question, and I couldn't see my father's face, but I soon knew how he answered.

Nana ran onto the field, and for the rest of that half he was little more than a blur, moving not with the elegance my father associated with soccer, but with pure fury. A fury that would come to define and consume him. He scored goal after goal, even stealing the ball from his own teammates at certain points. No one checked him. The angry parent's rage was written in the bright red of his face, but even he didn't say anything else, though I'm sure his son paid the price for that rage in the car on the way home.

By the end of the game, Nana was spent. His shirt was so drenched in sweat that it clung to his body, so tight you could see the outline of his ribs as he panted and panted.

The Chin Chin Man stood up as the referee blew the closing whistle. He brought his hands to his mouth and let out a loud, long cheer. *"Mmo, Mmo, Mmo. Nana, wayɛ ade."* He picked me up and danced me around the bleachers, our dance not elegant or precise but messy, exuberant, loud. He kept cheering this cheer—Good job, Good job, Good job— until Nana, embarrassed, cracked a smile. The fury fled. Though the occasion for this moment was a somber one, the moment itself was joyful. Getting in the car that day, Nana and I were so happy, glowing in the warmth of our father's pride, delighted by Nana's accomplishments. Looking at us then, two laughing, playful children and their warm, doting father, it would be easy to assume that we'd all but forgotten what that man had yelled. That we'd forgotten we had any cares at all. But the memory lingered, the lesson I have never quite been able to shake: that I would always have something to prove and that nothing but blazing brilliance would be enough to prove it.

13

When Nana started playing soccer, my parents started fighting about food. There was, as was typical of team sports, a rotating snack schedule. Every third week, it was my family's turn to provide the oranges, grapes, and Capri Suns that all the moms called "Rocket Fuel" for the sixteen other boys on the team. At halftime, the Rockets would suck the juice from the orange wedges, leaving the flesh of the fruit behind. "Such waste," my mother said whenever she came to a game to find the sidelines littered with wedges, little land mines of uneaten fruit, of privilege. My family was always attuned to such waste: chicken left on the bone by diners too polite to eat with their hands, crusts cut off of sandwiches for children who took only a single bite and left the rest. I was at an age where I was trying picky eating on for size, pushing all the tomatoes to the edges of my plate in silent refusal. My mother let this go on for two days. On the third day she put a switch on the table and stared me down. She didn't have to say a word. I had gotten the switch only once before, the day I'd whispered "damn" into the silent sanctuary of the

First Assemblies. The word had echoed through that holiest of holies; the echo found my mother; my mother found the switch. Afterward, her hands had trembled so violently, I thought she would never do it again, so when the switch appeared on the table that night, I suspected she was bluffing. I eyed her, eyed the switch, eyed the clock. By midnight, six hours after I'd begun my dinner, with tears in my eyes and terror in my heart, I ate the last of the tomatoes.

Nana had never been a picky eater. To feed his height, he ate everything he could. Nothing was safe. My mother knew, down to the cent, what every scrap of food in our house cost. After every trip to the grocery store, she would sit at the kitchen table and pore over the receipts, highlighting numbers and making lists. If the Chin Chin Man was there, she would shout some figure at him and say, "These children are going to eat us out of home and house."

She and the Chin Chin Man started watering down the orange juice. Like chemists performing a punishing experiment, they would collect the empty gallon jugs, fill them a quarter of the way with orange juice, and flood the rest with water, until the color of the liquid inside could no longer be called orange, until the drink could no longer be called juice. Nana and I stopped drinking it, but Nana didn't stop eating. Cereal, granola bars, fruit, the leftover rice and stew. He ate and ate and ate, and seemed to grow taller with every bite.

My parents started hiding whatever food could be hidden. Open a drawer and look in the very back and you might find an Ovaltine cracker. Nestled between stacks of clothing in their closet were the bananas.

"Here's what we do," Nana said when the Cheerios went missing one day when both of our parents were at work and the two of us were left to our own devices, to our hunger. "We'll split up. You check the low places and I'll check the high places."

We opened every drawer, looked atop every shelf, and collected our booty in the middle of the living room. There were all the things we'd expected to be hidden, and many more things we didn't even know we had. At age four, I was already a fiend for Malta. I liked to suck down the bitter foam from the top of the bottle and drink in large gulps. I would have had one every day, for every meal, if I could have, but I'd been told it was a party drink only, unavailable on regular days. But now there it was, along with all the other forbidden fruits.

Nana and I tore into the food and drinks, giggling. We had only about an hour before the Chin Chin Man returned home, and we knew that all the food would need to go back exactly where we'd found it. Nana ate chocolate and Cheerios, I sipped a Malta slowly, savoring the sweet barley taste, and at dinner that night, seated across the table from each other while our parents passed around bowls of light soup, we would catch each other's eyes and grin, sharing our tasty secret.

"Who did this?" my mother said, pulling an empty granola bar wrapper from the trash. The jig was up. Nana and I had been careful, but clearly not careful enough. Even the trash wasn't safe from our mother's exacting eye.

"Who did this? Where did you find it?"

I burst into tears, giving us away. I was ready to confess to all of our crimes, but the Chin Chin Man chimed in.

"Leave the kids alone. Do you want them to starve? Is that what you want?"

My mother pulled something out of her purse. A bill? A receipt? "We will all starve if we don't start making more money. We can't afford to live like this any longer."

"You were the one who wanted to come here, remember?"

And so it went. Gently, gently, Nana took my hand and led me out of the room. We went to his bedroom and he closed the door. He pulled a coloring book from his bookshelf and grabbed me the crayons. Before long I wasn't listening anymore.

"Good job, Gifty," he said as I showed him my work. "Good job," and outside the sound of chaos swirled on.

14

Toward the middle of my first year of graduate school, Raymond and I started seeing each other more seriously. I couldn't get enough of him. He smelled like vetiver and musk and the jojoba oil he put in his hair. Hours after I'd left him, I would find traces of those scents on my fingers, my neck, my breasts, all those places where we had brushed up against each other, touched. After our first night in bed together, I'd learned that Raymond's father was a preacher at an African Methodist Episcopal church in Philadelphia, and I'd laughed. "So that's why I like you," I said. "You're the son of a preacher man."

"You like me, huh?" he said with that deep voice, that sly grin, as he moved toward me so that we could begin again.

It was my first real relationship, and I was so smitten that I felt like I was a living lily of the valley, a rose of Sharon. *Like an apple tree among the trees of the forest is my beloved among the young men. I delight to sit in his shade, and his fruit is sweet to my taste.* My friend Bethany and I used to read passages from Song of Solomon to each other, crouched beneath the pale blue pews in the empty sanctuary of the First Assemblies of God. It felt illicit to read about all of that flesh—breasts like fawns, necks like ivory towers—in the pages of this holy book. It was an incongruous thrill, to feel that flush of desire well up between my legs as Bethany and I giggled through those verses. *Where is all of this pleasure coming from?* I'd think, my voice getting huskier and huskier with each chapter. Raymond was the closest I'd come to recapturing that feeling, the pleasure as well as the sense of forbiddenness. The fact that he wanted to be with me at all made me feel like I was getting away with some con.

He lived on campus, in an Escondido Village low-rise, and pretty soon I was spending most of my time there. He liked to cook these sumptuous meals, five-hour braises with homemade bread and salads of shaved radishes and fennel. He'd invite all of his colleagues from Modern Thought and Literature, and they would have intense, detailed conversations about things I had never heard of. I'd nod and smile at the mentions of the use of allegory in Ben Okri's *Stars of the New Curfew* or generational trauma among diasporic communities.

Afterward, I would wash the dishes the way my mother taught me, turning off the water as I soaped down the pots and pans, trying to get rid of the elaborate mess Raymond's cooking always left behind.

"You're so quiet," he said, coming up behind me to wrap his arms around my waist, to kiss my neck.

"I haven't read any of the books y'all were talking about."

He turned me around to face him, grinned. I almost never let a "y'all" slip from my lips, and when I did Raymond seemed to savor it like a drop of honey on his tongue. That word used sparingly, thoughtlessly, was the only remaining evidence of my Alabama years. I'd spent a decade carefully burying everything else.

"Talk about your own work, then. Let us know how the mice are doing. I just want them to get to know you a little better. I want everyone to see what I see," he said.

What did he see? I wondered. I'd usually bat him away so that I could finish washing the dishes.

That year was the beginning of my final thesis experiment. I put the mice in a behavioral testing chamber, a clear-walled structure with a lever and a metal tube. I trained the mice to seek reward. When they pressed the lever, Ensure would flood into the tube. Pretty soon they were pressing the lever as often as possible, drinking up their reward with abandon. Once they'd gotten the hang of this, I changed the conditions. When the mice pressed the lever, sometimes they got Ensure, but sometimes they got a mild foot-shock instead.

The foot-shock was randomized, so there was no pattern for them to figure out. The mice just had to decide if they wanted to keep pressing the lever, keep risking that shock in the pursuit of pleasure. Some of the mice stopped pressing the lever right away. After a shock or two, they did the mouse equivalent of throwing up their hands and never went near the lever again. Some of the mice stopped, but it took time. They liked the Ensure enough to keep holding out hope that the shocks would stop. When they realized they wouldn't, those mice, reluctantly, gave up. Then there was the final group of mice, the ones who never stopped. Day after day, shock after shock, they pressed the lever.

. . .

My parents started fighting every day. They fought about money, how there was never enough. They fought about time, about displays of affection, about the minivan, about the height of the grass in the lawn, about Scripture. *But at the beginning of creation God made them male and female. For this reason a man will leave his father and mother and be united to his wife, and the two will become one flesh. So they are no longer two, but one flesh. Therefore what God has joined together, let no one separate.*

The Chin Chin Man hadn't just left his father and his mother; he'd left his country as well, and he wouldn't let my mother forget it.

"In my country, neighbors will greet you instead of turning their heads away like they don't know you."

"In my country, you can eat food fresh from the ground. Corn, hard on its cob, not soft like the spirits of these people."

"In my country, there is no word for half-sibling, step-sibling, aunt, or uncle. There is only sister, brother, mother, father. We are not divided."

"In my country, people may not have money, but they have happiness in abundance. In abundance. No one in America is enjoying."

These mini-lectures on Ghana were delivered to the three of us with increasing frequency. My mother would gently remind my father that Ghana was her country too, our country. She nodded and agreed. America *is* a difficult place, but look at what we've been able to build here. Sometimes Nana would come into my room and pretend to be him. "In my country, we do not eat the red M&M's," he'd say, throwing the red M&M's at me.

It was hard for Nana and me to see America the way

our father saw it. Nana couldn't remember Ghana, and I had never been. Southeast Huntsville, northern Alabama, was all we knew, the physical location of our entire conscious lives. Were there places in the world where neighbors would have greeted us instead of turning away? Places where my classmates wouldn't have made fun of my name—called me charcoal, called me monkey, called me worse? I couldn't imagine it. I couldn't let myself imagine it, because if I did, if I saw it—that other world—I would have wanted to go.

It should have been obvious to us. We should have seen it coming, but we didn't see what we didn't want to see.

"I'm going home to visit my brother," the Chin Chin Man said, and then he never came back.

In those first few weeks, he called every once in a while. "I wish you could see how brilliant the sun is here, Nana. Do you remember? Do you remember it?" Nana ran home from school every Tuesday in order to make their 3:30 telephone calls.

"When are you coming back?" Nana asked.

"Soon, soon, soon."

If my mother knew that soon, soon, soon was a lie, she didn't let on. I suppose if it was a lie, it was one she wanted to believe. She spent most of her mornings on the phone with him, speaking in hushed tones as I prattled on to my favorite doll. I was four, oblivious to the lurch my father had left us in and to the deep pain my mother must have been feeling.

If I've thought of my mother as callous, and many times I have, then it is important to remind myself what a callus is: the hardened tissue that forms over a wound. And what a wound my father leaving was. On those phone calls with the

Chin Chin Man, my mother was always so tender, drawing from a wellspring of patience that I never would have had if I were in her shoes. To think of the situation now still makes me furious. That this man, my father, went back to Ghana in such a cowardly way, leaving his two children and wife alone to navigate a difficult country, a punishing state. That he let us, let her, believe that he might return.

My mother never spoke an ill word about him. Not once. Even after soon, soon, soon turned into maybe, turned into never.

"I hate him," Nana said years later, after the Chin Chin Man had canceled yet another visit.

"You don't," my mother said. "He hasn't come back because he is ashamed, but it doesn't mean he doesn't care about you. And how could you hate him when he cares so much? He cares about you, he cares about me and Gifty. He cares about Ghana. How could you hate a man like that?"

The mice who can't stop pushing the lever, even after being shocked dozens of times, are, neurologically, the ones who are most interesting to me. By the time my mother came to stay with me in California, my team and I were in the process of identifying which neurons were firing or not firing whenever the mice decided to press the lever despite knowing the risks. We were trying to use blue light to get the mice to stop pressing the lever, to "turn on," so to speak, the neurons that weren't functioning properly in warning those mice away from risk.

I talked about the lever experiment at the next dinner party that Raymond threw. He'd made cassoulet, rich with pork and duck and lamb, glistening with oil and so delicious and sinful that everyone in the room let out audible sighs after their first bites.

"So it's a question of restraint," one colleague, Tanya, said. "Like how I can't restrain myself from eating more of this cassoulet, even though I know my waistline isn't going to be happy about it."

Everyone laughed as Tanya rubbed her stomach like Winnie-the-Pooh upon finding a pot of honey.

"Well, yes," I said. "But it's a bit more complicated than that. Like even the idea of a 'you' that can restrain 'yourself' doesn't quite get at it. The brain chemistry of these mice has changed to the point where they aren't really in control of what they can or can't control. They aren't 'themselves.'"

They all nodded vigorously, as though I'd said something extremely profound, and then one of them mentioned King Lear. *We are not ourselves when nature, being oppressed, commands the mind to suffer with the body.* I hadn't read Shakespeare since high school, but I nodded along with them, pretending for Raymond's sake to be interested in the conversation. After they left that night, all those dishes in their wake, I could tell that he was happy to see me finally opening up to his friends. I wanted to be happy too, but I felt like I was lying somehow. Whenever I listened to his friends speak about issues like prison reform, climate change, the opioid epidemic, in the simultaneously intelligent but utterly vacuous way of people who think it's important simply to weigh in, to have an opinion, I would bristle. I would think, *What is the point of all this talk? What problems do we solve by identifying problems, circling them?*

I said my goodbyes and then I rushed home and threw up and I never could eat that dish again.

15

When I was still in elementary school, my children's church pastor told us that sin was defined as anything you think, say, or do that goes against God. She pulled out these two puppets that looked like little monsters and had them demonstrate sin. The purple monster would hit the green monster, and our pastor would say, "Hey, hitting is a sin." The green monster would wait until the purple monster's back was turned and then steal a Hershey's Kiss from the purple monster's hand. Everyone thought this move was hilarious, so hilarious that our pastor had to remind us that it was sinful to steal.

I was a good, pious child, committed to not sinning, and the definition that our pastor gave confounded me. It was easy enough to not do anything wrong or say anything wrong. But to not think sinfully? To not think about lying or stealing or hitting your brother when he comes into your room intent on torturing you, was that even possible? Do we have control over our thoughts?

When I was a child this was a religious question, a question of whether it was possible to live a sinless life, but it is also, of course, a neuroscientific question. That day, when the children's church pastor used her puppets to teach us about sin, I realized, with no small amount of embarrassment, that my secret goal of becoming as blameless as Jesus was in fact impossible, and perhaps even blasphemous. My pray-without-ceasing experiment had all but proven the impossibility of controlling my thoughts. I could control one layer, the most readily available layer, but there was always a sublayer lurking. That sublayer was truer, more immediate, more essential, than anything else. It spoke softly but constantly, and the things it said were the very things that allowed me to live and to be. Now I understand that we have a subconscious life, vibrant and vital, that acts in spite of "ourselves," our conscious selves.

In the book of Matthew, Jesus says, *"You shall love the Lord your God with all your heart and with all your soul and with all your mind."* Here is a separation. Your heart, the part of you that feels. Your mind, the part of you that thinks. Your soul, the part of you that is. I almost never hear neuroscientists speak about the soul. Because of our work, we are often given to thinking about the part of humans that is the vital, inexplicable essence of ourselves, as the workings of our brains—mysterious, elegant, essential. Everything we don't understand about what makes a person a person can be uncovered once we understand this organ. There is no separation. Our brains are our hearts that feel and our minds that think and our souls that are. But when I was a child I called this essence a soul and I believed in its supremacy over the mind and the heart, its immutability and connection to Christ himself.

The week before Buddy the dog died, his golden hair

started falling out in tufts. You'd pet him and come away with fistfuls of that luster. It was clear that he was coming to his end, but before he did, I went over to Ashley's house and prayed for him. "Dear God, bless this dog and let his soul be at rest," I said, and Ashley and I knelt down next to Buddy and cried into his soft body, and I had a vision of Buddy in the vet's office, his soul rising out of that golden shell and floating up toward Heaven. It comforted me then to believe in a soul, a separate self, to picture Buddy's soul alive and well, even if he wasn't.

At times, my life now feels so at odds with the religious teachings of my childhood that I wonder what the little girl I once was would think of the woman I've become—a neuroscientist who has at times given herself over to equating the essence that psychologists call the mind, that Christians call the soul, with the workings of the brain. I have indeed given that organ a kind of supremacy, believing and hoping that all of the answers to all of the questions that I have can and must be contained therein. But the truth is I haven't much changed. I still have so many of the same questions, like "Do we have control over our thoughts?," but I am looking for a different way to answer them. I am looking for new names for old feelings. My soul is still my soul, even if I rarely call it that.

I have only a few memories of the Chin Chin Man from before he left, and even those are memories that might have been created from my mother's stories. Nana was ten and he remembered everything about our father. I would ask him question after question, about his hair, the color of his eyes, the size of his arms, his height, his smell. Everything. In the beginning Nana would answer patiently, always ending with "You'll see for yourself soon."

In that first year, when we all thought the Chin Chin Man was coming back, we did everything we could to keep our lives the same, to make our home a place our patriarch would recognize when he returned. My mother, who was always the disciplinarian except in extreme cases, would sometimes find herself in those extreme cases shouting, "Just wait until your father gets home!" Those words still sparked fear in us, were still enough to convince us to behave.

Nana started playing even more soccer. He tried out for the advanced league and made the team. They practiced every day and had games that took them to Atlanta, Montgomery, Nashville. It was a huge strain on my mother, as all of the parents were expected to pay for the equipment and uniforms and travel expenses. Worse still, they were expected to chaperone at least one of the away games.

The day of the Nashville game, she had no one to watch me. She'd already taken the day off work. At that point she was a home health aide for two families, the Reynoldses and the Palmers, and though neither family was as abusive as Mr. Thomas, her work doubled but her pay didn't keep pace. My father's job had kept more regular hours, and so he was the one who acted as my caretaker while my mother went from the Reynoldses to the Palmers and back again. When he left, my mother resorted to paying an old Bajan woman whose daughter she knew from the home health company. I loved this old woman, whose name I have since forgotten. She smelled like fresh ginger and hibiscus, and for years any whiff of those things would conjure up an image of her. I loved to sit in her lap and snuggle into the pillow of her fat stomach and feel it expand as she breathed. She kept ginger candies on her at all times, and she fell asleep so often that it was easy enough for me to rifle through her purse and steal one. If she woke up and caught me, she'd spank me or she'd shrug and laugh and I'd laugh too. It was our little game, and I usually won. But the day of the Nashville game, she'd gone back to Barbados to attend her friend's funeral.

I rode the team bus to Nashville on my mother's lap. She had packed a cooler of oranges and grapes and Capri Suns and mini water bottles. The night before, she'd washed Nana's jersey by hand because a grass stain hadn't come out in the washing machine. She didn't trust washing machines. She didn't trust dishwashers either. "When you want something done right, do it," she would often say.

Nana's team was called the Tornados. There was one other black kid on the team and two Koreans, so Nana didn't have to worry as much about bearing the full brunt of taunts from angry, racist parents. He was still the best kid on the team, still the reason so many parents got red cards, but it was a comfort to him to not feel so alone.

On the bus ride that day, I wouldn't sit still. This was the summer before I started kindergarten, nearly a year after the Chin Chin Man left, and I could feel the end of my freedom encroaching. I was wilder than usual. On more than one occasion I'd been brought home by a neighbor after getting into some mischief, and my mother had long since stopped telling me to wait until my father got home. I ran up and down the aisle of the bus. I tugged the hair of the child in front of me until he yelped. I flailed like a fish in my mother's arms until she released me. The drive from Huntsville to Nashville only takes about two hours, and I was determined to make every passenger feel every minute of it.

My mother kept apologizing to the other chaperones and sending me a look that I knew well. It was her *I cannot beat you in front of all these white people, but just you wait* look. I didn't care. If a beating was inevitable, why stop? I spent the last fifteen minutes of the bus ride sing-shouting "The Wheels on the Bus," while the soccer team plugged their ears and groaned. Nana ignored me. By that point he was an expert at that.

Two referees in impractical cowboy hats waited for us as we pulled into the parking lot of the soccer fields.

The boys and their parents rushed off the bus, no doubt eager to get away from me, but I had already stopped my singing and returned to my calmer, more peaceful self. Nana was seated next to the emergency exit window, his head leaned against the red bar in a way that looked uncomfortable.

"Come on, Nana," some of the kids said as they made their way out, but Nana didn't get up from the seat. He lightly banged his head against that red bar, over and over and over, until everyone left, and it was, finally, just the three of us. My mother, Nana, and me.

My mother squeezed into the seat beside Nana and pulled me up onto her lap. She took his chin in her hand and turned him to face her. "Nana, what's bothering you?" she said in Twi.

Nana had tears in the corners of his eyes that were threatening to spill, and he was making a face that I've only ever seen in young boys, a face that is the façade of a man, hiding a boy who has had to grow up far too fast. I have seen that faux tough look on boys as they pushed shopping carts, walked siblings to school, bought cigarettes for their parents who waited in their cars. It breaks my heart now, to see that face, to recognize the lie of masculinity sitting atop the shoulders of a young child.

Nana blinked his tears back. He sat up a little straighter, gently lifted our mother's hand from his face, and returned it to her lap. "I don't want to play soccer anymore," he said.

Just then one of the referees came onto the bus. He saw the three of us squeezed into those small seats and gave us a sheepish grin, lifting that cowboy hat off his head and placing it onto his heart, as though my family was the national anthem, the yellow school bus a ballpark. "Ma'am, we're 'bout ready to get this game started and there are a bunch of boys out there saying their star player's still on this bus."

My mother didn't even turn to look at the referee. She kept her eyes trained on Nana. We all remained perfectly quiet and still, and finally the man took the hint, put his cowboy hat back on, and got off the bus.

"You love soccer," my mother said once we heard the sound of the referee's cleats crunching the gravel of the lot.

"No, I don't."

"Nana," she said sharply, and then she stopped and exhaled for so long I wondered where she had been keeping all of that air. She could have told Nana that she'd lost a day's paycheck to chaperone this trip, that she was already on thin ice with the Reynoldses for missing work two weeks before when I wouldn't stop vomiting and had to be taken to the emergency room. She could have told him how that emergency room bill was higher than she'd expected, even though we had insurance, that the night she'd opened that envelope she sat there at our dining room table crying into her scrubs so that we wouldn't be able to hear her. She could have told him that she had already had to take on some extra work cleaning houses to afford the fees for the advanced soccer league, and that those fees were nonrefundable and she couldn't get her time back either. All that time she'd spent working to afford a trip on a bus with a loud daughter and son who'd somehow realized in the two-hour-long bus ride that his father wasn't coming back.

"We'll find another way home," she said. "We don't have to stay here for one more second, Nana, okay? You don't have to play if you don't want to."

We walked to the Greyhound station, our mother holding our hands the entire time. We took that bus home, and I don't think Nana made a single noise. I don't think I did either. I could feel that something had changed among the three of us and I was trying to learn what my role in this new configuration of my family might be. That day was the end of my naughtiness, the beginning of my good years. If our mother was angry or upset at us, me for being a terror, Nana for changing his mind, she didn't let on. She wrapped us up in her arms during that long ride home, her face inscrutable. When we got home, she put all of Nana's soccer gear into a box, sealed the box, and dumped it into the nether regions of our garage, never to be seen again.

16

I asked Katherine to lunch at the little Thai restaurant in the basement of the psychology building. I ordered from the brusque woman, who could sometimes make eating there feel like a punishment despite how good the food was, and wandered out to sit in the courtyard while I waited for Katherine to arrive. It was a sunny, beautiful day. The kind of day I often took for granted living in a place where the beauty of the school, of nature, seemed to come so effortlessly. This was in stark contrast to my time on the East Coast, where beauty was hard won, where every brilliant day had to be savored, the memories of them stored like acorns buried underground by industrious squirrels, just to get you through those punishing winters. That first winter in Massachusetts, with snow piled up to my knees, I'd missed Alabama with an intensity I hadn't thought possible. I craved heat and light the way other people craved coffee and cigarettes. Sick and sluggish, I got a SAD lamp from mental health services and sat staring at it for hours, hoping it would fool me into believing I was back in the place where

I assume my ancestors first instilled this need for warmth—
in Ghana on a beach just above the equator.

Katherine was half an hour late. I started eating and
watched two undergrads argue in front of the bike stand
across the way. It was clear they were a couple. One of the
women circled her U-lock around her wrist while the other
woman shouted, "I have a PSET due at three, Tiffany. You
know that." Tiffany didn't seem to know, or maybe she just
didn't care. She was on her bike, zooming off within seconds, and the other woman just stood there, stunned. She
looked around, trying to see if the fight had had any wit-
nesses. I should have looked away, given her some privacy in
her embarrassment, but I didn't. We made eye contact, and
her face grew so red I could almost feel the heat coming off
of it. I smiled at her, but that only seemed to make her feel
worse. I remembered what it was like to be that age, so aware
of yourself and the theater of your private little shames. "I
have my shit too," I wanted to say. "I have worse shit than a
PSET due at three, worse shit than Tiffany, even." She narrowed her eyes at me as though she'd heard my thoughts,
and then she stormed off.

Katherine finally arrived. "Sorry, sorry," she said, slipping into the seat across from me. "The Caltrain just decided
to stop running for some reason."

Even in that haggard, breathless state, she looked beautiful. Long black hair piled messily on the top of her head,
those braces-straight teeth—a telltale sign of someone
who'd grown up with money and attention. They gleamed
brilliant every time she smiled. I glanced at her stomach.
Nothing. "That's okay," I said, and then I clammed up. I
had invited Katherine on the pretense that I wanted to talk
about our work. There were so few women in our field, and

though it was important to have role models and mentors, I had done very little to connect with the other women in my department. I was the typical graduate student, clamoring for the attentions of the hotshot male scientists, the ones who had discovered this thing, won that award. I wanted my name spoken in the same breath as theirs, my work written about in the same journals. Katherine, brilliant though she was, liked to wear a sweatshirt with the word STEMINIST splashed across the front. Every year, she manned a booth at the undergraduate career fair for women considering a career in science. When she'd asked me, my first week at Stanford, if I wanted to join the Women in STEM group she led, I'd said no without a second thought. I'd had a professor in college laugh when I asked if he'd be my advisor the year I declared my major. True, I had never taken a class with him, and true, he was the preeminent microbiologist on campus, but still, in that split second of laughter before he caught himself and said, "Why sure, dear," I'd wanted nothing more than to turn into dust, to sink into the ground and disappear forever. I didn't want to be thought of as a woman in science, a black woman in science. I wanted to be thought of as a scientist, full stop, and it mystified me that Katherine, whose work was published in the best journals, was content to draw attention to the fact of her womanhood. Even this question of a baby, of the little ovulation "o's" her husband had snuck into his calendar just at the moment when Katherine's career was set to take off, was itself a reminder of the millstone of womanhood we wore around our necks.

I didn't want to wear mine, and I wasn't really interested in talking to Katherine about the research that she was doing. What I wanted to talk about was my mother, her sleepy breath hum and weight loss, her vacant eyes, her slop-

ing back. My dinnertime visits had done nothing to draw
her out. After three days, I'd given up that tack and tried a
different one. I called Pastor John and held the phone to my
mother's ear while he prayed.

"Father God, we ask that you rouse this woman from
her slumber," he said. "Jesus, we pray that you lift her spirits. Remind her that all of her crosses belong to you."

He kept going like this for some time, and my hand
started to shake as I held the phone. I might as well have
been casting spells over her for all the good this was doing.
After he had finished, I hung up and slumped down onto
the edge of the bed, sunk my head into my hands. I wanted
to cry but I couldn't. Behind me, my mother's breath continued its hum. The sound reminded me of the video of the
black mamba I'd watched when I was a child, even though
that snake hadn't made a sound. The hum was the only lively
thing about my mother, and so I'd come to be grateful for it,
whatever it was.

What was the ethical thing to do? Was it right of me
to let her stay in that bed courting death, practicing for it,
even? I turned this question over in my head every day, playing out the possible scenarios, the things I could do, should
do. I knew the statutes for involuntary commitment in
California, and my mother didn't meet those burdens. She
wasn't threatening to hurt herself or anyone else. She wasn't
hearing voices or having visions. She was eating, though
only sporadically and only when she knew I wouldn't be
home to see her do it. It had only been a week, but the days
dragged on, weighed on me. She told me she was "tired"
and that she needed "rest." I'd heard that before, but every
time I thought of getting someone to intervene I thought of

the last time and my courage failed me. The last time, when she'd gotten out of the hospital after her commitment, she'd looked at me and said, "Never again," and I knew what she meant.

I should have said all of this to Katherine. She was a great doctor, an empathetic person, but when I tried to broach the topic of my mother, my words turned to ashes in my mouth.

"Are you all right, Gifty?" Katherine asked.

She was giving me what must have been her psychiatrist's stare, intense and questioning. I couldn't hold her gaze.

"Yeah, I'm just a little stressed. I want to get this paper submitted before the end of the quarter, but I can't seem to make myself work on it these days," I said. I stared out at the palm trees as a quick wind blew through their branches, causing the fronds to sway.

Katherine nodded at me, but her gaze didn't change. "Okay," she said softly. "I hope you're taking good care of yourself."

I nodded, but I didn't even know what it would mean to take good care of myself, what that would look like. The only thing I was managing to take care of was my mice, and even they had had their bloody scuffle just weeks before. Me, my mother, my mice—we were all a little scuffed up, but trying in whatever ways we knew how. I thought about the winter day my freshman year at Harvard when I'd finally walked into counseling and mental health services to ask for a SAD lamp.

"I think it's the weather. I just feel kind of sad. Not all the time," I said to the receptionist, though she had only asked for my name. When she handed me the lamp, she asked if I wanted to start seeing a counselor. "Freshman year

can be tough," she said. "You're far from home, your classes
are more rigorous than they were in high school. It can be
helpful to talk to someone."

I hugged the lamp to my chest and shook my head. The
rigor, the toughness, I'd wanted those things.

17

My sophomore year at Harvard was particularly brutal. The magic of my SAD lamp had worn off and I spent much of that winter trudging to class through snow that came up to my waist. I'd taught my mother how to make video calls on her computer, and so sometimes I would call her, thinking I would tell her how unhappy I was, but then her face would greet me on the screen, confused and annoyed by the technology, and I'd lose my resolve, not wanting to add my burdens to her own.

To make matters worse, I was barely hanging on in my Integrated Science course. I did fine on the homework and tests, but the course had a project lab component that required working in small groups, and every day, as I sat mutely in class, I watched my participation points plummet.

"The class would really benefit from hearing your thoughts," my professor would sometimes write on the top of my assignments. Later, in my dorm room, I would rehearse the kinds of things I might say, telling my reflection about all of my project ideas, but then class time would roll around, and my professor's eyes would fall on me and I would clam up. My small group started ignoring me. Some-times, when the class split up to work on our projects, my group would form a circle with me on the outside. I'd shoulder my way in or, more often than not, wait for someone to notice.

Most of the semester passed this way. Yao, who had established himself as the leader of our small group, would order everyone around, doling out our assignments for the night and shutting down any of the ideas proposed by women. He was tyrannical, misogynistic, but the rest of the group—Molly, Zach, Anne, and Ernest—were easygoing and funny. I enjoyed being around them, even though they merely tolerated me.

Zach was the clown. At five foot two, he was shorter than both Molly and me, but he used his humor and his intelligence to fill up whatever room he was in. Most days he spent half of our group time trying out little bits on us as though we were judges on a stand-up comedy reality show. It made it hard for us to know when he was being genuine or when he was setting up an elaborate joke, and so, though he was funny, everyone approached anything he said with some amount of discomfort.

"I passed by these dudes in the quad who were handing out little orange Bibles," Zach said one day.

"They're so pushy," Molly said. "They practically shoved one into my pocket." Molly was both smart and striking, but she was often dismissed because her voice, with its lilting, questioning sound, made people assume they could ignore anything she had to say.

"If they touched you, you could scream sexual harass-ment," Ernest said. "I mean, it wouldn't be the first time someone used Christianity as a cover-up for sexual assault. This is Boston, after all."

"Oof, harsh, dude," Yao said. He turned to Zach. "Did you take the Bible?"

"Yeah, I took it and then I climbed onto John Harvard's lap and just started waving it around shouting 'GOD DOESN'T EXIST! GOD DOESN'T EXIST!'"

"How do you know God doesn't exist?" I said, interrupting their laughter.

They all turned to face me. *The mute speaks?* their faces said.

"Um, you're not serious, are you?" Anne said. She was the smartest one in our group, though Yao would never admit it. Before this, I'd sometimes catch her watching me, waiting to see if my silence harbored brilliance, but now she looked at me as though I had finally confirmed her suspicions that I was a complete idiot, a mistake of the admissions process.

I liked Anne, the way she would sit back and listen to the rest of the group fumble before swooping in at the last second with the right answer, the most clever idea, leaving Yao grumbling and huffy. I was embarrassed to have earned her ire, but also, I couldn't help myself. I doubled down. "I just don't think it's right to make fun of other people's beliefs," I said.

"I'm sorry, but believing in God isn't just ridiculous, it's fucking dangerous too," Anne said. "Religion has been used to justify everything from war to anti-LGBT legislation. We aren't talking about some harmless thing here."

"It doesn't have to be that way. Belief can be powerful and intimate and transformative."

Anne shook her head. "Religion is the opiate of the masses," she said, and I shot her a killing look.

"Opioids are the opiates of the masses," I said. I knew what I sounded like. Wild, crazed.

Anne looked at me as though I were a lizard molting before her very eyes, as though she was finally seeing me, some spark of life. She didn't press.

Yao cleared his throat and moved the group on to a safer topic, but I had already exposed myself. A backwoods bama, a Bible thumper. I thought of the religious student groups on campus that spent some of their days hanging up flyers in the dorms' common rooms, inviting people to worship. Those flyers had to compete with the hundreds of other flyers, for dance marathons, Greek parties, spoken-word shows. They didn't stand a chance. And, though I hadn't worked out how I felt about the Christianity of my childhood, I did know how I felt about my mother. Her devotion, her faith, they moved me. I was protective of her right to find comfort in whatever ways she saw fit. Didn't she deserve at least that much? We have to get through this life somehow.

My outburst broke the dam, and after that day I started speaking up more in class. My grade recovered, though my small group didn't bother hiding their disdain for me. I don't think any of my ideas were ever taken seriously until someone else repackaged them as their own. After all, what could a Jesus freak know about science?

18

I have been saved and baptized in the Spirit, but I have never been baptized in water. Nana was baptized in water as a baby at my parents' church in Ghana, where they have a more capacious attitude toward the rules and conventions of Protestantism than most American Pentecostal churches have. There was a kind of "more is more" attitude toward religion at my mother's home church. Bring on the water, the Spirit, the fire. Bring on the speaking in tongues, the signs and wonders. Bring on the witch doctor, too, if he cares to help. My mother never saw any conflict between believing in mystics and believing in God. She took stories about vipers, angels, tornadoes come to destroy the Earth literally, not metaphorically. She buried our umbilical cords on the beach of her mother's sea town like all the mothers before her, and then she took her firstborn to be blessed. More is more. More blessing, more protection.

When she had me in Alabama, she learned that many Pentecostals here do not believe in baptizing babies. The denomination is characterized by the belief in one's ability to have a personal relationship with Christ. To choose the

Lord, to choose salvation. A baby could not choose to accept
Jesus Christ as her Lord and Savior, so while Pastor John
would be happy to say a prayer for me, he wouldn't baptize
me until I chose it myself. My mother was disappointed by
this. "Americans don't believe in God the way we do," she
would often say. She meant it as an insult, but still, she liked
Pastor John, and she followed his teachings.

When my friend Ashley's little brother was born, my
family was invited to his christening. Ashley stood onstage
in a white dress and white shoes with crystal kitten heels. I
thought she looked like an angel. Colin cried the entire time,
his face red, his mouth sputtering. He didn't seem to like
it very much, but his entire family was radiating happiness.
Everyone in the room could feel it, and I wanted it.

"Can I be baptized?" I asked my mother.

"Not until you're saved," she said.

I didn't know what it meant to be saved, not in the context of religion. Back then, when people at church talked
about salvation, I took the word literally. I imagined that I
needed to be near death in order for salvation to take hold.
I needed to have Jesus rescue me from a burning building
or pull me back from the edge of a cliff. I thought of saved
Christians as a group of people who had almost died; the
rest of us were waiting for that near-death experience to
come so that God could reveal himself. I suppose I'm still
waiting for God to reveal himself. Sometimes, the children's
church pastor would say, "You have to ask Jesus to come
into your heart," and I would say those words, "Jesus, please
come into my heart," and then I would spend the rest of the
service wondering how I would ever know if he'd accepted
my invitation. I'd press my hand to my chest, listen and feel
for its thumping rhythm. Was he there in my heartbeat?

Baptism seemed easier, clearer somehow than almost dying or heart-listening, and after Colin's baptism I became obsessed with the idea that water was the best path to knowing that God had taken root. At bath time, I would wait for my mother to turn her back and then I would submerge myself in the water. When I lifted myself up, my hair would be wet, despite the shower cap, and my mother would curse under her breath.

Black girl sin number one: getting your hair wet when it wasn't wash day.

"I don't have time for this, Gifty," my mother would say as she brushed out my curls, braided my hair. After my third surreptitious DIY baptism, I got a spanking so bad I couldn't sit without pain for the rest of that week. That put an end to that.

When the wounded mouse finally died, I held his little body. I rubbed the top of his head, and I thought of it as a blessing, a baptism. Whenever I fed the mice or weighed them for the lever-press task, I always thought of Jesus in the upper room, washing his disciples' feet. This moment of servitude, of being quite literally brought low, always reminded me that I needed these mice just as much as they needed me. More. What would I know about the brain without them? How could I perform my work, find answers to my questions? The collaboration that the mice and I have going in this lab is, if not holy, then at least sacrosanct. I have never, will never, tell anyone that I sometimes think this way, because I'm aware that the Christians in my life would find it blasphemous and the scientists would find it embarrassing, but the more I do this work the more I believe in a kind of holiness in our connection to everything on Earth. Holy is the mouse. Holy is the grain the mouse eats. Holy is the seed. Holy are we.

I started playing music around the apartment, songs that I knew my mother liked. I wasn't really optimistic that music would get her out of bed, but I hoped that it would, at the very least, soothe something inside of her. I played schmaltzy pop-country songs like "I Hope You Dance." I played boring hymnals sung by tabernacle choirs. I played every song on Daddy Lumba's roster, imagining that by the end of "Enko Den" she would be up, boogying around the house like she used to when I was a child.

I also started cleaning the apartment more, because I figured she probably liked the familiar scent of bleach, the way it clung to your nose hairs hours after you'd used it. I'd spray the toxic all-purpose cleaner onto the windowsill in the bedroom and watch the mist of it float off and away. Some of those particles probably reached her in the bed.

"Gifty," she said one day, after I'd wiped the window to gleaming. "Would you get me some water?"

Tears sprung to my eyes as I said, "Yes, of course," with so much glee you'd have thought she was asking me to accept a Nobel Prize. I brought a glass of water back to her and watched her sit up to drink it. She looked tired, which seemed improbable to me given that she'd done nothing but rest since she got here. I never thought of her as old, but in a little more than a year she would be seventy, and all of those years were beginning to write themselves onto her sunken cheeks, her hands, hardened from labor.

I watched her drink the water slowly, so slowly, and

then I took the glass from her after she'd finished. "More?" I asked.

She shook her head and started to sink back down under the covers and my heart sank with her. Once the duvet was completely draped over her, covering her body, nearly to her chin, she looked at me and said, "You need to do something about your hair."

I stifled my laughter and brought my hands up to my dreadlocks, wrapped them around my fingers. My mother didn't speak to me for a month the summer I came home with the beginnings of locks. "People will think you were raised in a dirty home," she argued before falling silent for nearly the entire length of my stay, and now those locks had her speaking again, if only to chastise me. Holy is the black woman's hair.

19

In college I took a poetry class on Gerard Manley Hopkins to satisfy a humanities requirement. Most of the other science majors I knew took intro to creative writing courses to fulfill the requirement. "It's an easy A," one friend said. "You just, like, write down your feelings and shit and then the whole class talks about it. Literally everyone gets an A." The idea of an entire classroom full of my peers talking about the feelings I'd somehow cobbled into a story terrified me. I decided to take my chances with Hopkins.

My professor, an incredibly tall woman with a lion's mane of golden curls, walked into the classroom ten minutes late every Tuesday and Thursday. "All right, then, where were we?" she'd say, as if we'd already been talking about the poems without her and she wanted us to catch her up. No one ever responded, and she'd usually glare at us with her piercing green eyes until someone surrendered and stammered out something nonsensical.

"Hopkins is all about a delight in language," she said one day. "I mean, listen to this: 'Cuckoo-echoing, bell-swarmed, lark-charmed, rook-racked, river-rounded.' He's taking so much pleasure out of the way these words fit together, out of the sound of them, and we, the readers, get equal pleasure reading it."

She looked ecstatic and pained as she said this, like she was halfway to orgasm. I wasn't getting equal pleasure from reading it. I wasn't even getting a quarter of the pleasure my professor seemed to be getting simply from talking about it. I was intimidated by her and I hated the poetry, but I felt a strange sense of kinship with Hopkins every time I read about his personal life, his difficulty reconciling his religion with his desires and thoughts, his repressed sexuality. I enjoyed reading his letters and, inspired to some romantic ideal of the nineteenth century, tried writing letters of my own to my mother. Letters in which I hoped to tell her about my complicated feelings about God. "Dear Ma," they started, "I've been thinking a lot about whether or not believing in God is compatible with believing in science." Or, "Dear Ma, I haven't forgotten the joy I felt the day you walked me down to the altar and the whole congregation stretched out their hands, and I really, truly felt the presence of God." I wrote four such letters, all of which could have been a different petal on the flower of my belief. "I believe in God, I do not believe in God." Neither of these sentiments felt true to what I actually felt. I threw the letters away, and I gratefully accepted my B– in the course.

Nana had always been conflicted about God. He hated the youth pastor at First Assemblies, a man in his early twenties who had just finished Masters Commission, a kind of training camp for future spiritual leaders, and who insisted that everyone call him P.T. instead of Pastor Tom.

P.T. was interested in relating to the youth on their level, which for his relationship with Nana meant that he was constantly making up slang terms that he assumed black teenagers were using. "Whattup, broseph?" was a favorite greeting of his. Nana could hardly even look at him without rolling his eyes. Our mother chided him for being disrespectful, but we could tell that even she thought that P.T. was kind of an idiot.

Nana was thirteen when he graduated from children's church and moved on to youth group services. I missed him during Sunday school when the children's church pastor pulled out her puppets and Nana reluctantly went across the hall to listen to P.T.'s teachings. I started to get a little restless in those services, squirming around in my seat and asking to go to the bathroom every five minutes, until finally the pastors decided it would be all right for me to go to Sunday school with Nana as long as I returned to children's church during regular service hours. In those early-morning classes, Nana sat about as far away from me as possible, but I didn't mind. I liked being in the same room as him, and I liked feeling older, wiser than the other children my age who were stuck listening to the children's church pastor's little sketches, which, by that time, had grown tiresome. I was, even then, desperate to prove my competence, my superiority, so being the youngest in the youth group felt like a kind of arrival, a demonstration of my goodness.

Like the children's church pastor, P.T. talked a lot about sin, but he wasn't partial to puppets. He paid little attention to me and interpreted Scripture as he saw fit.

He said, "If girls only knew what boys think about when they wear those low-cut things and those high-cut things, they wouldn't wear them anymore."

He said, "There are a lot of people out there who've never heard the Gospel, and they're just busy walking in sin until we spread the good news."

He said, "God glories in our commitment to him. Remember, he is our bridegroom and we are his bride. We must be faithful to none other."

P.T. was forever smirking and drumming his fingers on the lip of the table as he talked. He was the kind of youth pastor who wanted to make God hip in a way that almost felt exclusionary. His wasn't the God of bookworms and science geeks. He was the God of punk rock. P.T. liked wearing a shirt that proclaimed JESUS FREAK across the front. The word "freak" written there next to "Jesus" was purposefully combative, incongruous, as if to shout, "This isn't your mother's Christianity." If Jesus was a club, P.T. and other youth pastors like him were the bouncers.

One day Nana called bullshit on an exclusionary God. He raised his hand, and P.T. paused his drumming, tilted his seat back. "Shoot, bro," he said.

"So what if there's a tiny village somewhere in Africa that is so incredibly remote that no one has found it yet, which means no Christians have been able to go there as missionaries and spread the Gospel, right? Are all of those villagers going to Hell, even though there's no way that they could have heard about Jesus?"

P.T.'s smirk set in and his eyes narrowed at Nana a bit. "God would have made a way for them to hear the good news," he said.

"Okay, but hypothetically."

"Hypothetically, dude? Yeah, they're going to Hell."

I was shocked by this answer, by the smugly satisfied way in which P.T. had consigned an entire helpless village of Africans to eternal damnation without so much as a blink. He didn't spend even the length of an exhale thinking about Nana's question, working on a way out. He didn't say, for example, that God doesn't deal in hypotheticals, a perfectly reasonable answer to a not entirely reasonable question. His willingness to play into Nana's game was itself a sign that he saw God as a kind of prize that only some were good enough to win. It was like he *wanted* Hell for those villagers, like he believed there were people for whom Hell is a given, deserved.

And the part that bothered me most was that I couldn't shake the feeling that the people P.T. believed deserved Hell were people who looked like Nana and me. I was seven, but I wasn't stupid. I had seen the pamphlets that proclaimed the great need for missionaries in various other countries. The children in those pamphlets, their distended bellies, the flies buzzing around their eyes, their soiled clothing, they were all the same deep, dark brown as me. I already understood the spectacle of poverty, the competing impulses to help and to look away that such images spurred, but I understood, too, that poverty was not a black and brown phenomenon. I had seen the way the kids at school who came from the trailer park walked around, their short fuses sparked by a careless word about their tight shoes or "flooding" pants, and I had seen the rotted-out barns and farmhouses off the back roads in the Podunk towns just minutes outside my city. "Don't let our car break down in this dirty village," my mother would pray in Twi whenever we passed through one of these towns. She used the word *akuraase,* the same word she would use for a village in Ghana, but I had already been conditioned to see America as somehow elevated in relation to the rest of the world, and so I was convinced that an Alabama village couldn't be an *akuraase* in the same way that a Ghanaian village could. Years after P.T.'s remarks I started to see the ridiculousness of that idea, the idea of a refined and elevated American poverty that implies a base, subhuman third world. The belief in this subhumanity was what made those posters and infomercials so effective, no different really from the commercials for animal shelters, the people in these infomercials no better than dogs. P.T.'s unconsidered answer was no doubt just a careless thought from a man who was not accustomed to thinking too deeply about why he held fast to his faith, but for me, that day, his words set that very kind of thinking into motion.

I watched P.T. set his chair legs back down on the ground and continue his teaching, being careful not to let his eyes fall on Nana. Across the room, Nana also had a smug look on his face. He didn't go to youth services much after that.

20

Dear God,
Buzz says that Christianity is a cult except that it started
so long ago that people didn't know what cults were yet.
He said we're smarter now than we were back then. Is
that true?

Dear God,
Would you show me that you're real?

21

My apartment smelled like oil, like pepper, like rice and plantains. I set my bag down in the entryway and rushed to the kitchen to find a sight as familiar to me as my own body: my mother cooking.

"You're up," I said, and immediately regretted the choked excitement in my voice. I didn't want to frighten her. I'd seen videos of cornered black mambas, striking before slipping away, faster than a blink. Was my mother capable of the same?

"You don't have eggs. You don't have milk. You don't have flour. What do you eat?" she said. She was wearing a robe she must have found in one of my drawers. Her left breast, deflated from the weight loss and shriveled with age, peeked out through the thin fabric. When we were children, her propensity for nakedness had embarrassed Nana and me no end. Now, I was so happy to see her, all of her, I didn't care.

"I don't really cook," I said.

She sucked her teeth at me and continued working, slicing the plantains, salting the jollof. I heard the sizzle of the oil, and that smell of hot, wet grease was enough to make my mouth water.

"If you had spent time in the kitchen with me, helping me, you would know how to make all of this. You would know how to feed yourself properly."

I held my breath and counted to three, waiting for the urge to say something mean to pass. "You're here now. I can learn now."

She snorted. So, this was how it would go. I watched her lean over the pot of oil. She grabbed a handful of plantains and dropped them in, her hand so low, so close to the oil. The oil sputtered as it swallowed the plantains, and when my mother lifted her hand from the pot, I could see glistening specks from where the oil had spit at her. She wiped the spots with her index finger, touched her finger to her tongue. How many times had she been burned like this? She must have been immune.

"Do you remember that time you put hot oil on Nana's foot?" I asked from my spot at the counter. I wanted to get up and help her, but I was nervous that she would make fun of me or, worse, tell me how every move I made was wrong. She was right that I had avoided her kitchen my entire childhood, but even now, even with my small sample size of days spent cooking with her, it's her voice I hear, saying, "You clean as you go, you clean as you go," whenever I cook.

"What are you talking about?"

"You don't remember? We were having a party at the house and you put oil—"

She sharply turned to face me. She was holding a mesh strainer in her hand, high up in the air like a gavel she could bring down at any moment. I saw panic in her face, panic that covered the blankness that had been there since she'd arrived.

"I never did that," she said. "I never, *never* did that."

I was going to press her but then I looked into her eyes and knew immediately that I had made a mistake. Not in the memory, carried back to me through that smell of hot oil, but in the reminder.

"I'm sorry. I must have dreamed it," I said, and she brought the gavel down.

My mother rarely threw parties, and when she did, she spent the entire week leading up to them in enough of a cooking/cleaning frenzy to make you wonder if we were hosting royalty. There were a handful of Ghanaians in Alabama who made up the Ghana Association, and many of them had to drive upward of two hours to come to any of the gatherings. My mother, never the life of the party, only went to a meeting if the drive was under an hour, and she only hosted if she had four days off in a row, a rare enough occurrence to mean that she only hosted twice.

She'd bought me a new dress and Nana new slacks. She pressed them in the morning and then laid them out on our beds, threatening death if we so much as looked at them wrong before it was time to get into them, and then she spent the rest of the day cooking. By the time the first guests arrived, the house was practically sparkling, fragrant with the scents of Ghana.

It was the first time many of the other Ghanaians were seeing us since the Chin Chin Man's departure, and Nana and I, already outcasts for our taciturn mother, were dreading the party, the stares, the unsolicited advice from the grown-ups, the teasing from the other kids.

"We'll stay for five minutes and then we can fake sick," Nana whispered through his smile as we greeted an auntie who smelled like baby powder.

"She'll know we're lying," I whispered back, remembering her CIA-level interrogation into the mystery of who had stolen a Malta from the back of her closet.

It didn't come to that. By the time the other children showed up, Nana and I had moved from enduring to enjoying the party. My mother had made bofrot, puff-puff, balls of fried dough, and before long all of the children were engaged in an all-out war, the bofrot as our weapon. The rules were ill-defined, but the general idea of the game was that if you were hit with a flying bofrot then you were out.

Nana was, as usual, an expert player. He was fast, he had a good arm, and he was especially adept at escaping detection, for we all knew that if the adults caught us wasting food by throwing it at each other, the game, and our lives, would surely end. I knew I wasn't fast enough to outrun Nana, and so I hid behind our couch, waiting with my pile of bofrots, listening for the frustrated sighs and giggles of the other children who'd been pelted out. That couch, the only couch I'd ever known, was so old, so ugly, that it was slowly giving up on itself. The seams on one of the cushions had burst, leaving its stuffing, like guts, spilling out from the sides. The left arm of the couch had a decorative wooden piece nailed in, but every so often the piece would fall off, nails out, and Nana, my mother, or I would have to shove it back into the upholstery. I must have knocked the wooden piece off to get behind the couch that day, because it wasn't long before I heard Nana scream. I slunk out from behind the couch to find him with the wooden piece nailed to the bottom of his foot.

Every uncle and auntie in the room came over to hold court. My mother could hardly shove her way through before everyone had offered up their solutions to the problem. I quickly ate my bofrots, hiding the evidence of my involvement, as the adults in the room got louder and louder. Finally, my mother got to Nana. She sat him down on that treacherous couch and, without a hint of ceremony, pulled the wooden piece, nail and all, from Nana's foot, leaving behind a perfect, bleeding hole.

"Lockjaw, my sister," one of the aunties said.

"It's true, that nail might give him lockjaw. You can't take any chances."

The din started up again as the adults discussed tetanus prevention. Nana and I rolled our eyes at each other, waiting for the grown-ups to stop their posturing, slap a Band-Aid on his foot, and call it a day. But there was something about their talk, the way they were working themselves up with memories and ideas of Ghana, their old home. It was like they were turning themselves on with these mentions of folk remedies, turning themselves on and showing each other up, proving that they hadn't lost it, their Ghanaianness.

My mother scooped Nana up into her arms and carried him into the kitchen, the entire party trailing after her. She put a small pot of oil on the stove and dipped a silver spoon in it and, with Nana screaming, the grown-ups encouraging, and the children looking on in fear, she touched the hot oiled spoon to the hole in Nana's foot.

Could my mother have forgotten that? The time she had stopped believing in the powers of a tetanus vaccination and had instead left Nana's health up to folk wisdom. Nana had been so angry at her afterward, so angry and confused. Surely, she remembered.

I set the table while my mother scooped rice and fried plantains onto two plates. She sat down next to me and the two of us ate in silence. That food was better than anything I had eaten in months, years even, better still for having been the one sign of life from a woman who had done nothing but sleep since her arrival. I ate it hungrily. I accepted seconds and did the dishes while my mother looked on. Evening came, and she got back into bed, and by the time I left for the lab the next morning, she still had not gotten up.

22

A mouse with a fiber-optic implant on its head looks like something out of a science-fiction movie, though I suppose any creature with a fiber-optic implant on its head would. I often attached such implants to my mice's heads so that I could deliver light into their brains during my experiments. Han came into the lab one day to find me attaching a fiber-optic patch cord to one of my mice's implants. Both Han and the mouse didn't seem the least bit interested in what I was doing.

"Don't you think it's weird how quickly we get used to things?" I said to Han. The patch cord was connected to a blue LED that I would use to deliver light the next time the mouse performed the lever experiment.

Han hardly looked up from his own work. "What do you mean?" he said.

"I mean that if anyone else walked in here and saw this mouse with all of this intense hardware fastened onto its head they'd find it a little strange. They'd think we were creating cyborgs."

"We are creating cyborgs," he said. And then he paused, looked at me. "I mean, there's some debate about whether nonhumans can be considered cyborgs, but given the fact that 'cyborg' itself is an abbreviation of 'cybernetic organism,' I think it's safe to say you can extend the definition to any organic matter that's been biomechanically engineered, right?"

I'd brought this on myself. I spent the next fifteen minutes listening to Han talk about the Future of Science Fiction, which was perhaps the most I'd ever heard him talk about anything. I was bored by the conversation at first, but it was nice to see him so animated by something that I ended up getting caught up in it despite myself.

"My brother always said he wanted bionic legs so that he could be faster on the basketball court," I said without thinking.

Han pushed up his glasses and leaned in closer to his mouse. "I didn't know you had a brother," he said. "Does he still play basketball?"

"He, um. He . . ." I couldn't seem to get the words out. I didn't want to see Han's ears turn red, that telltale sign of mortification or pity. I wanted to remain who I was to him, without coloring our relationship with stories of my personal life.

Han finally looked up from his work and turned to face me. "Gifty?" he said.

"He died. It was a long time ago."

"Jesus, I'm so sorry," Han said. He held my gaze for a long time, longer than either of us was used to, and I was grateful that he didn't say anything more. That he didn't ask, as so many people do, how it happened. It embarrassed me to know that I would have been embarrassed to talk about Nana's addiction with Han.

Instead I said, "He was incredible at basketball. He didn't need the bionic legs."

Han nodded and flashed me a sweet, quiet smile. Neither of us really knew what to do or say next, so I asked Han who his favorite science-fiction writers were, hoping that a change of subject might melt away the lump that was forming in my throat. Han took the hint.

A year or so after my mother shoved the box of Nana's cleats and jerseys and soccer balls into the corner of our garage, Nana came home from school with a note from his P.E. teacher. "Basketball tryouts on Wednesday. We'd love to see Nana there," the note said.

That summer, Nana had hit six feet tall at just thirteen years old. I'd helped my mother measure him on the wall just off the kitchen, climbing up onto her shoulders and placing the faint pencil mark where Nana's head touched. "Ey, Nana, we'll have to lift the ceiling soon," my mother teased once the tape measure snapped back into its case. Nana rolled his eyes, but he was smiling, proud of his genetic luck.

Basketball was, of course, a logical sport for a tall, athletically gifted child, but we were a soccer family in football country. It never really occurred to any of us. And, though we never admitted it to ourselves or to each other, we all felt like a change in sport would be an insult to the Chin Chin Man, who had once said that his time would be better spent watching giraffes in the wild than watching basketball players on television.

But, clearly, Nana missed sports. His body was of a kind that needed to be in motion for him to feel at ease. He was always fidgeting, bouncing his legs, rolling his neck, cracking his knuckles. He wasn't meant to sit still, and those of us who had loved to watch him play soccer knew that there was something right, true, real about Nana in motion. He was himself, beautiful. My mother signed the consent form.

It was clear right away that this was the sport that he was intended to play. It was like something, in his body, in his mind, clicked into place once he held that basketball in his hands. He was frustrated with himself for being behind the other players, having not started the sport when he was younger, and so my mother bought a hoop she couldn't really afford and assembled it, with the help of Nana and me. It stood there in our driveway, and the very second it was erected it became like a totem for Nana. He was out there every day for hours, worshipping it. By his third game he was his team's fifth-highest scorer. By the end of the season he was the best.

My mother and I used to attend his games and sit in the very back. We weren't versed in the sport and neither of us ever bothered learning the rules. "What's happening?" one of us would whisper to the other whenever a whistle blew, but it was pointless to ask questions when we didn't really care what the answers were. It didn't take long for people to notice Nana, then us. Parents started cozying up to my mother, trying to get her to sit closer to the front, next to them, so that they could say things like "Boy, does he have a future ahead of him."

"What kind of nonsense is that?" my mother would say in the car on the way back. "Of course he has a future ahead of him. He has *always* had a future ahead of him."

"They mean in basketball," I said.

She glared at me through the rearview. "I know what they mean," she said.

I didn't understand why she was upset. She had never been like the stereotypical immigrant parents, the ones who smack their kids around for anything less than an A, who won't let their children play sports or attend dances, who pride themselves on their oldest, who is a doctor, their middle, who is a lawyer, and are overly worried about their youngest, who wants to study finance. My mother certainly wanted us to be successful, to live in such a way that we wouldn't end up having to work tiring, demanding jobs like she did. But that same tiring, low-paying work meant that she was often too busy to know if we were making good grades and too broke to get us help if we weren't. The result of this was that she had taken to simply trusting us to do the right thing, and we had rewarded that trust. It insulted her, I think, that people were so keen to talk about Nana's basketball prowess as the key to his future, as though he didn't have anything else to offer. His athleticism was a God-given talent, and my mother knew better than to question what God gives, but she hated the idea that anyone might believe that this was Nana's only gift.

Sometimes, when Nana was feeling generous, he'd let me play HORSE with him in the driveway. I liked to think that I held my own in those weekend afternoon games, but I'm sure Nana went easy on me.

We lived in a rented house at the end of a cul-de-sac, and the top of our driveway, where the basketball hoop stood, was the peak of a small hill. Whenever one of us missed a shot, if we weren't fast enough, the ball would bounce off the backboard and launch down that hill, gathering speed as it went. Though I was an energetic child, I was lazy, lousy at sports. I dreaded chasing the ball down the hill and would make little bargains with Nana so that he would do it instead. When I missed my "S" shot, I promised him I would wash all of his dishes for a week. It took Nana five long strides to get down to the bottom, six strides to get back up.

"Do you think the Chin Chin Man would have liked basketball if he'd grown up playing it?" I asked.

I was setting up a shot from inside the frame of the garage. It was physically impossible to get the ball as high as I would need to in order to sink it from there, but I hadn't yet studied physics, and I had an abundance of misplaced confidence in my skills. I missed the shot by several feet and chased it down before it could start its descent.

"Who?" Nana said.

"Daddy," I said, the word sounding strange to my ears. A word from a language I used to speak but was forgetting, like the Twi our parents had taught us when we were small but then had grown too tired to keep up.

"I don't give a fuck what he thinks," Nana said.

My eyes widened at the use of the swear word. They were all understood to be forbidden in our house, though our mother used the Twi ones with abandon because she thought we didn't know what they meant. Nana wasn't looking at me. He was setting up his shot. I stared at his long arms, the veins tracing their way from biceps to hand, pulsing, exclamation points on those newly formed muscles. He hadn't answered my question, but it didn't really matter. He was answering his own question, one whose large, looming presence must have been something of a burden to him, and so he lied to try to get out from under its weight. *I don't care,* he told himself every time he spoke to the Chin Chin Man on the phone. *I don't care,* when he scored twenty points in a game, looked up to the stands to find his bored sister and mother and no one else. *I don't care.*

Nana made the shot from the crest of our driveway's hill. It was a shot he knew I couldn't make. He threw the ball at me, hard. I caught it against my chest and told myself not to cry as I walked to the spot where Nana had stood. I stared at the little red target on the backboard and tried to channel everything I had toward it. A couple of months later, Nana would climb a ladder and scrape that red rectangle off, hoping that he would learn to make his shots by feel, by sense memory. I bounced the ball a couple of times and looked at Nana, whose expression was indiscernible. I missed the shot, and the game ended. Well after the sun set that night, Nana was still out in our driveway, shooting free throws against the backdrop of the moon.

In Hamilton and Fremouw's 1985 study on the effects of cognitive behavioral training on basketball free-throw performance, researchers asked three college basketball players with low game-to-practice free-throw ratios to listen to tape recordings with instructions for deep muscle relaxation. The men were also tasked with watching videotapes of themselves playing basketball, while attempting to reconstruct the thoughts they were having in each moment that played back to them. The researchers wanted them to identify any moments when they experienced negative self-evaluation and to instead try to cultivate positive self-statements. So, instead of thinking "I'm the worst. I've never been good at anything in my life. How did I even make it onto this team?" they were to aim for "I got this. I'm capable. I'm here for a

reason." By the end of the training program, all three subjects had improved by at least 50 percent.

I don't know what thoughts ran through Nana's mind in
those days. I wish I did. Because of my career, I would give
a lot to be able to inhabit someone else's body—to think
what they're thinking, feel what they're feeling. For a copy
of Nana's thoughts, from birth to death, bound in book
form, I would give absolutely anything. Everything. But
since accessing his mind has never been possible, I resort to
speculating, assuming, feeling—modes of logic with which
I have never been entirely comfortable. My guess is that it
wasn't just Nana's body that couldn't sit still. He had a mind
that was always thrumming. He was curious, intense, often
quiet, and when he asked a question there were a hundred
more lurking behind it. This constant striving for exact-
ness, the right position for his legs, the right thing to say,
was what made him someone who could shoot free throws
for hours on end, but it also made him someone who had a
harder time changing the narrative—getting from a negative self-statement to a positive one. When he said, "I don't
give a fuck what he thinks," he said it in such a way that it
was abundantly clear to me that this was precisely what he
cared most deeply about. And because Nana cared deeply,
thought deeply, I imagine that these were the kinds of negative statements he would reconstruct if he were to have
watched a video of himself playing basketball or simply living his life. It didn't hurt his game any, but it hurt him in
other ways.

Maybe it would have helped if we were the kind of family who talked about our feelings, who indulged in an "I
love you," a little *aburofo nkwaseasɛm,* every now and again.

Instead, I never told Nana how proud I was of him, how much I loved seeing him on the basketball court. On the game days when our mother was at work, I would walk to Nana's high school to watch him play, and then I would wait for him to finish talking to the other players and come out of the locker room so that he and I could walk back home together. "Good job, Nana," I would say when he finally came out in a fog of Axe body spray. Nana's coach always left as soon as the final whistle blew, so the only adult who would still be around was the night janitor, a man whom both Nana and I avoided because his job always made us think about our father.

"Y'all sure don't act like any siblings I've ever seen," the janitor said that one night. "I mean, 'Good job, Nana,' like he's your employee or your student or something. You should be giving him a hug."

"Come on, man," Nana said.

"I'm serious, y'all act like you don't hardly know each other. Go on, give your sister a hug," he said.

"Nah, man, we're good," Nana said. He started walking toward the door. "Let's go, Gifty," he said, but I was still standing there, looking at the janitor, who was giving me a kids-these-days kind of head shake.

"Gifty!" Nana shouted without turning, and I ran to catch up.

I'd left our house when it was still light out, but by the time the two of us got outside it was a hot and humid night. Fireflies flashed their greetings all around us. Nana's long strides meant I had to hustle to keep up with him, a half-shuffle, half-jog that I had perfected over the years.

"Do you think it's weird we don't hug?" I asked.

Nana ignored me and quickened his pace. These were the Nana-ignores-everybody days, when my mother and I would steal commiserating glances at each other after one of his moody groans. To Nana, my mother would say, "You think you and me are size? Fix your face." To me she would say, "This too shall pass."

We lived about a mile and a half away from the school, an easy walk by our mother's standards, but one we dreaded. Sidewalks in Huntsville were mostly decorative. People drove their SUVs to grocery stores two blocks away, their air-conditioning on full blast. The only people who walked were people like us, people who had to walk. Because they had one car, one parent who worked double shifts even on game days. Because walking was free and public transportation was either nonexistent or unreliable. I hated the honking, the slurs yelled out through rolled-down windows. Once, while I was walking by myself, a man in a pickup truck had driven slowly next to me, staring at me so hungrily I grew afraid and ducked into the library, hid among the books until I was certain he hadn't followed me. But I liked walking with Nana on those spring nights when the weather was just starting its quick turn from pleasant to oppressive, when the cicadas' songs gave way to those of the katydids. I loved Alabama in the evenings, when everything got still and lazy and beautiful, when the sky felt full, fat with bugs.

Nana and I turned onto our street. One of the streetlamps was out, and so there was a minute-long stretch of near darkness. Nana stopped walking. He said, "Do you want a hug?"

My eyes were still adjusting to that patch of dark. I couldn't see his face, couldn't tell if he was serious or just making fun of me, but I considered the question carefully anyway. "No, not really," I said.

Nana started laughing. He walked those last couple of blocks unhurriedly, at my pace so that I could walk beside him.

23

I dreaded going back to my apartment and finding, always finding, that little had changed, and so I started spending more and more time in my lab. I thought of it as "communing with the lab mice," but there was hardly anything interesting, let alone spiritual, about my humdrum days and long afternoons. Most of my experiments didn't even require me to do much other than check in on them once a day to make sure no major mishaps had occurred, so I mostly just sat in my frigid office, staring, shivering, at my blank Word document, trying to conjure up the motivation to write my paper. It was boring, but I preferred this familiar boredom to the kind I found at home. There, boredom was paired with the hope of its relief, and so it took on a more menacing tint.

In the lab, at least, I had Han. He was using brain-mapping tools to observe mouse behaviors, and he was the only person I knew who spent more time in the lab than I did.

"Are you sleeping here now?" I asked Han one day when he walked in with a toothbrush case. "Don't you ever worry you're going to die here and no one will find your body for days?"

Han shrugged, pushed up his glasses. "That Nobel Prize isn't going to win itself, Gifty," he said. "Besides, you'd find me."

"We have got to get out more," I said, and then I sneezed. The problem with spending so much time at the lab around my mice was that I was allergic to them. A common allergy in my field. Years of coming into contact with their dander, urine, saliva, had left my immune system battle-weary and weakened. While most people's symptoms included the regular itchy eyes/runny nose combination, I had the particular pleasure of bursting into a bloom of itchy rashes anytime I so much as touched my skin without washing my hands. Once the rash had even appeared on my eyelid.

"Stop scratching," Raymond said whenever I absent-mindedly reached for the ever-present patch on my upper back or underneath my breasts. We had been together for a couple of months, and though some of the shine had come off, there was still nothing I loved more than watching him move through the kitchen with such grace—flicking salt, chopping peppers, licking sauce from the tip of his index finger. That morning, I was sitting on a stool in his kitchen, watching him slowly stir his scrambled eggs, the movement of his wrist so hypnotic, I hadn't noticed what I was doing to my own body.

I had asked Raymond to warn me if he caught me scratching, but that didn't stop me from being incredibly annoyed with him whenever he did. *Don't tell me what to do. It's my body,* my mind would scream at him, but my mouth would say, "Thank you."

"Maybe you should see a doctor," he said one day after he watched me swallow my breakfast of Benadryl and orange juice.

"I don't need to see a doctor. They'll just tell me what I already know. Wear gloves, wash my hands, blah blah blah."

"Blah blah blah? You've been clawing your legs in your sleep." Raymond was eating a proper breakfast—eggs with toast, coffee. He offered me a bite, but I was always running late in those days. No time to eat, no time to waste. "You know, for someone in the med school, you're really funny about doctors and medicine," he said.

He was referring to the time, a few months before, when a particularly nasty case of strep throat had led a doctor at the urgent care clinic to prescribe me hydrocodone in addition to the usual antibiotics. Raymond had gone with me to pick up the medicine from the pharmacy, but when we got home I flushed the painkillers down the toilet.

Now, I said, "Most people's immune systems are highly capable and efficient. Overprescription is a huge problem in this country, and if we don't take charge of our own health, we're susceptible to all kinds of manipulation from pharmaceutical companies who profit off of keeping us ill and—"

Raymond threw his hands up in surrender. "I'm just saying, if a doctor prescribes me the good stuff, I'm taking it."

The good stuff. I didn't say anything to Raymond. I just walked out of the apartment, got in my car, and drove to the lab, my skin screaming, weeping.

I had grown more careful about how I handled the mice after my first year of graduate school. I washed my hands more often. I never touched my eyes. It was rare for me to get reactions as serious as the ones I used to get back when I thought I was invincible, but still, spending hours there communing with the mice left me a little worse for wear by the time I finished up each day.

Staying in the lab for that long worked on my mind as well. The slowness of this work, the way it takes forever to register even the tiniest of changes, it sometimes left me asking *What's the point?*

What's the point? became a refrain for me as I went through the motions. One of my mice in particular brought those words out every time I observed him. He was hopelessly addicted to Ensure, pressing the lever so often that he'd developed a psychosomatic limp in anticipation of the random shocks. Still, he soldiered on, hobbling to that lever to press and press and press again. Soon he would be one of the mice I used in optogenetics, but not before I watched him repeat his doomed actions with that beautifully pure, deluded hope of an addict, the hope that says, *This time will be different. This time I'll make it out okay.*

"What's the point of all of this?" is a question that separates humans from other animals. Our curiosity around this issue has sparked everything from science to literature to philosophy to religion. When the answer to this question is "Because God deemed it so," we might feel comforted. But what if the answer to this question is "I don't know," or worse still, "Nothing"?

24

According to a 2015 study by T. M. Luhrmann, R. Padma-vati, H. Tharoor, and A. Osei, schizophrenics in India and Ghana hear voices that are kinder, more benevolent than the voices heard by schizophrenics in America. In the study, researchers interviewed schizophrenics living in and around Chennai, India; Accra, Ghana; and San Mateo, California. What they found was that many of the participants in Chennai and Accra described their experiences with the voices as positive ones. They also recognized the voices as human voices, those of a neighbor or a sibling. By contrast, none of the San Mateo participants described positive experiences with their voices. Instead, they described experiences of being bombarded by harsh, hate-filled voices, by violence, intrusion.

"Look, a crazy person," my aunt said to me that day in Kumasi, as casually as if she were pointing out the weather. The sea of people in Kejetia didn't part for him, didn't back away in fear. If his presence was weather, it was a cloud on an otherwise clear day. It wasn't a tornado; it wasn't even a storm.

. . .

My mom would often tell me and Nana about a ghost that used to haunt her cousin's apartment in those early days of her living in the United States.

"I would turn the light off and he would turn it back on. He would move the dishes around and shake the room. Sometimes I could feel him touching my back and his hand felt like a broom brushing my skin."

Nana and I laughed at her. "Ghosts aren't real," we said, and she chided us for becoming too American, by which she meant we didn't believe in anything.

"You don't think ghosts are real, but just wait until you see one."

The ghost my mother saw came around only when her cousin was out of the apartment, which was fairly often, as she was a full-time student who also worked part-time at a Chick-fil-A. My mother had been struggling to find a job. She spent most of those days at home alone with baby Nana. She was bored. She missed the Chin Chin Man and ran up her cousin's phone bill making calls to him, until her cousin threatened to kick her out. Her house rules: don't cost me money and don't have any more babies. My mother stopped phoning Ghana, leaving her sex life an ocean away. This was around the time she started seeing the ghost. Whenever she told the two of us stories about the ghost, she spoke about him fondly. Though he frustrated her with his little tricks, she liked that broom-brushed feeling on her back; she liked the company.

. . .

I read the Luhrmann study the day it came out in the *British Journal of Psychiatry*, and I couldn't stop thinking about it. What struck me was the relational quality between the Ghanaian and Indian participants and the voices they heard. In Chennai they were the voices of family; in Accra, the voice of God. Maybe the participants accepted the experiences as positive because they understood these voices as real—a real and living god, kith and kin.

My mom had been staying with me for about a week and a half when it occurred to me that there was something more I could be doing. Before I left for work in the morning, when I brought her a bowl of soup and a glass of water, I would sit with her for a while and brush my hand along whatever portion of skin went uncovered by the blanket. If I was feeling bold, I'd pull the blanket down just slightly so that I could rub her back, I'd squeeze her hand, and sometimes, a few precious times, she would squeeze my hand back.

"Look at you becoming soft like an American," she said one day. Her back was turned to me and I had just finished pulling the covers up over her bare shoulders. Mockery was her preferred way of displaying affection, a sign of her old self surfacing. I felt like I was finding a single tooth of a titanosaur fossil, excited but overwhelmed by the bigger bones that were yet buried.

"Me? Soft?" I said with a little laugh, but my voice mocked her back, said, "You, you're the soft one."

My mother turned with great effort so that she was facing me. Her eyes narrowed for a second and I braced myself, but then her face softened; she even smiled a little. "You work too much."

"I learned that from you," I said.

"Well," she said.

"Do you want to come to the lab sometime? You could see what I do. It's boring usually, but I'll do a surgery the day you come so it'll be interesting."

"Maybe," she said, and that was enough for me. I reached out my hand to hers. I squeezed, but this was the last bone I would find today, maybe for weeks longer. She left her hand limp.

25

Before my mother came to stay with me, I realized that I no longer had a Bible. I knew she was in bad shape and probably wouldn't notice, but it nagged at me to think of her reaching for one and not being able to find it. I went to the campus bookstore and purchased a New King James Version with the same amount of embarrassment and fear of being caught that one might have when purchasing a pregnancy test. No one batted an eye.

At first, I kept the Bible on the nightstand, where my mother had always kept our Bibles, but, as far as I could tell, she never touched it. It rested on that nightstand in the same position, day in, day out, gathering dust. After a while, when I came in to sit with her, I would pick it up and start to flip through it, reading passages here and there, quizzing myself to see whether or not I could remember all of those hundreds of Bible verses I had committed to memory over the years. In college, whenever I struggled to remember all of the proteins and nucleic acids I needed to know intimately for my major, I would think about the surfeit of Bible verse knowledge taking up space in my brain and wish that I could empty it all out to make room for other things. People would pay a lot of money to someone who could turn the brain into a sieve, draining out all of that now-useless knowledge—the exact way your ex liked to be kissed, the street names of the places you no longer live—leaving only the essential, the immediate. There are so many things I wish I could forget, but maybe "forget" isn't quite right. There are so many things I wish I never knew.

The thing is, we don't need to change our brains at all. Time does so much of the emptying for us. Live long enough and you'll forget almost everything you thought you'd always remember. I read the Bible as if for the first time. I read at random, the rich and grandiose storytelling of the Old Testament, the intimate love letters of the Gospels, and I enjoyed it in a way that I hadn't when I was a child, when I had such a hawkish approach to memorizing Scripture that I almost never took the time to think about what I was reading, let alone savor the words. While reading from 1 Corinthians, I found myself moved by the language. "This is actually quite beautiful," I said to myself, to my mother, to no one.

Here's a verse from the book of John: *In the beginning was the Word, and the Word was with God, and the Word was God.* I wrote about this verse in my childhood journal. I wrote about how writing itself made me feel closer to God and how my journal keeping was a particularly holy act, given that it was the Word that was with God, that *was* God. In those days my journal was my most prized possession and I took my writing very seriously. I took words seriously; I felt like those opening words of John's were written just for me. I thought of myself as a lost apostle, my journal as a new book of the Bible. I was young when I wrote that entry, maybe seven or eight, and I was so very smug about it. Proud of how well it was written. I was almost tempted to show it to my family or to Pastor John.

So it was a bit of a shock, years later, when P.T. delivered a sermon, one of his few memorable ones, in which he told us all that the word "Word" was translated from the Greek word *Logos,* which didn't really mean "word" at all, but rather something closer to "plea" or even "premise." It was a small betrayal for my little apostle's heart to find out that I had gotten my journal entry wrong. Worse still, I felt then, was the betrayal of language in translation. Why didn't English have a better word than "Word" if "Word" was not precise enough? I started to approach my Bible with suspicion. What else had I missed?

Even though I felt ambushed, I did like the ambiguity that the revelation introduced into that verse. In the beginning there was an idea, a premise; there was a question.

My junior year of college, I went to a church service by myself. I wore a simple black dress and a big floppy hat with which I could easily hide my face, though a woman in a hat at a university church service was a strange enough sight that I probably drew more attention to myself, not less. I went to the very last pew, and I hadn't but bent my knees to sit down before I felt sweat start to bead on my brow. The prodigal daughter returns.

The reverend that day was a woman, a professor in the Harvard Divinity School whose name I've forgotten now. She preached on literalism in the church and she began the sermon by asking the congregation to ponder this question: "If the Bible is the infallible word of God, must we approach it literally?"

When I was a child, I would have said yes, emphatically and without a moment's thought. What I loved best about the Bible, particularly the outlandish moments in the Old Testament, was that thinking about it literally made me feel the strangeness and dynamism of the world. I can't tell you how much sleep I lost over Jonah and that whale. I used to pull my covers up all the way over my head and shimmy down into the dark, breath-damp cavern it created, and I would think of Jonah on that ship to Tarshish and I would think of the punitive, awful God who ordered him thrown overboard to be swallowed whole by a giant fish. And I would feel my breath shorten in that confined space and I would be amazed, truly amazed by God, by Jonah, by the whale. The fact that these sorts of things didn't ever seem to happen in the present did nothing to keep me from believing that they happened in the age of the Bible, when everything was weighted with import. When you're that young, time already seems to crawl. The distance between ages four and five is forever. The distance between the present and the biblical past is unfathomable. If time was real, then anything at all could be real too.

The reverend's sermon that day was beautiful. She approached the Bible with extraordinary acuity, and her interpretation of it was so humane, so thoughtful, that I became ashamed of the fact that I very rarely associated those two things with religion. My entire life would have been different if I'd grown up in this woman's church instead of in a church that seemed to shun intellectualism as a trap of the secular world, designed to undermine one's faith. Even

Nana's hypothetical question about villagers in Africa had been treated as a threat instead of as an opportunity. The P.T. who had revealed that in the beginning was the Logos, the idea, the question, was the same P.T. who had refused to think about whether or not those hypothetical villagers could be saved and in so doing refused the premise, the question itself.

When Pastor John preached against the ways of the world, he was talking about drugs and alcohol and sex, yes, but he was also asking our church to protect itself against a kind of progressivism that for years now had been encroaching. I don't mean progressive in a political sense, though that was certainly a part of it. I mean progress in the sense of the natural way in which learning something new requires getting rid of something old, like how discovering that the world is round means that you can no longer hang on to the idea that you might one day fall off the edge of the Earth. And now that you have learned that something you thought was true was never true at all, every idea that you hold firm comes into question. If the Earth is round, then is God real? Literalism is helpful in the fight against change.

But while it was easy to be literal about some teachings of the Bible, it was much harder to be literal about others. How, for instance, could Pastor John preach literally about the sins of the flesh when his own daughter got pregnant at seventeen? It's almost too cliché to be believable, but it happened. Mary, as she was ironically named, tried to hide her condition for months with baggy sweatshirts and fake colds, but it wasn't long before the entire congregation caught on. And soon Pastor John's sermons about the sins of the flesh took on a different weight. Instead of a punitive God, we were told of a forgiving God. Instead of a judgmental church, we were encouraged to be an open one. The Bible did not change, but the passages he chose did; the way that he preached did as well. By the time Mary's due date rolled around, she and the baby's father were married and all was forgiven, but I never forgot. We read the Bible how we want to read it. It doesn't change, but we do.

I became deeply interested in the idea of Logos after P.T.'s sermon. I started writing in my journal more often, but the nature of my entries changed. Whereas before, they were simply recordings of my day and the things I wanted God to do, after, they became lists of all the questions that I had, all the things that didn't quite make sense to me.

I also started paying more attention to my mother. When she spoke Fante on the phone with her friends, she became like a girl again, giggling and gossiping. When she spoke Twi to me, she was her mother-self, stern and scary, warm. In English, she was meek. She stumbled and was embarrassed, and so to hide it she demurred. Here's a journal entry from around that time:

> Dear God,
> The Black Mamba took me and Buzz out to eat today.
> The waitress came over and asked what we wanted to
> drink and TBM said water, but the waitress couldn't
> hear her and asked her to repeat herself but she didn't
> and so Buzz answered for her. Maybe she thought the
> waitress didn't understand her? But she was talking so
> quietly it was like she was talking to herself.

There were other moments like this, where the woman whom I thought of in my head as fearsome shrank down to someone I could hardly recognize. And I don't think she did this because she wanted to. I think, rather, that she just never figured out how to translate who she really was into this new language.

26

Mary, the pastor's pregnant daughter, was the subject of gossip around our small evangelical community for nine months and beyond. As her belly swelled, so did the rumors. That she had conceived the baby in the First Assemblies' baptismal one Sunday evening after hours. That the baby was fathered by a NASCAR driver whose mother was a member of our congregation. When Pastor John pulled Mary out of school to be homeschooled by her mother, we all assumed that the school had something to do with the pregnancy. Maybe it had happened there. Throughout all of this conjecture, Mary didn't say a word. When the father, a sweet, shy boy from a neighboring church, finally revealed himself, the two of them, child bride and bridegroom, were married before her third trimester. The whisperings slowed but they didn't stop.

The problem was that it wasn't just Mary who had gotten pregnant. That year, four other fourteen- to sixteen-year-old girls from our church made revelations of their own. Not to mention the girls from churches around town.

I was twelve. The most sex ed I had gotten was earlier that year in middle school when a woman from a Baptist church in Madison had visited our science class two days in a row to tell us that our bodies were temples that shouldn't allow just anyone in. Then she assigned homework, an essay with the prompt "Write about why patience is a virtue." All of the language was vague and metaphorical. Our holy temples; our silver boxes; our special gifts. I don't think she said the words "penis" or "vagina" once. I left with no idea what sex actually was. But sin I was familiar with, and as I watched all the older girls carry their sins on their bellies for the entire world to see, I understood that for these girls to be young, unmarried, pregnant, meant that a particular kind of shame had descended on my congregation.

Soon after Melissa, the last of the five girls, announced her pregnancy, my church had an intervention of sorts. I wasn't told where we were going, but I and all the other preteen girls climbed into the church van and were driven downtown to an old warehouse building that looked like it was ready to be torn down.

There were several other girls already there. Most of them were older than us; one was visibly pregnant. The room was set up as though for a board meeting, and at the head of the table sat a woman with dishwater-blond hair. She looked like someone who had probably been pretty and popular only a couple of decades before but then had left high school, where admiration had come easily and plenti-fully, and had suffered in the real world.

"Come on in, girls, grab a seat," she said.

I and my fellow church girls took seats at the end of the table. "Do you know what's going on?" we whispered to each other. The girls who were already there glared at us, mean in their boredom.

"How many of you have already had sex?" the woman asked once we had settled in.

Everyone looked around but no one raised their hand, not even the pregnant girl.

"Come on, now. Don't be shy," she said.

Slowly hands started to go up all around me. I made my silent judgments.

"This here building used to be a place where women came to kill their babies, but God saw fit to turn it around. He laid it on my pastor's heart to use this place for good instead of for evil, and so now we bring girls like you in here to teach y'all about how God wants you to wait. I'm telling you girls, even if you've already had sex before, you can ask God to forgive. You can leave here better than when you came in. Amen?"

For the next eight hours, Miss Cindy, as she asked to be called, took us through her course on abstinence. She showed us slideshows of the spotted, oozing, stop-sign-red genitalia afflicted by STDs. She spoke about her own teen pregnancy. ("I love my daughter and I believe everything happens for a reason, but if I could go back and tell my younger self to keep her legs closed, I would.") The only good part about all of this was when we got Steak-Out for lunch.

At one point, six hours in, Miss Cindy said, "If you and I were neighbors and we went into a covenant agreement so that our lambs could graze freely on each other's land, we would have to seal that covenant by slaughtering one of our lambs. A covenant is not a promise. It's so much more than that. A covenant requires bloodshed. Remember that the Bible says that marriage is a covenant and when you sleep with your husband on your wedding night and your hymen breaks, that blood is what is sealing your covenant. If you've already had sex with other men, you've already made promises you can't keep."

We spent the rest of our time wide-eyed with fear, looking at the wreckage of this woman and wondering who, what, had wrecked her.

I have made promises I can't keep, but it took me a while to make them. For years, Miss Cindy's words were enough to keep me from exploring the "secret world" between my legs lest I destroy my imaginary marriage before it even began. Not too long after my eight-hour session in the abandoned abortion clinic, I started my period. My mother placed her hand on my shoulder and prayed that I'd be a good steward of my womanhood, and then she handed me a box of tampons and sent me on my way.

It's ridiculous to me now to think about how limited my understanding of human anatomy was back then. I stared at the tampon applicator. I put it against my outer labia and pushed. I watched the white tail of the tampon slip out of the applicator as both fell to the ground. I repeated this with half of the box before I gave up, decided it was best to keep some things a mystery. It wasn't until my freshman year in college, in biology class, that I learned what and where a vagina truly was.

In class that day, I stared at the diagram in wonder, the secret world, an inner world, revealed. I looked around at my classmates and could see in their business-as-usual faces that they already knew all of this. Their bodies had not been kept from them. It was neither the first nor the last time at Harvard that I would feel as though I was starting from behind, trying to make up for an early education that had been full of holes. I went back to my dorm room and tentatively, furtively pulled out a hand mirror and examined myself, wondering all the while how, if I hadn't left my town, if I hadn't continued my education, this particular hole, the question of anatomy, of sex, would have been filled. I was tired of learning things the hard way.

"Sorry for being kind of a bitch back there. It's just weird to hear people talk about Jesus in a science class, you know?"

Anne from my small group had caught up with me after my outburst in Integrated Science. I didn't bother telling her that I hadn't mentioned Jesus at all. I just quickened my pace through the quad, which was eerily empty at that hour. She kept walking with me until we reached my building, and then she stood there and stared at me.

"Do you live here too?" I asked.

"No, but I thought we could hang out."

I didn't want to hang out. I wanted her to leave. I wanted that class to end, school to end, the world to end, so that everyone could forget about me and what a fool I had made of myself. I looked at Anne as if for the first time. Her hair was piled up on top of her head in a messy bun pierced through with chopsticks from the dining hall. Her cheeks were red from walking or the weather. She looked tired and a little mean. I let her in.

That year the two of us became inseparable. I don't know how it happened, really. Anne was a senior. She and her group of many-gendered, multiracial friends made me feel like maybe there was a place for me in that East Coast tundra. Anne was funny, strange, beautiful, and mordant. She didn't suffer fools, and sometimes I was the fool.

"It's ridiculous. Like do you have to spend the rest of your life flagellating yourself for all the shit you think you've done wrong that 'God' doesn't approve of?" she said one day toward the middle of our spring semester, when the winter weather had started to relent and a few flowers were just beginning to break ground, stretch toward the sun. We were sitting on my bed while Anne skipped class and I waited for my next one to start. Sometimes she would spend the whole day in my room. I'd finish all my classes and come back to find her curled up in my bed, laptop warming her stomach as she binge-watched *Sex and the City* for the millionth time.

Anne always said "God" with air quotes and an eye roll. Her father was Brazilian and her mother was American. They had met at a Buddhist meditation retreat in Bali before abandoning religion altogether and moving to Oregon to raise their two children godlessly. Anne looked at me as one might look at an alien who had dropped from the sky and needed to be taught how to assimilate into human life.

"I don't flagellate myself. I don't even believe in God anymore," I said.

"But you're so rigid with yourself. You never skip class. You don't drink. You won't even *try* drugs."

"That's not because of my religion," I said with a look that I hoped said, *Drop it.*

"You're weird about sex."

"I'm not weird about sex."

"You're a virgin, aren't you?"

"Lots of people are virgins."

Anne moved over on the bed so that she was facing me. She leaned in so close to me that I could feel her breath on my lips.

"Have you ever been kissed?" she asked.

27

Basketball season started in November, but for Nana the sport was year-round. He went to basketball camp in the summers, played on his school team during the season, and spent all year long in our driveway or heading over to the outdoor courts in and around Huntsville so that he could play pickup games with the kids there. My mother and I were subjected to hours upon hours of watching basketball on television. When Nana had friends over, all of them would shout at the television loudly and unintelligibly, as though the players on the screen owed them something. Nana joined in when others were there, but when it was just him, he watched silently and with intense concentration. Sometimes, he even took notes.

It wasn't long before college recruiters started showing up to his games. Alabama, Auburn, Vanderbilt, UNC. Nana played well regardless of who was watching. My mother and I made more of an effort to learn the rules so that we could better share in his victories, but even as we tried, we knew it didn't matter. Nana was the triumph. It was only the beginning of his sophomore year's season, and he had broken records statewide. All the practices and workouts and away games made it easy for Nana to worm his way out of Wednesday-night and Sunday-morning services at First Assemblies. I knew it hurt my mother to see Nana choosing ball over God, so, instead of heading to youth group, I started going to "big church." I wanted to sit beside her, to have her feel like at least one of her children still cared about what she cared about.

I was eight, then nine. I was bored. If I fell asleep, as I often did, my mother would pinch my arm and stage-whisper, "Pay attention."

I don't remember the sermons very well, but I remember the altar calls that came at the end of them every Sunday. Pastor John's speech was always the same. To this day I can recite it from memory:

"Now, I know someone out there is sitting with a heavy heart. I know someone out there is tired of carrying a cross. And I'm telling you now, you don't have to leave here the same as when you came in. Amen? God's got a plan for you. Amen? All you have to do is ask Jesus into your heart. He'll do the rest."

Pastor John would say this, and then the worship leader would rush up to the piano and start to play.

"Is there anyone who'd like to come down to the altar today?" Pastor John would ask, the music filling up the room. "Is there anyone who'd like to give their life to Christ?"

After a few months of big church, I noticed my mother sneaking glances at me whenever Pastor John made his altar call. I knew what those glances meant, but I wasn't ready for that long walk down to the altar, for the entire congregation to train their eyes on me, praying that Jesus take my sins away.

I still wanted my sins. I still wanted my childhood, my freedom to fall asleep in big church with little consequence. I didn't know what would become of me once I crossed the line from sinner to saved.

Nana couldn't decide on a school. He would often talk through his pro/cons list with me while our mother was at work. He wanted to stay in the South but he didn't want to feel like he had barely left home. He wanted to go pro eventually, but he also wanted to have a good, normal college experience.

"Maybe you should call Daddy and see what he thinks," I said.

Nana glared at me. The Chin Chin Man had recently called to tell us that he was remarrying, and since then Nana had stopped talking to him. It hadn't occurred to either of us that he and my mother had gotten divorced. He was, until that day, our long-distance father, her long-distance husband. Now who would he be?

On the days when he called, which were fewer and further between, my mother would pass the phone to me and I would spend my requisite two minutes making small talk about the weather and school, until the Chin Chin Man asked if I would put Nana on the line.

"He has basketball," I would say, as Nana stared at me, furiously shaking his head. After I hung up the phone, I would wait for our mother to chastise me for lying or Nana for refusing to talk, but she never did.

She had to work the day of Nana's game against Ridgewood High. It wasn't a big game. Ridgewood was ranked second to last in the state, and everyone was expecting an easy win for Nana's team.

I made a quick snack for myself and then walked to the game. The stands were nearly empty and so I chose a seat in the middle and pulled out my homework. Nana and his teammates did their warm-ups, and occasionally he and I would make eye contact and shoot each other silly faces.

The first half of the game went as expected. Ridgewood was down fifteen and Nana's team was taking it pretty easy, treating the game like it was practice. I finished my math homework right around when the buzzer rang for halftime. I waved at Nana as he and his team went to the locker room, and then I picked up my science homework.

I was in the fourth grade, and our science unit for that month was on the heart. For homework, we were to draw a picture of the human heart with all its ventricles and valves and pulmonary veins. While I enjoyed science, I was a horrible artist. I had brought along my pack of colored pencils and my textbook. I spread them out on the bleachers next to me and began to draw, staring from my blank sheet of paper to the example heart in my book. I started with the pulmonary veins, then the inferior vena cava. I messed up the right ventricle and started to erase, just as the second half of the game kicked off. I got frustrated with myself easily, even in those days, whenever I felt I wasn't getting something exactly right. That frustration sometimes led to quitting, but something about being at Nana's game, watching him and his teammates win so effortlessly, made me feel like I could draw the perfect heart if only I stuck with it.

I was staring at my heart when I heard a loud shout. I couldn't see what happened at first, but then I spotted Nana

on the ground, hugging his knee to his chest and motion-
ing toward his ankle. I rushed down to the court and paced,
unsure of how to make myself useful. The medic came onto
the court and started asking Nana some questions, but I
couldn't hear anything. Finally, they decided to take him to
the emergency room.

I rode with him in the back of the ambulance. We
weren't a family who held hands, but we were a family who
prayed. I bowed my head and whispered my prayers as Nana
stared blankly at the ceiling.

Our mother met us at the hospital. I didn't dare ask who
was watching Mrs. Palmer, but I remember being as worried
about my mother being able to keep her job as I was about
Nana. He was still in pain but attempting to be stoic about
it. He looked more annoyed than anything else, no doubt
already thinking about the games he would have to miss, the
time he would have to take off.

"Nana," the doctor said when he came into the room.
"I'm a big, big fan. My wife and I saw you in the game
against Hoover, and you were just on fire." He looked too
young to be a doctor, and he had that thick, slow drawl some
southerners have, as though each word has to wade through
molasses before it can leave the mouth. Both my mother and
I kept looking at him with no small amount of distrust.

"Thank you, sir," Nana said.

"The good news is nothing's broken. Bad news is you've
torn some ligaments in your ankle. Now there's not much
we can do for that area, other than have you rest it and ice
it. Should heal up on its own. I'll prescribe you some Oxy-
Contin for the pain and then have you follow up with your
primary care doctor in a few weeks to see how it's coming

along. We'll get you back out on the court in no time, all right?"

He didn't wait for any of us to speak. He just got up and left the room. A nurse came in behind him with some aftercare instructions, and the three of us made our way to the car. I don't really remember much else from that day. I don't remember going to the pharmacy to pick up the pills. I don't remember if Nana got crutches or a brace, if he spent the rest of the day sprawled out in our living room with his foot elevated, eating ice cream while our mother waited on him as though he were a king. Maybe all of those things happened; maybe none. It was a bad day, but the nature of its badness was utterly ordinary, just regular old shit luck. Ordinary is how I'd always thought of us, our foursome that had turned into a trio. Regular, even if we stuck out like sore thumbs in our tiny corner of Alabama. I wish now, though, that I could remember every detail of that day, because then maybe I could pinpoint the exact moment we shifted away from ordinary.

28

I was getting too attached to the mouse with the limp. I couldn't help feeling sorry for it every time it hobbled toward that lever, ready for punishment and pleasure. I watched its little tongue poke out, lapping up the Ensure. I watched it shake off the foot-shocks, then go back for more.

"Have you ever tried Ensure?" I asked Han one day at the lab. After nearly a year of working together, we had finally broken the ice. The fire-hydrant-red, telltale discomfort of his ears had become a thing of the past.

He laughed. "Do I look like an old lady or a mouse to you?"

"I think I'm going to buy some," I said.

"You're joking."

"Aren't you even a little bit curious?"

He shook his head, but I'd made up my mind. I left the lab and drove to the nearest Safeway. I bought two of the original, one in chocolate and one in butter pecan just for the novelty of it. I had stopped coming to this Safeway because of the cashier I wanted to sleep with, but I faced her boldly, Ensure in hand. I gave her a look that I hoped said

I'm trying to take control of my own health. For a brief second I imagined her thinking, *What a strong woman,* imagined her getting turned on by my unlikely but empowered choice of beverage and then sneaking me into the storage room to show me more. Instead, she didn't even make eye contact.

Afterward, I speeded all the way back to the lab. There were often cops patrolling this little patch of road for speeders, but my Stanford Medical School bumper sticker had gotten me out of at least one ticket. The policeman that day had collected my license and registration, all while making small talk.

"What do you study?" he asked.

"What?"

"Your bumper sticker. What kind of doctor are you?"

I didn't bother correcting him. Instead I said, "I'm a neurosurgeon."

He whistled and handed me back my things. "You must be real smart," he said. "You should protect that brain of yours. Go slower next time."

Han started laughing the second he saw me walk in with the bottles.

"You sure I can't tempt you?" I asked. "Don't you want to know what all the fuss is about?"

"You're pretty weird," Han said, as though this was just then occurring to him for the first time, and then he shrugged, resigned himself to my strangeness and the experiment. "You know just as well as I do that even after we drink this, we still won't understand what the fuss is about. We're not mice. We can't get addicted to this stuff."

He was right, of course. I wasn't expecting to get high

from drinking fortified chocolate milk. I wasn't really expecting anything other than a little fun and, silly as it was, a base point from which I could relate to that limping mouse who had caught my attention.

I shook the bottle of chocolate and then cracked it open. I gulped down some of it and then handed it to Han, who took a couple of sips.

"Not bad," he said, and then, seeing the look on my face, "What's wrong, Gifty?"

I swallowed another sip of Ensure. Han was right. It wasn't bad, but it wasn't good either. "My brother was addicted to opioids," I said. "He died of an overdose."

The first time I saw Nana high, I didn't understand what I was seeing. He was slumped down on the couch, his eyes rolled back, a faint smile on his face. I thought he was half asleep, dreaming the sweetest of dreams. Days went by like this, then a week. Finally, I figured it out. No dream could wreak the havoc this wreaked.

It took me a while to gather the courage, but I once asked Nana if he could describe what it felt like when he took the pills or shot up. He was six months into his addiction, two and a half years away from his death. I don't know what emboldened me to ask a question like that. Up until that point I had exercised a "don't dare mention it" kind of policy, figuring that if I avoided any talk of drugs or addiction, then the problem would go away on its own. But it wasn't just that I avoided mentioning Nana's addiction because I wanted it to go away; it was that it was so everpresent that mentioning it felt ridiculous, redundant. In just that short amount of time, Nana's addiction had become the sun around which all of our lives revolved. I didn't want to stare directly at it.

When I'd asked Nana what it felt like to be high, he had smirked at me a little and rubbed his forehead.

"I don't know," he said. "I can't describe it."

"Try."

"It just feels good."

"Try harder," I said. The anger in my voice surprised us both. Nana had already become accustomed to all the yelling and pleading and crying from our mother as she tried to urge him to stop, but I never yelled. I was too scared to be angry, too sad.

Nana couldn't bring himself to look at me, but when he finally did, I looked away. For years before he died, I would look at his face and think, *What a pity. What a waste.*

Nana sighed and said, "It feels amazing, like everything inside my head just empties out and then there's nothing left—in a good way."

29

My mother had to work the Sunday night after Nana's accident. The bottle of OxyContin had not yet started to dwindle at a rate faster than it should have, and so we didn't yet know to worry about anything other than his ankle. She had taken the week off to care for him, until an angry voice mail from her boss sent her back to the Palmer house.

I asked her if she would take me to church on her way to her night shift, and she was so excited to see me *wanting* to go to church on my own, without her prodding, that she didn't even seem to mind that it was out of her way.

There weren't that many people there that evening. I chose a seat in the middle pew and urged myself to stay awake. The worship leader that night was the woman with the warbling voice.

"To hiiiiim whooo siiiiiits onnnnn the thronnnnneeeee," she sang, her vibrato so strong that it threw her a half step off beat.

I clapped along, fighting the urge to plug my ears until some other soloist got a chance to shine.

After worship, Pastor John went up to the pulpit. He

preached from the book of Isaiah, a short, dull sermon that did little to move the few congregants who had decided to get some God in before their workweek. Even Pastor John seemed bored by his own message.

He cleared his throat and said a quick closing prayer, and then he made the altar call.

"Now, I know someone out there is sitting with a heavy heart. I know someone out there is tired of carrying a cross. And I'm telling you now, you don't have to leave here the same as when you came in. Amen? God's got a plan for you. Amen? All you have to do is ask Jesus into your heart. He'll do the rest. Is there anyone who'd like to come down to the altar today? Is there anyone who'd like to give their life to Christ?"

The sanctuary was quiet. People started looking at their watches, packing up their Bibles, counting down the number of hours they had left until Monday came and work beckoned.

I didn't move at all. Something came over me. Something came over me, filled me and took hold. I had heard that altar call hundreds of times and felt absolutely nothing. I had prayed my prayers, written my journal entries, and heard only the faintest whisper of Christ. And that whisper was one I distrusted, because maybe it was the whisper of my mother or of my own desperate need to be good, to please. I hadn't expected to hear the loud knocking on my heart's door, but that night I heard it. I heard it. These days, because I have been trained to ask questions, I find myself questioning that moment. I ask myself, "*What* came over you?" I say, "Be specific."

I had never felt anything like it before, and I have never felt anything like it since. Sometimes I tell myself that I made it all up, the feeling of my heart full to bursting, the desire to know God and be known by him, but that is not true either. What I felt that night was real. It was as real as anything a person can feel, and insofar as we know anything at all, I knew what I needed to do.

I was in the fourth grade. I raised my hand as I had been taught to do in school. Pastor John, who had been closing his Bible, saw me in that tiny crowd, in that center pew.

"Praise God," he said. "Praise God. Gifty, come on down to the altar."

I walked that long, lonely walk of trembling. I knelt down before my pastor as he placed a hand on my forehead and I felt the pressure of his hand like a beam of light from God himself. It was almost unbearable. And the smattering of congregants in the sanctuary of the First Assemblies of God stretched out their hands toward me and prayed, some under their breaths, some shouting, some in tongues. And I repeated Pastor John's prayer, asking Jesus to come into my heart, and when I stood up to leave the sanctuary, I knew, without even the slightest of doubts, that God was already there.

30

Being saved was incredible. Every day I would head to school, and look at my classmates with delicious pity, worrying over their poor, poor souls. My salvation was a secret, a wonderful secret, burning hot in my heart, and what a shame it was that they didn't have it too. Even Mrs. Bell, my teacher, was the recipient of one of my benevolent smiles, my lunchtime prayers.

But this was Alabama, and who was I kidding? My secret wasn't mine at all. As soon as I told Misty Moore that I was saved, she told me that she'd been saved two years before, and I felt embarrassed by what little joy I'd carried for a week. Consciously, I knew it wasn't a contest, but subconsciously, I thought I had won, and to hear that Misty Moore, a girl who had once lifted up her shirt at recess so that Daniel Gentry could see the rumor of her breasts, had been sanctified before me, a girl with no rumors to speak of, stung. The shine wore off, but I did my best to hold on to the feeling of all those hands stretched out toward me, the sanctuary buzzing with prayers.

My mother was back at work, and Nana was always

asleep on the couch. There was no one to share my good
news with. I started volunteering at my church in an attempt
to make use of my salvation. There wasn't much that needed
to be done at the First Assemblies. Occasionally, I would
pick up the hymnals that had been left in the pews and put
them back in their places. About once every two months my
church would take a van down to the soup kitchen to help
serve, but more often than not, I would be the only person to show up. P.T., who drove the van for those trips,
would take one look at me, standing in my raggedy jeans
and T-shirt, and sigh. "Just you today, huh?" he'd ask, and
I'd wonder who else he'd been expecting.

The First Assemblies of God also had a fireworks stand,
just off the highway at the Tennessee border, called Bama
Boom! I still don't understand why we had it. Maybe we
got it under the guise of ministry. Maybe it was about earn-
ing a little extra money. I suspect now that Pastor John just
had a fireworks kink and used our church to live it out. I
was technically too young to volunteer at the stand, but it
wasn't as though people came around to check ID, so once in
a while I would put my name on the sign-up sheet and head
to the border with P.T. and the older youth group kids, who
were much more interested in hanging out at the stand selling rocket blasters than they were in ladling soup for the
homeless.

I could tell that P.T. and the youth didn't really want
me around, but I was used to keeping quiet and out of the
way. They put me at the register because I was the only one
who could ring people up without having to use the head-
sized calculator we kept under the counter. I would sit at the
counter working my way through my huge stack of books
while P.T. set off fireworks outside. We weren't supposed

to use the merchandise without paying, so every time P.T. skulked off with a box of Roman candles, I would clear my throat loudly and make sure that he knew that I knew.

Ryan Green was one of the youth volunteers. He was Nana's age, and he'd been over at our house for a couple of Nana's parties. I knew him well enough to dislike him, but if I'd known him better, known that he was the biggest dealer at the high school, I probably would have hated him. He was loud, mean, dumb. I never signed up to volunteer if I saw his name on the sheet, but he was P.T.'s protégé, and, as such, he got to come sometimes even when the list was full.

"Hey, Gifty, when's your brother gonna get back on the court? We're getting our asses whooped without him."

It was two months after Nana's injury. The doctor said that he was healing up nicely, but he was still being cautious with his right side, favoring his other ankle, scared to get hurt again. Our mother and Nana's doctor had cut him off from the pain pill refills, but still, we would find him on the couch more often than not, watching television, or simply looking ahead with that dreamy stare. He had started going back to practice, but he still wasn't putting much weight on that leg and he always came home complaining of pain.

"I don't know," I said to Ryan.

"Well, shit. Tell him we need him."

I made a noncommittal noise and went back to my book. Ryan looked outside to make sure P.T. wasn't heading back in. He was different in front of P.T., still loud and obnoxious, but with a prayerful edge. He didn't curse or spit. He raised both hands during worship and closed his eyes tightly, singing loudly and swaying softly. I disliked him, not just because of his duplicitousness, but because he always carried an empty plastic water bottle around so that he could spit his dip into it. And I would see that thin brown liquid sloshing around in the bottle, and I would see the way he looked at me as though I were no better than the sludge he spit from his mouth, and it would force me to remember that there was an imbalance in my world.

"Hey, why you always reading them books?" he asked.

I shrugged.

"Be better if you tried sports like your brother." He raised his hands up in mock surrender, though I hadn't said anything. "Don't call the NAACP on me or nothing, but them books ain't gonna get you nowhere and sports just might do it. Too bad Nana don't play football though. That's a real game."

He reached across the counter and shut my book. I opened it and he shut it again. I kept the book closed and looked up at him with all of my fury, and he laughed and laughed.

P.T. finally came in, and Ryan immediately straightened up.

"Anybody come in here yet?" P.T. asked.

I was burning mad, but I knew that telling on Ryan would only make my life worse. He pulled out that water bottle and spit into it, still smiling from the memory of his devilment. In church that Sunday, I saw Ryan up in the first pew standing next to P.T., his arms stretched up toward Heaven and tears streaming down his face as the worship leader asked, "How great is our God?" I tried to focus on the music. I tried to focus on Christ, but I couldn't stop looking at Ryan. If the Kingdom of Heaven allowed someone like him in, how could there also be a place for me?

31

I miss thinking in terms of the ordinary, the straight line from birth to death that constitutes most people's lives. The line of those drug-addled years of Nana's life is not so easy to draw, so direct. It zigs and it zags and it slashes.

Nana got hooked on the OxyContin; that much became clear to my mother about two months in, when he asked to go back to the doctor for a second refill. She said no, and then she found more hidden in his light fixture. She thought the problem would just go away, because what did we know about addiction? What, other than the "just say no" campaigns, was there to guide any of us through the jungle of this?

I didn't really understand what was going on yet. I just knew that Nana was always sleepy or sleeping. His head was always nodding, chin to chest, before rolling or bouncing violently back up. I would see him on our couch with this dreamy look on his face and wonder how an ankle injury had knocked him so flat. He, who had always been in motion, how could he now be so still? I asked my mother for money, and the few times she gave it to me, I walked to

Publix and picked up instant coffee. No one in our house had ever touched coffee, but I had heard the way people talked about it at church, how rapturously they approached the dispensers in the Sunday school classroom. I fixed the coffee in our kitchen, following the instructions on the back of the package. I stirred the powder into the water until it turned a deep, dark brown. I tasted it and found it disgusting and so figured it would be sufficiently medicinal. I'd present it to Nana, push his shoulder, his chest, try to rouse him long enough for him to drink it. He never did.

"Can you die from sleeping?" I asked my fourth-grade teacher, Mrs. Bell, after school one day.

She was sitting at her desk, shuffling the papers from the homework assignment we had all turned in. She gave me a funny look, but I was used to getting funny looks for the questions I asked. Always too many, too strange, off topic.

"No, sweetie," Mrs. Bell said. "You can't die from sleeping."

I don't know why I put my faith in her.

Nana sweat so much that his shirts were drenched through mere minutes after he put them on. This was after my mother cleaned out his light fixture, throwing away the last of the prescription pills that he had squirreled away. He had to keep a trash can nearby at all times because he was constantly vomiting. He was constantly shaking. He shit himself more than once. He looked like walking, breathing misery, and I was more scared for him then, sick in his sobriety, than I had been when he was high.

My mother wasn't scared at all. She was a caregiver by profession, and she did what she had always done when a patient was in distress. She would hoist Nana up, lifting him by the armpits, and lower him into the bathtub. She always closed the door, but I could hear them. Him, embarrassed and angry; her, down-to-business. She washed him the way she had when he was a child, the way I knew she must have washed Mr. Thomas, Mrs. Reynolds, Mrs. Palmer, and everyone else in between.

"Lift your leg," I'd hear her command, and then softer, gentler, *"Ebeyeyie."* It will be all right.

There must be some Oedipal shame about lying in the bathtub at sixteen, crying as your mother washes the shit and vomit and sweat off your body. I would avoid Nana for several hours after one of these cleanings, because I knew that somehow my being witness made him feel all the worse. He'd skulk off to his room and hide there until the entire event had to be repeated.

But if I saw my mother in the moments after she'd cleaned her firstborn child, I would go stand by her, be buoyed by her and this wellspring of strength she seemed so capable of drawing from. She never had even the faintest hint of shame. She would see me, my worry and fear and embarrassment and anger, and she would say, "There will come a time when you will need someone to wipe your ass for you," and that would be that.

My mother was accustomed to sickness. She knew what it meant to be close to death, to be around it. She knew that there was a sound to it, that raspy, gurgling noise that comes out and up from whatever part of the body where death hides, lurking, waiting its turn, waiting for life to tag out.

She was with Mrs. Palmer in her final hours. Like my

mother, Mrs. Palmer had been a pious, churchgoing woman, and she'd requested that my mother be at her bedside to read her Scripture before she went on to receive her reward.

"This is what death sounds like," my mother said, and she imitated that crackling noise. "You shouldn't be afraid of it, but you should know it. You should know it when you hear it, because it is the last sound and we all make it."

Mrs. Palmer had been given morphine to ease her pain. She had smoked all her life, even in that final week, and her lungs had become ornamental. Instead of an exhale there was collapse, and every inhale was a whisper. Morphine didn't reshape her lungs into the air-filled sponges they were meant to be, but it offered a distraction, telling the brain, "Instead of air, I can give you a kind of freedom from need."

"That's what drugs are for," my mother lectured Nana and me the first night she returned home from Mrs. Palmer's bedside. "To ease pain."

Nana rolled his eyes and stomped off, and my mother sighed a heavy sigh.

I was afraid of death and of pain. I was afraid of old people. When my mother came home from Mrs. Palmer's house, I wouldn't go near her until after she had taken a shower, washed off whatever it was I worried was clinging to her skin. When she smelled like my mother again, I would go to her, sit beside her and listen to her talk about Mrs. Palmer's decline as though I were gathering before a campfire waiting for the woman holding a flashlight to her face to tell ghost stories.

Where shall I go from your Spirit? Or where shall I flee from your presence? If I ascend to heaven, you are there! If I make my bed in Sheol, you are there! If I take the wings of the morning and dwell in the uttermost parts of the sea, even there your hand shall lead me,

and your right hand shall hold me. My mother would read me
the Scriptures that she had read to Mrs. Palmer, and this one
in particular always stood out. To this day, it brings tears to
my eyes. You are not alone, it says, and that is a comfort, not
to the dying, but to those of us who are terrified of being
left behind.

Because really, it wasn't Mrs. Palmer's death that I was
afraid of; that wasn't the reason my mother had started
trying to teach us about the sound and the relief of pain.
I was scared for Nana. Scared of Nana and the death rattle
that none of us wanted to acknowledge we were listening
for. I have seen people who suffer from addiction and the
family and friends who love them in various places and at
various points in my life. I've seen them sitting on stoops
and on park benches. I've been with them in the lobbies of
rehab centers. And the thing that always strikes me is how
there is always someone in the room who is listening for the
sound, waiting for the arrival of that rasping rattle, knowing
that it will come. Eventually, it will come. The Scriptures
my mother read were as much for us as they were for Mrs.
Palmer. My mother and I wanted blessed assurance because
Nana couldn't offer us assurances of any kind.

I don't know how she did it, but my mother convinced Nana
to accompany us to the First Assemblies one Sunday. He was
still detoxing, too weak to protest. The three of us walked
into the sanctuary, but we didn't take our regular seats. We
sat in the back with Nana at the aisle so that he could get up
and head to the bathroom if he needed to. He looked better than he had in days. I knew this because I couldn't stop
looking at him.

"Jesus, Gifty," he'd say whenever he caught me staring at him for those long stretches, drinking him in. It was like my gaze hurt him, which should have been enough to get me to leave him alone, but I couldn't make myself look away. I felt like I was watching some major natural event—newly hatched sea turtles heading toward the lip of the ocean, bears coming out of hibernation. I was waiting for Nana to emerge, new, reborn.

In the church I grew up in, people cared about rebirth. For months on end, all across the South, all over the world, revival tents are erected. Preachers stand at pulpits promising people that they can rise from the ashes of their lives. "Revival fire fall," I used to sing along with the choir, jubilantly asking that God raze everything to the ground. I stole glances at Nana at the end of our pew, and I thought, *Surely the fire has fallen?*

"Nana?" Ryan Green said as he entered the sanctuary. He clapped Nana on the shoulder, and Nana shrank from his touch. "When are you getting back out on the court?" he asked. "I mean, it's great to see you in church and everything, but church ain't where we need you." He laughed to himself.

"I'll be back soon," Nana said. "My ankle's healing up."

Ryan looked at him skeptically. "Like I said, we're getting killed without you. Prayer ain't helping the guys we got out there playing now. I'd be happy to help you out if there's anything you need in order to get you back on the court."

My mother shot Ryan a killing look. "You don't talk to my son," she said.

"Hey, I'm sorry, Mrs.—"

"Get away from us," she said, so loud this time that a few people in the pew in front of us turned.

"I didn't mean any disrespect, ma'am," Ryan said, amused.

When he left, Nana leaned against the edge of the pew. My mother put her hand on his shoulder, and he shrugged it away.

32

Dear God,
At church today, Bethany said her mom doesn't want
her coming over to our house after service anymore. I told
Buzz, but he didn't care.

I knew without asking that my mother expected us to keep Nana's addiction close to the chest, and the secret ate away at me like moths in cloth. I wished for a priest, a confessional booth, but finally I just settled for my friend Bethany. The Sunday after I confessed, she told me she wasn't allowed to play with me anymore, and suddenly, I knew: addiction was catching, shameful. I didn't talk about Nana's addiction again until college, when one of my lab mates asked me how I knew so much about the side effects of heroin. When I told her about Nana, she said, "This would make such a good TED Talk." I laughed but she kept going. "Seriously, Gifty, you're amazing. You're like taking the pain from losing your brother and you're turning it into this incredible research that might actually help people like him one day." I laughed a little more, tried to shrug her off.

If only I were so noble. If only I even *felt* so noble. The truth is there were times when my mother and I had been driving all over Huntsville for hours searching for Nana, times when I saw him strung out in front of the carp-filled pond at Big Spring Park when I would think, *God, I wish it was cancer,* not for his sake but for mine. Not because the nature of his suffering would change significantly but because the nature of my suffering would. I would have a better story than the one I had. I would have a better answer to the questions "Where's Nana? What happened to Nana?"

Nana is the reason I began this work, but not in a whole-some, made—for—TED Talk kind of way. Instead, this sci-ence was a way for me to challenge myself, to do something truly hard, and in so doing to work through all of my mis-understandings about his addiction and all of my shame. Because I still have so much shame. I'm full to the brim with it; I'm spilling over. I can look at my data again and again. I can look at scan after scan of drug-addicted brains shot through with holes, Swiss-cheesed, atrophied, irreparable. I can watch that blue light flash through the brain of a mouse and note the behavioral changes that take place because of it, and know how many years of difficult, arduous science went into those tiny changes, and still, *still,* think, *Why didn't Nana stop? Why didn't he get better for us? For me?*

He was on a bender the day we found him sprawled out in Big Spring Park. On the grass, spread out like that, he'd looked like an offering. To whom, for what, I couldn't say. He'd been sober for maybe a couple of weeks, but then he didn't come home one night, and we knew. One night turned into two, turned into three. My mother and I couldn't sleep for waiting. As the two of us drove around looking for him, I thought about how tired Nana must have been, tired of our mother washing him in the bathtub like he'd reverted to his original state, tired of all the nothing in a bad way. I don't know who he scored from after our doctor stopped writing him prescriptions, but it must have been easy enough that day in the park because he was gone, just gone.

My mother wanted me to help her get him in the car. She hoisted him up by the armpits and I grabbed his legs but I kept dropping them, and then I would start crying and she would yell at me.

The thing I will never forget is that people were watching us do all of this. It was the middle of a workday and there were people out in that park drinking coffee, taking their smoke breaks, and no one lifted a finger. They just watched us with some curiosity. We were three black people in distress. Nothing to see.

By the time we got Nana in the car, I was doing that snuffling non-cry cry of children who've been told to stop crying. I couldn't stop crying. I was sitting in the back with Nana's head in my lap and I was certain that he was dead, and I was too scared to tell my mother because I knew I would get in trouble for even hinting at his death, and so I just sat there, snuffling, with a dead man on my lap.

Nana wasn't dead. We got him to the house and he woke up, but in that zombie-like way that people who got a little too high wake up. He didn't know where he was. My mother pushed him and he stumbled backward.

"Why do you keep doing this?" she screamed. She started slapping him and he didn't even lift his hands to his face. By that point he was twice her size. All he would have had to do was grab her arm, push her back. He did nothing.

"This has to stop," she kept saying as she hit him. "This has to stop. This has to stop." But she couldn't stop hitting him and he couldn't stop being hit. He couldn't stop any of it.

My God, my God, how ashamed I still am.

33

Most of the time in my work, I begin with the answers, with an idea of the results. I suspect that something is true and then I work toward that suspicion, experimenting, tinkering, until I find what I am looking for. The ending, the answer, is never the hard part. The hard part is trying to figure out what the question is, trying to ask something interesting enough, different enough from what has already been asked, trying to make it all matter.

But how do you know when you are nearing a true end instead of a dead end? How do you finish the experiment? What do you do when, years into your life, you figure out that the yellow brick road you've been easing down leads you directly into the eye of the tornado?

My mother hit Nana, and Nana stood still. Finally, I stepped in between them, and when the first of my mother's slaps landed on my face, she withdrew her hands, flattened them to her sides, looking all around the room in a crazed panic.

She didn't believe in apologizing to children, but this,

the flattened hands and look of horror, was the closest she had ever come.

"This ends here," she said. "This ends today." She stood there for a while longer, watching her two children. My face was stinging from the slap, but I didn't dare lift my hand to soothe it. Behind me, Nana was dazed, still high, hurting. He hadn't spoken.

Our mother left the room, and I eased Nana toward the couch. I pushed him a little and he fell onto it, crumpled into a ball at the armrest, his head nestled near the spot where the treacherous wooden piece had once been. I took off his shoes and looked at his foot, healed scar-less, leaving no trace of nail, of oil. I draped a blanket over him and sat down, and we stayed like that for the rest of the night. For the rest of the night, I watched him come down, nod off, whimper. *This is it,* I thought, because surely none of us could take another day like this.

By morning our mother had come up with a solution. She had been awake all night making calls, though I don't know who she talked to, who she trusted with the addiction that we had been doing our best to keep secret. Nana, sober now, was all apologies, repeating the old mantra: I'm sorry. It will never happen again. I promise you, it will never happen again.

Our mother listened patiently to all of those words we had heard before and then she said something new. "There's a place in Nashville that will take you. They're coming to pick you up and they'll be here in five minutes. I've already packed a bag for you."

"What place, Ma?" Nana said, taking a step back.

"It's a good, Christian place. They'll know what to do. They can help you so you won't be as sick as last time."

"I don't want to go to rehab, Ma. I'll quit. I promise, I'm done. Really, I'm done."

Outside, we heard a car pull up. Our mother went into the kitchen and started packing food into Tupperware. We could hear her prattling around, shuffling through all those lids she kept in perfect order, stacked by size and labeled.

"Gifty, please," Nana hissed, turning to me for the first time. "Say something to her. I—I can't . . ."

His voice trailed off and his eyes filled with tears. The sound of my name, the tenderness with which he'd spoken it, made me feel as though I'd been dunked in cold water.

Our mother packed the Tupperware into what she still called "polythene bags," grocery bags that she collected and reused like they would run out one day. She brought the food and a suitcase into the living room and stood before us.

"We shouldn't keep them waiting," she said.

Nana trained his pleading eyes on me. He looked at me, and I looked away, and outside, the car horn beeped.

Before I started my thesis project, I had floundered a bit, trying to figure out what to do. I had ideas and impressions but I couldn't make them coalesce, I couldn't figure out the right question. I would waste months on one experiment, find that it led nowhere, then backtrack only to end up in the same place as before. The real problem was the fact that I didn't want to look at the question that was staring me right in the face: desire, restraint. Though I had never been an addict, addiction, and the avoidance of it, had been running my life, and I didn't want to give it even one more second of my time. But of course, there it was. The thing I really wanted to know. Can an animal restrain itself from pursuing a reward, especially when there is risk involved? Once I had that question figured out, everything else started to fall into place.

The rehab in Nashville was a thirty-day program. The facility didn't allow visitors, but, after Nana's detox period ended, every Friday we were allowed to call and talk to him for a few minutes. The calls were depressing. "How are you?" I would ask. "Fine," Nana would say, and then silence would hang in the air, counting us down to the end of the phone call. It was the Chin Chin Man all over again, and I worried that this would be the way of things, that Nana and I would spend a lifetime of silent minutes, strangers on the phone.

I'm glad I didn't get a chance to talk to Nana while he was detoxing. I don't think I could have withstood watching him sweat out his addiction again. As it was, those sober Friday calls were enough to break my heart. Every week the sound of his voice changed. He was still angry at our mother and me, still feeling betrayed, but every week, his voice got a little clearer, a little stronger.

My mother and I drove to Nashville to pick him up on his last day there. After thirty days of shitty rehab food, he told us that all he wanted to eat was a chicken sandwich. We pulled into the nearest Chick-fil-A, and Nana and I sat at the booth while our mother ordered. Thirty days, three Friday phone calls, and we had so little to say to each other. When our mother came back with our orders, the three of us ate, making the same dull small talk we'd made before.

"How are you feeling?" my mother asked.

"Good."

"I mean, how—"

Nana took our mother's hand in his. "I'm good, Ma," he said. "I'm going to stay sober. I'm focused and I really, really want to get better, okay?"

"Okay," she said.

Has anyone ever been watched with as much intensity as a beloved family member just out of rehab? My mother and I looked at Nana as though our gazes were the only thing that would keep him there, rooted in the bright red seat, dipping waffle fries in sweet-and-sour sauce. Above his head, there was the Chick-fil-A cow urging us to "eat mor chikin." I'd always found those ads clever, and I'd always had a strange southern pride in this place that retained its Christian values even as it grew. Years later, after my politics and religion had changed, when friends were protesting the restaurant I couldn't make myself do it. All I could think about was that Saturday with Nana, how happy I'd felt to be with my family, to say a quick prayer of healing over our trays of fast food.

As we finished eating, Nana told us about how the staff at the rehab had taken them through morning prayers and taught them meditation. Nana was the youngest one there by a mile, and the staff had been kind and encouraging. In group therapy meetings every evening, the patients talked not simply about their troubles but also about their hopes for the future.

"What did you say?" I asked. The future was something I hadn't allowed myself to think about for some time. While Nana was sick, our lives moved in slow motion and at great speed simultaneously, making it impossible to see what direction things might take.

"I just said that I want to get right, you know. Play basketball, spend time with y'all. That kind of thing."

. . .

How does an animal restrain itself from pursuing a reward, especially when there is risk involved? By the time my mother came to stay with me in California, I had started to get a clearer picture of the answer to this question that I had been obsessing over for most of my graduate career, this test to which I had submitted many mice and many hours of my life. I'd found hints of the two different neural circuits mediating reward-seeking behavior, and I had looked at the neurons to see if there was any detectable difference in pattern. Once I'd confirmed a difference, I used calcium imaging to record the mice's brain activity so that I could determine which of the two circuits was important to the behavior. Finally, at the end of all of this, I had almost enough information to write a paper that showed that if one were to use optogenetics to stimulate the mPFC→NAc risk-encoding cells, then, yes, it was possible to suppress reward seeking.

All of this behavior manipulation, all of this tweaking and adjusting, injecting and imaging, to find out that restraint was *possible,* that it could, through arduous science, be done. All of this work to try to get to the bottom of the thing that had no bottom: Nana relapsed just fourteen hours after leaving rehab.

34

Opioids work on the reward circuits of the brain. The first time you take them, your brain is so flooded with dopamine that you are left thinking that, like food, like sex, opioids are good for you, necessary for the very survival of your species. "Do it again! Do it again!" your brain tells you, but every time you listen, the drugs work a little less and demand a little more, until finally you give them everything and get nothing in return—no rush, no surge of pleasure, just a momentary relief from the misery of withdrawal.

I attended a lecture Han was giving about the process of imaging cells involved with reward expectation. The lecture hall wasn't packed, so Han spotted me as soon as I walked in. He shot me a little wave.

I took a seat in the back as Han got started. On the projector screen, dopamine neurons spun purple with small green flashes throughout.

"The green that you're seeing up there are the active release sites on the dopamine neurons," Han said, using his laser pointer to indicate the spots. "The mesocortical, meso-limbic, and nigrostriatal dopamine pathways are what we call the reward pathways, all right? They're the ones that activate when we're expecting or receiving a reward."

Han scanned the room, and I gave him a thumbs-up when his eyes landed on me. He grinned, then coughed to cover up the grin. He continued lecturing, and I looked around the room. Ambitious undergrads mostly, attending a midday neuroscience lecture perhaps for class credit, or perhaps because they wanted to pursue a career in the field, or perhaps just out of plain old curiosity.

When Han finally finished, I waited for the room to clear. I sat in my seat as he started shuffling the papers on his desk. I raised my hand, but he wasn't looking at me so I cleared my throat loudly. "Excuse me, Professor?" I said.

He started laughing, leaned against the desk. "Yes, Gifty?"

"Are you telling me that when I get a 'like' on my Face-book posts, dopamine is released?"

"Why yes, right you are," he said.

"What about when I do something bad?" I asked.

Han shrugged. "Depends. What kind of thing? How bad are we talking?"

"Bad, bad," I said, and he just laughed and laughed.

35

Dear God,
I wish Nana would just die already. Please, just let this
be over.

36

All of the self-help literature I've read says that you have to talk about your pain to move through it, but the only person I ever felt like I wanted to talk to about Nana was my mother and I knew she couldn't handle it. It felt unfair, to pile my pain on top of hers, and so I swallowed it instead. I wrote journal entries that grew increasingly frantic, increasingly desperate, until I reached that one, heinous line.

"God will read what you write, and he will answer your writing like prayers," my mother once said. The night I wished for my brother's death I thought, *Good, so be it,* but by the light of morning, when I realized that I had written a sentence for which I would never forgive myself, I ripped it out of my notebook, tore it to shreds, then flushed it down the toilet, hoping God would forget. What had I done? When Nana relapsed, I burrowed in my shame. I went quiet.

I went quiet and my mother went insane. She became a kind of one-woman child hunter, driving up and down the streets of Huntsville searching for my brother. At church she would move up to the altar during praise and worship and dance around like a woman possessed. If the song made any mention of "falling on one's knees" she would take it literally, thudding down immediately in a way that seemed painful.

Church gossip is as old as the church itself, and oh how my church loved to gossip. Years later, Mary, the pastor's daughter, would become the worship leader. Her toddler would run around the sanctuary every morning before she took him to the nursery, and everyone would smile sweetly at him, all the while remembering the circumstances under which he came to be. That gossip was as juicy as a peach. My congregation got fat on it, but when Mary got married we starved. Before that there was Nana and my mother's ridiculous dances at the altar. If Mary's pregnancy was a peach, then Nana had been a feast.

Everyone knew that Nana had gotten hurt in a game, but it took them a while to catch up to his addiction. Every Sunday, when Pastor John asked for prayer requests, my mother and I would put Nana's name in the basket. Pray for his healing, we said, and, at first, it was easy for everyone to assume we meant his ankle. But how long does it take God to heal a sprained ankle?

"I heard he's on drugs," Mrs. Cline said. She was a deacon at the First Assemblies. Fifty-five years old, unmarried, straight as a broom with lips so thin they looked like a slit across her face.

"No," Mrs. Morton gasped.

"Oh yes, honey. Why do you think he doesn't come around here anymore? He's not playing this season, so we know he's not too busy."

"That's sad. That's sad he's on drugs."

"It is sad, but—and I really do hate to say this—their kind does seem to have a taste for drugs. I mean, they are *always* on drugs. That's why there's so much crime."

"You're right. I have noticed that."

I had been studying my Bible verses in the Sunday school room when I overheard that conversation in the hallway. If I'd heard it today, I know what I would have done. I would have marched outside and told them that there is no data to support the idea that black people are biologically more given to drugs or crime than any other race. I would have marched out of that church and never looked back.

But I was ten years old and I was ashamed. I sat stock still in my chair and hoped that they couldn't hear me on the other side of the door. I gripped the open flaps of my Bible so tightly that I left marks pressed into the pages. When they left, I let out the breath I was holding, and pinched the skin between my thumb and index finger, a trick I'd picked up to help keep me from crying. In that moment, and for the first time in my life really, I hated Nana so completely. I hated him, and I hated myself.

I am not a psychologist or a historian or a social scientist. I can examine the brain of a depressed animal, but I am not given to thinking about what circumstances, if any, led up to that depression. Like everyone else, I get a part of the story, a single line to study and recite, to memorize.

When I was a child, no one ever said the words "institutionalized racism." We hardly even said the word "racism." I don't think I took a single class in college that talked about the physiological effects of years of personally mediated racism and internalized racism. This was before studies came out that showed that black women were four times more likely to die from childbirth, before people were talking about epigenetics and whether or not trauma was heritable. If those studies were out there, I never read them. If those classes were offered, I never took them. There was little interest in these ideas back then because there was, there *is,* little interest in the lives of black people.

What I'm saying is I didn't grow up with a language for, a way to explain, to parse out, my self-loathing. I grew up only with my part, my little throbbing stone of self-hate that I carried around with me to church, to school, to all those places in my life that worked, it seemed to me then, to affirm the idea that I was irreparably, fatally, wrong. I was a child who liked to be right.

We were the only black people at the First Assemblies of God Church; my mother didn't know any better. She thought the God of America must be the same as the God of Ghana, that the Jehovah of the white church could not possibly be different from the one of the black church. That day when she saw the marquee outside asking, "Do you feel lost?" that day when she first walked into the sanctuary, she began to lose her children, who would learn well before she did that not all churches in America are created equal, not in practice and not in politics. And, for me, the damage of going to a church where people whispered disparaging words about "my kind" was itself a spiritual wound—so deep and so hidden that it has taken me years to find and address it. I didn't know what to make of the world that I was in back then. I didn't know how to reconcile it. When my mother and I made prayer requests for Nana, did the congregation really pray? Did they really care? When I heard the gossip of those two women, I saw the veil lift and the shadow world of my religion came into view. Where was God in all of this? Where was God if he was not in the hushed quiet of a Sunday school room? Where was God if he was not in me? If my blackness was a kind of indictment, if Nana would never be healed and if my congregation could never truly believe in the possibility of his healing, then where was God?

My journal entry from the night I heard Mrs. Morton and Mrs. Cline talking:

Dear God,
Please hurry up and make Buzz better. I want the whole
church to see.

I knew, even as I was writing that entry, that God didn't work that way, but then I wondered, how exactly did he work? I doubted him, and I hated myself for doubting him. I thought that Nana was proving everyone right about us, and I wanted him to get better, be better, because I thought that being good was what it would take to prove everyone wrong. I walked around those places, pious child that I was, thinking that my goodness was proof negative. "Look at me!" I wanted to shout. I wanted to be a living theorem, a Logos. Science and math had already taught me that if there were many exceptions to a rule, then the rule was not a rule. Look at me.

This was all so wrongheaded, so backward, but I didn't know how to think any differently. The rule was never a rule, but I had mistaken it for one. It took me years of questioning and seeking to see more than my little piece, and even now I don't always see it.

. . .

My mother went insane when Nana relapsed, and I went quiet. I burrowed inside my own mind, hiding there, feverishly writing in my journal, hoping for Rapture. These were in fact the end times, not of the world but of my belief. I just couldn't see it yet.

I was quiet, and I was angry at just how easily and quickly everyone in our lives had turned on Nana. Even sports could no longer protect him. When Nana was king, Pastor John would sometimes call him up onto the stage on Sundays, and the congregation would stretch out our hands and pray for his upcoming week, for victory in all the games that he was about to play. Up there, with his head bowed, our hands outstretched in coronation, Nana received every blessing. And when game time came and his team won, all of us were gratified. "How great is our God?" we would sing during praise and worship, and we would believe it.

On the days, rare though they were, when Nana's team lost, I would listen to that spark of rage rush through the crowd.

"C'mon."

"Get your head in the game."

This was basketball in Alabama, not football. People didn't care as much, and yet still, this was the nature of their caring. Before Nana had made his team important in our state, the stands had been nearly empty at every game, but when his team got good, every spectator became an expert.

Nana played exactly two games during his addiction. He was a mess out there, sloppy and unfocused. He missed shot after shot; he dropped the ball and sent it careening toward the bleachers.

"Where'd this fucking coon learn how to play?" one

angry fan shouted, and I couldn't believe how fast the fall, how quick the turn.

When Nana was down, Pastor John stopped calling him up to the altar to receive our prayers, our outstretched hands. He played those two games as though he had just recently heard what basketball was. On the night of the last game he ever played, he was booed by everyone in the stands. Both sides, both sets of fans, joined their voices in chorus. Nana threw the ball as hard as he could against the wall when the referee made a call he didn't like. The ref kicked him out of the game and everyone cheered as Nana looked around, raising his middle fingers at all of us and storming off the court. In the stands that night, booing, I saw Ryan Green. I saw Mrs. Cline. I saw my church, and I couldn't unsee.

Love the Lord your God with all your heart and with all your soul and with all your mind and with all your strength . . . Love your neighbor as yourself. There is no commandment greater than these. I thought about that verse a lot in those days. Three pages of my childhood journals are filled with that verse, copied over and over again until my handwriting gets sloppy, lazy. I was trying to remind myself to love God, to love my neighbor.

But the instruction is not simply to love your neighbor. It is to do so in the same way as you love yourself, and herein was the challenge. I didn't love myself, and even if I had, I couldn't love my neighbor. I had begun to hate my church, hate my school, my town, my state.

Try though she might, my mother couldn't convince Nana to come to church with us again after our Sunday in the last pew. I was relieved, but I didn't share that with her.

I didn't want everybody staring at us, making their judgments. I didn't want further proof of God's failure to heal
my brother, a failure that I saw as unbelievably cruel, despite
a lifetime of hearing that God works in mysterious ways.
I wasn't interested in mystery. I wanted reason, and it was
becoming increasingly clear to me that I would get none of
it in that place where I had spent so much of my life. If I
could have stopped going to the First Assemblies altogether,
I would have. Every time I thought I might, I would picture
my mother up there at the altar, twirling and falling, singing with praise, and I knew that if I didn't go to our church
with her she would simply go alone. That she would simply
be alone, the last person on Earth who still believed that God
might heal her son, and I couldn't imagine anything lonelier
than that.

37

Now I want to write about Nana's addiction from inside it. That's how I want to know it, as though it were my own. I took meticulous notes of his final years in my journal. I wrote like an anthropologist with Nana as my sole subject. I can tell you what his skin looked like (sallow), what his hair looked like (uncombed, uncut). I can tell you that he, always too skinny, had lost so much weight that his eyes started to bulge against the sunkeness of his orbital sockets. But all of this information is useless. The ethnography of my journal is painful to read and unhelpful besides, because I can never know the inside of my brother's mind, what it felt like to move through the world in his body, in his final days. My journal entries were me trying to find a way into a place that has no entrances, no exits.

Nana started stealing from our mother. Small things at first, her wallet, her checkbook, but soon the car was gone and so was the dining room table. Soon Nana was gone too. For days and weeks at a time he went missing, and my mother went after him. It got to be so that she and I knew the names of every receptionist and every cleaning lady of every motel in Huntsville.

"You can give up if you want to," my mother would sometimes hiss at the Chin Chin Man over the phone, "but I will never give up. I will never give up."

The Chin Chin Man called regularly in those days. I'd talk to him on the phone for a few minutes, answering his boring questions and listening to the way time and guilt had changed his voice, and then I would hand the phone over to my mother and wait for the two of them to finish fighting.

"Where were you?" my mother once said to him over the phone. "Where have you been?" It was the same thing she said to Nana on the nights when he would slink in through the back door, coming down from a high, reeking to high Heaven, not expecting to find our mother holding vigil in the living room.

Those were the days of the broken things. Nana punched a hole through the wall. He smashed the television down onto the floor, and shattered every picture frame and lightbulb in the house. He called me a nosy cunt the night I caught him raving downstairs, and my mother ran up so that the two of us could hide from him.

We blocked the door to my bedroom with a chair, but soon he was pounding against it. "Fuck you both," he said, and we could hear the sound of his shoulder smashing against the door, and we could see the way the door wanted to give from its hinges, wanted to let him in. And my mother answered, loud in prayer, "Lord, protect my son. Lord, protect my son." I was afraid and I was angry. Who would protect us?

It was almost better when he was high. When he was high, he wasn't sick; he wasn't angry. He was subdued, quiet, gone. I saw him shoot up only once. On the couch, in the living room of our house, he plunged a needle into the crook of his elbow, and then he slipped away somewhere, oblivious to me and to everything else around him. I have never seen a needle since without thinking of him. I have preferred the flesh of mice to that of humans because I never want to put a needle into an elbow. I cannot see a median cubital vein and not see my brother nodding off and away on our couch.

How do I talk about the day he died? I don't remember that morning, and my journal entry from the night before says only: *Buzz looked tired but good!* I've read that line so many times in the years since, and the exclamation point still mocks me. I must have gone to school that day. I must have come home, made myself a snack, and waited for my mother to get home. I didn't expect to see Nana, but I had seen him the night before and I wasn't worried.

I do remember that my mother didn't come home on time. She was with the Foster family, new to her since Mrs. Palmer's passing. She was back on day shift, so she usually got in by seven o'clock. Instead, that night, she shuffled in at eight, apologizing while unloading the car. Mr. Foster's daughter was in town and the woman had talked her ear off.

I'd made myself dinner and I offered some to my mother. We both stared at the clock, and then the door, the clock and then the door. He didn't come in. We had developed a routine, an unspoken rule. Nana got two days before we hopped in the car and searched for him. He got four days before we called the police, but it had only come to that once, and that night was day one. We weren't there yet.

We didn't know to worry, so when the police knocked on our door at about nine o'clock to tell us that Nana had overdosed on heroin and died in the parking lot of a Starbucks, we were blindsided. We'd thought our routine would save us, save him.

I didn't write anything in my journal that night or for many years thereafter.

38

I ran into Katherine at the sandwich shop about a week after I'd bumbled through our lunch. I saw her bent over before a wire rack of chips, trying to pick out which ones she wanted, and I turned on my heels to escape.

"Gifty!" she shouted. I'd almost made it to the door. She jogged over toward me, a bag of sour cream and onion in hand. "How are you doing?" she asked.

"Oh hi, Katherine. I'm doing great, thanks," I said.

"Why don't you join me for lunch?"

"I've got a lot of work to do."

"It'll still be there after you eat," she said, reaching for my hand. "I insist."

She paid for the chips and my sandwich as well, and we headed over to the high-tops at the far end of the shop. It was almost empty save a few undergrads who had made their way over to this graduate student part of campus, probably for the quiet, the decreased chance of recognition. I'd once been like that, so lonely that I craved further loneliness. Even after I'd made a few friends in college, I would still go out of my way to create whatever conditions I needed that might allow me to be alone. If I'd done it right that day, I wouldn't be stuck eating with Katherine.

"Are you still having trouble writing?" Katherine asked.

"It's been a lot better," I said. I picked at my sandwich while Katherine popped open her bag of chips and started eating them slowly, one chip at a time.

We sat there quietly for some time. I wanted to escape the intensity of Katherine's gaze, and so I stared down at my food as though the key to life was stuffed between sourdough slices. Finally, Katherine broke the silence.

"You know, Steve is from the East Coast and he really wants to move back after I finish here, but why would anyone want to live anywhere that isn't California? I spent a summer in LA and now even the Bay Area is too cold for me. Seasons are overrated."

"Did you decide about the baby thing?"

She looked surprised. Clearly she didn't remember telling me about Steve's surreptitious ovulation calendar. "We haven't figured that out yet. He wants to start trying, but I want to wait until after my postdoc at least. I'm thirty-six, so it might be an uphill battle maybe, but that's true of my work too. I just don't know. What about you? Do you ever think about having kids?"

I shook my head quickly, too quickly. "I don't think I'd be a very good mother," I said. "Besides, I haven't had sex in like a year." Suddenly, I felt embarrassed by my revelation, but Katherine didn't seem even the least bit fazed. I felt like I'd shrugged the shoulder of my dress off, revealing skin. I'd lost some of my timidity around the subject of sex, but not all of it. For years I hadn't been able to reconcile wanting to *feel* good with wanting to *be* good, two things that often seemed at odds during sex, especially sex the way I liked it.

Every time, afterward, I would lie there staring at the ceiling, picturing my promises like little balloons floating up and away, ready to be popped.

I met Justin, the guy I officially lost my virginity to, at a mixer in New York called POC x Ivy League the summer after I'd graduated college. The first time we had sex, my body had been so rigid, my vagina so tense, that he looked at me uncertainly and said, "I don't think I can do this. Like literally, I don't think I can get it in."

"What should we do?" I asked, mortified but determined. I was taking the train back to Boston in a few hours, and I wanted this, wanted him. He left the room and came back with a jar of coconut oil, and after some massaging and encouraging, he was inside me. It hurt then, but by the end of that summer, we had found a delicious rhythm, visiting each other every few weekends just to spend a night or two together. I started to want more, more scratching, more talking.

"Are you a bad girl?" Justin would ask in bed. I was heading to California soon for graduate school, and we both knew, had always known, that the end was near. "Are you a bad, bad girl?"

"Yes," I said through gritted teeth, enjoying the pleasure he gave me, but in my head, I thought, *No, no, no. Why can't I be good?*

Katherine finished eating her chips and wiped her hands on a napkin. "You're still in your twenties, right?" she said. "Jesus, you're so young, and so damn brilliant. I honestly can't wait to see what you do in like five years, and if kids aren't a part of that equation, who cares? Your work is going to be big. I can feel it. What got you into this field anyway?"

The question threw me off guard, which was probably

what she'd intended. I looked at Katherine. Powder from the chips had collected on her lips, giving them a pale white shimmer.

"My mom's depressed. She's staying with me at the moment. In my bed. She's suffered from depression in the past and had a bad experience with psychiatric care, so she's really resistant to getting help. So, yeah, she's been here with me for about two weeks now." The words rushed out of me and I was so happy, so relieved, once they were said.

Katherine stretched out her hand, placed it over my own. "I'm so sorry. This must be really hard for you," she said. "How can I help?"

Gye Nyame, I wanted to say. Only God can help me.

My mother took a week off of work after Nana died. She wanted to throw a big, Ghanaian-style funeral complete with food and music and dancing. She sent money and measurements to the Chin Chin Man so that he could have our mourning clothes made. When they arrived, I took mine out of the package and held it. It was bloodred and waxy to the touch, and I didn't want to wear it. I couldn't remember the last time I had been required to wear traditional dress, and I thought it would seem like a lie. I felt about as Ghanaian as apple pie, but how could I tell that to my mother?

What weeping, what gnashing of teeth. My mother was nearly unrecognizable to me. When the policemen left our house the night of Nana's overdose, she fell to the ground, rocking, clawing at her arms and legs until she drew blood, crying out the Lord's name, *"Awurade, Awurade, Awurade."* She had not stopped crying since. How could I tell her that I found my mourning clothes garish? That I didn't want the

attention this funeral would draw? I didn't want any attention at all, and in those first few weeks I was safe from it.
Nothing teaches you the true nature of your friendships like
a sudden death, worse still, a death that's shrouded in shame.
No one knew how to talk to us, and so they didn't even try.
I should never have been left alone with my mother in those
days after Nana died, and my mother should never have been
left alone with herself. Where was our church? Where were
the few Ghanaians, scattered through Alabama, whom my
mother had built friendships with? Where was my father?
My mother, a woman who hardly ever cried, cried so much
that first week she fainted from dehydration. I stood over
her body, fanning her with the closest thing I could find—
her Bible. When she came to and figured out what had happened, she apologized. She promised me that she wouldn't
cry anymore, a promise she wasn't yet capable of keeping.

Where was Pastor John in all of this? He and his wife
sent flowers to our house that first week. He came by after
church the third Sunday, the only three Sundays since join-
ing the First Assemblies that my mother had missed a service. I answered the door, and the first thing he did was put
his hand on my shoulder and start praying.

"Lord, I ask that you cover this young lady with your
blessings. I ask that you remind her that you are near, that
you walk with her as she walks through her grief."

I wanted to shrug his arm away, but I was so grateful to
see him, so grateful for his, for anyone's, touch that I stood
there and I received.

He came into the house. My mother was in the living
room, and Pastor John went to her, sat down beside her
on our couch. He put his hands on her shoulders, and she
crumpled. It looked as intimate to me as nakedness, and so I

left the room, giving them space to be with each other and with the Lord. Though I have not always loved Pastor John, I loved him dearly the day that he finally showed up. He has stayed in my life and my mother's life ever since.

I never told my mother that I hated the funeral cloth. I wore mine, and my mother wore hers, and the two of us welcomed the guests to the clubhouse my mother had rented for Nana's funeral. Ghanaians came—from Alabama and Tennessee and Ohio and Illinois. And in Ghana, at the funeral that the Chin Chin Man threw, Ghanaians came—from Cape Coast and Mampong and Accra and Takoradi.

My mother paced up and down the room, singing:

Ohunu mu nni me dua bi na masɔ mu
Nsuo ayiri me oo, na otwafoɔ ne hwan?

There is no branch which I could grasp
I am in swamped waters, where is my savior?

I didn't know the song, and even if I had, I'm not sure I would have joined in. I sat in the front row with the handful of other Ghanaians worthy of the receiving line and shook hands with all the mourners who passed through. As their hands gripped mine, all I could think about was how desperate I was to wash away each touch, to turn the faucet to scalding heat, to get clean, get rid.

We were at the Elks Lodge, the only facility large enough to hold the extravagant funeral my mother wanted to throw. But the Elks Lodge was no Kumasi funeral tent, and though we had invited everyone from Nana's basketball team, his old soccer teams, everyone from the church, the entirety of the little world my mother had managed to build in fifteen years, the space was still only half full.

My mother kept pacing and singing her song:

Prayɛɛ, mene womma oo
Ena e, akamenkoa oo
Agya e, ahia me oo

What will become of us
I am left alone
I am impoverished

The Ghanaians wept and paced, threw up their hands and questioned God. The Americans stood, baffled.

Before long, Pastor John took the microphone and went up to the makeshift pulpit at the front of the room in order to say a word.

"We know that Nana was a talented young man. Many of us in this room saw him on the basketball court, shooting that basketball toward the Heavens themselves. It brought us joy to watch him and to recognize in this young man the glory of the Lord. Now whenever a young person dies, it's easy for those of us who were left behind to get angry. We think, why would God do this? Nana had so much to give, God, why? It's normal to feel that way, but let me remind you, God doesn't make mistakes. I said, God doesn't make mistakes. Amen? God in his infinite wisdom saw fit to bring Nana home to him, and we have to believe that the Heaven where Nana is now is so much more wonderful than anything this world had to offer him. Nana is in a better place, with our Heavenly Father, and one day we will have the great joy, the great, great joy, of meeting him there."

I sat there listening to Pastor John's words, listening to the amens and hallelujahs that rose up in chorus around those words, thinking, *Nana would have hated all of this*. And that knowledge, and that roomful of people who knew my brother but didn't know him, who skirted around the circumstances of his death, talking about him as though only the portion of his life that had taken place before his addiction was worthy of examination and compassion, wrecked me and felled the long-growing tree of my belief. I sat there in that lodge, reduced to a stump, wondering what would become of me.

39

The Chin Chin Man had sent us pictures of Nana's Ghanaian funeral. There were hundreds of people gathered in a tent in Kumasi, wearing clothes similar to the ones my mother and I had worn. My father was in only one of the photos. He looked stately in his black-and-red wrapper. His face was an old, faded memory. I had never looked like him, but, staring at the photo, I could see myself in his bent head, his sad eyes.

"They had a good turnout," my mother said as she flipped through the photos. "Your father did well."

I didn't know any of the other people pictured. Most of them hadn't known Nana, but a few said that they could remember the baby he once was.

When the Chin Chin Man called to ask if we had received the photos, I talked to him for a few minutes.

"What did you tell everyone?" I asked him.

"What do you mean?"

"About how Nana died. What did you tell them? What did you tell your wife?"

He paused and I looked at the photo of him, waiting for an answer. "I said he was sick. I said he was sick. Is that not true?"

I didn't even hand the phone to my mother. I just hung up. I knew she would call him back and that the two of them would whisper about me before they went over every detail about the funeral. What was eaten, what songs were played, what dances danced.

"I don't like how you disrespected your father," my mother said later that day. She hadn't gone to work in two weeks, and it was strange for me to see her in the house at every hour, doing everyday things, coming to my room to dispense a parenting reproach an American child might get on television. In those first few weeks after Nana died, before my mother's crash, I'd felt as though I was living the same life, but upside down, backward. Things looked normal to the untrained eye, but when had my mother ever been home, awake, talking to me at three in the afternoon?

"Sorry," I said.

"They had a good turnout at the funeral," she said.

"You already said that."

She glared at me in warning and I remembered myself. Things hadn't gotten so backward that I could become a regular American preteen girl, mouthing off to her mother.

"Do you wish you could have been there?" I asked, changing course.

"In Ghana? No. Nana would not have wanted that."

She stood there leaning against my doorframe for a little while longer. In those days, and still, I was always wondering how to be with her. Should I have gotten up and forced her into a hug? She told me she was going to take an Ambien. She left the room, and I could hear her rustling around the bathroom searching for the sleeping pills she'd come to rely on to survive her many years of working the night shift. I could hear her get into bed. Little did I know.

The Ambien made my mother loopy and mean. She would take one, but she wouldn't fall asleep right away. Instead she would wander around the house, looking for trouble. Once, she found me in the kitchen making myself a peanut butter sandwich and she said, "You know I didn't want another child after Nana." On Ambien, her words were always slow, slurred, like each one was dipped in the shocked sleep of that drug before it escaped her lips.

"I only wanted Nana," she said, "and now I only have you."

I know how this makes her sound. She said those words and then she ambled back upstairs to her bedroom. Within minutes, I could hear her snoring. I was hurt by what she said, but I understood what she meant. I understood and I forgave. I only wanted Nana, too, but I only had my mother.

Whenever she woke up from the drug-induced sleep, she looked frantic, like a woman who had been dropped down onto some deserted island and told that she had only an hour to find water. Her eyes were wild. The pupils darted around, searching, searching. Watching her, I would feel like a lion tamer or a snake charmer. *Whoa there,* I'd think as she slipped slowly back into reality.

"Where am I?" she asked one day.

"You're at home. At your house in Huntsville," I said.

She shook her head, and her eyes stopped searching. Instead they found me out, found me wanting. "No," she said, and then louder still, "No." She went back upstairs, got back in bed. That was the beginning.

40

My mother in bed at fifty-two. My mother in bed at sixty-eight. When I lay the two images of her side by side, looking for the differences, at first there seem to be few. She was older, thinner, more wrinkled. Her hair, late to gray, was now sprouting a few silver strands here and there. These differences were subtle but present. Harder to spot: me at eleven—out of my depth; me at twenty-eight—still so.

Ambien is a drug meant only for the short term. It's a drug for shift workers, people who've long lost their circadian rhythm, but it's also used by people who just want to fall asleep a little easier. The drug is in a class known as hypnotics, and it seemed to me, that first day when I couldn't get my mother out of bed, that the hypnosis had simply worked too well.

I had been skipping church ever since Nana's funeral, and that first day of my mother's slumber I considered skipping school too. It was the only time in my life that I can remember not wanting to go to school, because while I hated the social aspects of my middle school, I loved school itself. I loved the classrooms, and I especially loved the library with its old, damp smell.

I couldn't get my mother up, so I decided to put off thinking about what to do and walk to school.

"Are you all right, Gifty?" Mrs. Greer, the librarian, asked when she saw me in the stacks. I was letting the sweat from my walk cool under the frigid blast of the air conditioner. I hadn't expected anyone to be in the library at that early hour. Even Mrs. Greer tended to show up a bit late, supersized Diet Coke in hand and a sheepish grin on the days I was there first, browsing while she booted up the computers for the checkout system. She was a librarian who was always thinking about ways to make reading hip and cool for young people. The problem was she said things like "Let's make reading hip and cool for all you young people" to the students themselves, which meant her plans would never work.

I didn't mind that the library was neither cool nor hip. I liked Mrs. Greer with her soda addiction and her dedication to the eighties perm. In fact, if there was anyone at school that year who would have honestly cared about my problems at home, who would have listened to my worries and found a way to help, it would have been Mrs. Greer.

"I'm fine," I told her, and as soon as the lie left my lips I knew that I was going to take care of my mother myself. I was going to nurse her back to health through the sheer force of my eleven-year-old will. I would not lose her.

My mother at sixty-eight and me at twenty-eight. Katherine started dropping by my office. She brought baked goods:

cookies and pies, fresh bread, a pound cake. She would sit in the corner of my office and insist that we tuck in to whatever it was she had brought right away, even if I was in the middle of writing, which was my usual excuse and almost never really true. "I've never tried this recipe before," Katherine would say, brushing off my faint protests. "Let's see if it's any good."

It was always good. I knew she was not exactly lying, but skirting the truth about the reason for her visits. These home-baked treats were her way of saying that she was there if I needed her. I wasn't ready to need her, but I ate everything she made. I brought the baked goods home to my mother, and, to my delight, she ate some of the things too. When Katherine came back, I would say, "I think my mom really liked the lemon pound cake," and the next day, there would be a fresh lemon pound cake in my mailbox, wrapped in cellophane and tied with ribbons, and so professional looking that I started calling them "Kathy's Cakes" in my head, capital letters and everything, like she was a one-woman bakery. I don't know how she found the time.

I rushed home from school early the first week of my mother's bedroom exile. Every afternoon was the same. I would push her arm and she would murmur softly, loudly enough to convince me that she was still alive. I made her peanut butter and jelly sandwiches, and when, hours later, I found them untouched, I threw them out and washed the plates. I cleaned everything I could think to clean—the bathroom, the garage, her bedroom and mine. I never went into Nana's room. Instead, I dragged the steam cleaner out from the nether reaches of the closet and steamed the living room carpet, emptying the grayish water into the bathtub over and over again. It soothed me to see all of the filth travel down the drain, leaving nothing but cleaner and cleaner water in its stead. I wanted my life to look like that process. I wanted my mother and me to come out of this difficult period clear, free.

I was accustomed to being alone at home but this, this false aloneness, was so much worse than any loneliness I had ever felt before. Knowing that my mother was in the house, knowing that she couldn't, wouldn't, get out of the bed to be near me, to help me in my sadness, made me angry and then my anger made me feel guilty, and so on and so on, in a terrible loop. To combat it, I kept the television on from the time I came home in the afternoons to the time I left in the mornings. I wanted my mother to hear it, to come out of her bedroom and yell at me about how much energy I was wasting. I wanted to hear her tell me, down to the cent, how much she paid in electricity every month, how much money my life was costing her—me, the child she had never wanted.

"Don't let the cold air out," she used to say when she caught me staring into the vortex of our refrigerator for too long, hoping the yet unknown thing I wanted to eat would magically reveal itself. "Do you know how much I pay for electricity?"

So, as she lay in bed, I kept the TV on. I let the cold air out.

Han knocked on the door of my office.

"Come in," I said. Kathy had dropped off one of her cakes earlier, and it sat there on my desk, beautifully wrapped, taunting me.

"I'm headed to Philz for a coffee. Can I get you anything?"

"Aw, thanks, Han," I said. "I'm actually going to go home soon."

"Wow, Gifty taking the rest of the day off?" he said. "What's the occasion?"

I swallowed hard. "My mom's in town," I said. "I was thinking we'd split this strawberry cake Katherine made."

I knew it was magical thinking, but it made me feel better to say it, to imagine my mother and me sitting on my small balcony with two forks and a fat slice of cake.

Han said, "See you tomorrow, then," and I packed up the rest of my stuff and drove home. When I got there, I set Kathy's Cake down on the nightstand next to my mother and picked up the Bible. I started reading to her from the book of John. It was her favorite Gospel, and, though it seemed like forever ago, it had been mine as well. I wanted to read to her about Lazarus, the man from Bethany whom Jesus had raised from the dead.

Even when I was a child, this miracle had seemed like a stretch to me, too miraculous an event in a book filled with miraculous events. David and Goliath, Daniel and the lion's den, even Jonah and the whale, had seemed plausible, but Lazarus, four days dead, then beckoned back to life with one "Come forth" from Jesus, seemed like a step too far.

The problem for me then wasn't that I didn't believe that Jesus could do it. It was that I didn't understand why he would. I'd spent every Easter of my childhood in a pastel-colored dress and white patent-leather shoes, scream-singing "He is ri-i-i-sen, HE IS RI-I-I-SEN, AND HE LIVES FOR-EVERMORE," celebrating with relish the resurrection of a man whom death could not conquer. And so what to make of Lazarus's coming forth? Why would Jesus steal his own thunder in that way, and why did we not sing songs for Lazarus, the man who God thought deserved to live again?

"Our friend Lazarus sleeps, but I go that I may wake him up," I read, but my mother didn't stir. I put the Bible away and went back into the kitchen to put a pot of tea on. Thinking about Lazarus has always led me to think about what it means to be alive, what it means to participate in the world, to be awake. When I was a child, I wondered how long Lazarus lived after he died. Was he still among us now? An ancient, a vampire, the last remaining miracle? I wanted an entire book of the Bible to be devoted to him and to how he must have felt to be the recipient of God's strange and amazing grace. I wondered if he was the same man he was before he cheated death or if he was forever changed, and I wondered how long forever was to a man who had once been asleep.

Looking back, I could see that I was so easily psychoanalyzable. I stirred my tea, thought about Katherine, thought about Lazarus, and played therapist to myself, recognizing the cliché of picking the book of John, picking Lazarus, for that particular moment in my life.

"Do you believe in the Gospel of Jesus Christ as evidenced by the Holy Spirit?" I asked myself, laughing alone in my kitchen. I didn't bother answering.

In *Philosophical Foundations of Neuroscience,* Bennett and Hacker write:

> What [neuroscience] *cannot* do is *replace* the wide range of ordinary psychological explanations of

human activities in terms of reasons, intentions, purposes, goals, values, rules and conventions by neurological explanations . . . For it makes no sense to ascribe such psychological attributes to anything less than the animal as a whole. It is the animal that perceives, not parts of its brain, and it is human beings who think and reason, not their brains. The brain and its activities *make it possible* for *us*—not for *it*—to perceive and think, to feel emotions, and to form and pursue projects.

While there were many "philosophy and the mind" or "philosophy and psychology" courses offered when I was an undergrad, there were few philosophy and neuroscience courses to be found. Bennett and Hacker's book was recommended to me my junior year by a TA named Fred who had once called me "unnerving and untraditional," which I took to mean that he thought I asked too many of the wrong kinds of questions. I'm fairly certain he gave me the book to get me out of his office hours, if not forever, then at least for the length of time it would take me to read it. I had never thought of my scientific questions, my religious questions, as philosophical questions, but nonetheless, I went back to my dorm's common room, opened the book, and read until I was bleary-eyed and exhausted. I was back in Fred's office the next week.

"I know that psychology and neuroscience have to work in concert if we want to address the full range of human behavior, and I really do love the idea of the whole animal, but I guess my question is that if the brain can't account for things like reason and emotion, then what can? If the brain makes it possible for 'us' to feel and think, then what is 'us'?

Do you believe in souls?" I was breathless. Fred's office was a long walk from my last class, and I had jogged there to try to catch him before he left for lunch.

"Gifty, I actually haven't read the book. I just thought you might like it."

"Oh," I said.

"I'll give it a read if you want to talk about it with me, though," he said.

"That's all right," I said, inching away. "Do you want the door open or closed?"

I took the long way home from Fred's office, wondering if it was too late to change my mind and become a doctor. At least then I could look at the body and see a body, look at a brain and see a brain, not a mystery that can never be solved, not an "us" that can never be explained. All of my years of Christianity, of considering the heart, the soul, and the mind with which Scripture tells us to love the Lord, had primed me to believe in the great mystery of our existence, but the closer I tried to get to uncovering it, the further away the objects moved. The fact that I can locate the part of the brain where memory is stored only answers questions of where and perhaps even how. It does little to answer the why. I was always, I am ever, unnerved.

This is something I would never say in a lecture or a presentation or, God forbid, a paper, but, at a certain point, science fails. Questions become guesses become philosophical ideas about how something should probably, maybe, be. I grew up around people who were distrustful of science, who thought of it as a cunning trick to rob them of their faith, and I have been educated around scientists and laypeople alike who talk about religion as though it were a comfort blanket for the dumb and the weak, a way to extol the virtues of a God more improbable than our own human existence. But this tension, this idea that one must necessarily choose between science and religion, is false. I used to see the world through a God lens, and when that lens clouded, I turned to science. Both became, for me, valuable ways of seeing, but ultimately both have failed to fully satisfy in their aim: to make clear, to make meaning.

"You're not serious," Anne said that day in Integrated Science when I revealed my former Jesus freak. She'd spent our entire friendship performing a kind of evangelism of her own, trying to disabuse me of my faith. I didn't need her help; I'd been doing that work on my own for years.

"Do you believe in evolution?" she asked one sunny spring day. We had dragged a couple of picnic blankets out onto the lawn so that we could study in the sunshine. It was among the happiest times of my life. And though we argued all the time and though we wouldn't stay friends for much longer, she knew me better than anyone had ever known me. Even my mother, flesh of my flesh, had never really seen me the way Anne saw me. Only Nana had known me better.

"Of course I believe in evolution," I said.

"Okay, but how can you believe in evolution and also believe in God? Creationism and evolution are diametrically opposed."

I plucked a weed from the grass at the edge of the blanket and started to crush its petals in my hand, smearing my fingers with yellow pigment, then presenting that color to Anne as though it were a gift. "I think we're made out of

stardust and God made the stars," I said. I blew and yellow
dust flew into the air, into Anne's hair, and she looked at me
like I was crazy, and she saw me.

I don't know why Jesus would raise Lazarus from the dead,
but I also don't know why some mice stop pressing the lever
and other mice don't. This may be a false equivalence, but
they are two questions that have emerged from my one,
unique mind at one point in my life or another, and so they
are two questions that have value to me.

I wasn't thinking about Lazarus much in the days after
Nana died. I had already stopped believing in the possibility
of extravagant miracles. But small miracles, everyday miracles, like my mother rising from her bed, those still seemed
worth hoping for.

"Please get up," I said to her each day before I left for
school, vigorously shaking her arm, her torso, her legs, until
she made some kind of noncommittal noise at me, some gesture that eased my mind, allowed me to believe that maybe,
maybe, that day would be the day.

She'd already lost her job, but I didn't know that. The
home health company called a hundred times or more, but
I had long since stopped answering the phone. I kept to my
routine like my routine would save me, and then on a Thursday, a week and a half in, I went into my mother's room and
she wasn't in her bed.

My heart soared. I had done it. Like Jesus, I had willed
a woman to come forth. I went to look for her in the living
room, the kitchen. Her car was still parked in the garage, and
it wasn't until I saw that little tan Camry there, its headlights
like eyes peering into my soul, that I knew what a grave mis-

take I had made. I ran back to my mother's bedroom, opened the door to the bathroom, and found her there, submerged in the bathtub with an empty bottle of Ambien resting on the counter.

I never wanted to see a policeman again, and so I called Pastor John.

"Slow down, honey," he said, and then panicked. "My God, my God. Just wait there."

The ambulance arrived before Pastor John did. The EMTs lifted my mother onto the stretcher. She couldn't look at me; she just kept saying "I'm sorry," and "I should have let him take him."

"What?" I asked. "Who?"

"He wanted to take Nana to Ghana and I said no. Oh, Awurade, why, why didn't I let him take him?"

Pastor John came in as they took my mother. We followed the stretcher out of the house, and I barely listened as Pastor John received instructions from the EMTs. I shut my eyes tightly, so tightly that I started to feel the tension in my forehead. I cried and I prayed.

41

Pastor John lived in a bright yellow house about three blocks away from the First Assemblies of God. The house had two empty bedrooms because their oldest sons had moved away, gone on to other churches in Alabama to be youth pastors and worship leaders themselves. I stayed in the oldest boy's room, while Mary, their daughter, stayed with an aunt. I'm still not sure why they sent Mary away. Maybe they thought my family's misfortune was catching.

My mother had been taken to the UAB psychiatric hospital in Birmingham. It was about an hour and a half's drive away, but she didn't want me to see her there, and so, though I had begged, Pastor John and his wife, Lisa, never made the drive out. Instead, I stayed in Billy's room. I walked to school. I spoke as little as possible and I refused to go to church on Sundays.

"I'm sure your mama would like it if you would say a prayer for her this Sunday," Lisa said. The night I'd arrived, she'd asked me what my favorite thing to eat was. I couldn't think fast enough so I'd told her spaghetti and meatballs, a dish I'd had only a handful of times. My family rarely ate out and my mother cooked only Ghanaian dishes. That night, Lisa made a big batch of spaghetti and meatballs and the three of us ate in near silence.

"I'm not going to church," I said.

"I know you're going through a lot, Gifty, but remember that God doesn't give us more than we can handle. You and your mama are warriors for Christ. You'll get through this."

I shoved an entire meatball into my mouth and chewed slowly so that I wouldn't have to respond.

My mother was at UAB for two weeks, so for two weeks I stayed at Pastor John's house, avoiding him and his wife as best I could. Eating cold meatballs from the fridge whenever I got a moment alone in their kitchen. At the end of the two weeks, my mother showed up. I'd expected her to look different, wilder somehow, more alive, but instead she looked the same. Just as tired, just as sad. She thanked Pastor John and Lisa but didn't say a word to me. We drove back to our house in silence, and when we pulled into the garage we sat there for a second, car idling.

"I'm sorry," my mother said. I was not accustomed to hearing her apologize, and now she was doing it for the second time that month. I felt like I was in the car with a stranger, an alien from a planet that I didn't care to visit. I kept my head down. I stared at my lap as though all the mysteries of the world were held there. My mother took my chin in her hand and pulled until I was facing her. "Never again," she said.

When my mother brought me home from Pastor John's house, I watched her carefully. She didn't go straight up to her bedroom. Instead she sat at our dining table, her elbows resting there, her head in her hands. I stood in the doorframe, suspicious. The last couple of years had taught me that no state of calm ever lasts. Nana's brief periods of sobriety in the wasteland of his addiction had been a kind of trick, lulling me into believing sobriety would be a permanent state. My mother was out of bed, but I wasn't falling for it. I knew a wasteland when I saw one.

"Gifty, I'm sick. I need your prayers now," she said.

I didn't answer. I stayed in the doorframe, watching her. She wasn't looking at me as she spoke. I knew that she was ashamed, in pain, and I wanted her to be.

"I bought you a plane ticket to Ghana. You'll go there when school lets out, so that I can focus on my healing."

"No," I said, and her head snapped toward me sharply.

Her eyes met mine, and she spoke in Twi. "Not you too," she said. "Don't you start speaking back to me. Don't you start acting up."

"I don't want to go," I whispered. "I can help you get better. I'll be good. I'll pray. I'll go to church again."

She wiped her hand over her face and shook her head. "You can go to church in Ghana. I need spiritual warfare. You'll be my warrior, won't you?"

And it was this last thing she said, "You'll be my warrior, won't you?" and the saccharine-sweet tone with which she said it, that finally made me realize that she was not the same woman I had once called mother. That woman was never coming back.

The summer I went to Ghana was the summer I discovered that I had an aunt. While the Chin Chin Man had spoken freely about every person and thing that he'd left behind in Ghana, my mother rarely talked about the past. In my memories she is always rushing out the door, too busy, too tired, to answer my endless questions.

"What's your mother's name?"

"How many siblings do you have?"

"Where were you born?"

Every question I asked was answered with silence. And then Nana died and I found myself on a plane, headed to a country I'd never been to before. When I arrived, I was met not by my father, but by a buxom, chatty woman whose face was the same as my mother's.

The first thing my aunt Joyce did when she saw me was inspect my arm, lifting it up and flopping it back down against my side. I would later see her do this with a chicken at the market, evaluating how much she was willing to pay for the meat by the sturdiness of its wing, the heft of its leg.

"You're too skinny," she said. "You get the skinniness from your father's side, as you can tell." To demonstrate, she lifted her shirt, grabbed a chunk of her stomach, and shook it at me. I was mortified to see her perform this act in the middle of that busy terminal. She had an outie, something I had never seen before, and I felt as though I was being shown a vestigial tail. I wanted my mother to get up from her bed, to see that outie flashing in her mind's eye like a glowing target, and come get me. I wanted my skinny arms to go unremarked upon. I wanted my brother.

Outside the airport, Aunt Joyce flagged down a man selling koko in pouches. She bought two for me and one for herself.

"Eat," she said, ready to commence the fattening-up process right there and then. I sucked the porridge from the plastic, urging myself not to cry, while my aunt, the stranger, watched me. She didn't look away, nor did she stop talking, until I had finished every drop in both bags.

"Your mother always thought she was better than us, but you see," she said, raising her eyebrows at me. What was I supposed to see? My too-skinny body? My presence in Ghana? Or maybe I was to see my mother, whom I could not see clearly that summer. No matter how hard I tried, I couldn't picture her face. My aunt Joyce and I sat outside the airport for an hour while she told me story after story after story about my mother, but all I could picture was the sloping curve of a woman's back.

42

"No weapon formed against me shall prosper. I said NO WEAPON. FORMED AGAINST ME. SHALL PROSPER."

The pastor of the largest Pentecostal church in Kumasi was stomping back and forth onstage, using his feet as exclamation marks. As he shouted, a chorus of Amens and Hallelujahs filled the sanctuary. A woman fell out in the Spirit and another rushed to fan her, shouting, "Thank you, Jesus," as her white handkerchief fluttered birdlike over the woman's body. I sat in the first pew with Aunt Joyce, who periodically nodded her head, pointed to the pastor, and said, "Enh-hnh. That's right," as though she and he were in private conversation with each other, not in the swelteringly hot sanctuary of a charismatic evangelical church in Kumasi with hundreds of other congregants all around them.

We were engaged in spiritual warfare. Or, at least, everyone else was. I was swooning in the Sunday sun, watching the sweat bead on my arms. Every time the pastor stomped, his own sweat would fling from his hair and baptize those of us who were sitting in the front row. I was disgusted every time a droplet landed on me, but then I would remember my wish of only a few years before—to be baptized in water—and I would have to stifle a laugh.

My laughter didn't fit with the pastor's message. "There are demons all around us," he said. "There are demons who have tried to take our children. We cast them out in Jesus's name."

To my left, the woman beside me put her hands to her chest, her stomach, her legs, before flinging them back into the air. Her face, almost angry in its intensity, told me everything I needed to know: she had demons in need of casting off.

This was not the First Assemblies of God in Huntsville, Alabama. This wasn't evangelicalism as I knew it. The noise of this worship service alone made the worship of my childhood church sound like the muffled, timid singing of a kindergarten choir. I had never heard Pastor John talk about demons and witches as though they were living, breathing beings, but this pastor spoke as if he could see them seated among us. My mother had grown up in a church like this, but she had not come back to Ghana to engage in spiritual warfare. She'd sent me as a kind of emissary. Sitting there, melting into a puddle at my own feet, I pictured my mother as I'd left her, and I knew that if her own faith, a living, breathing thing, could not save her, then my small portion would do nothing.

Aunt Joyce and I took a taxi from the service back to her house. I rolled the windows down and tried to let my body air out.

"That was a powerful service," Aunt Joyce said. "Powerful."

I looked out of the window and thought about how

much Nana would have liked to be here. To see this country of ours and to help me to navigate all of my own complicated feelings about it. "Very powerful," I told my aunt.

She smiled and took my hand. "Don't worry. Your mother will be feeling well again very soon."

That summer in Ghana, I learned to pound fufu. I learned to haggle at the market, to get used to cold-water bucket baths, to shake coconuts down from their trees. I developed an Encyclopedia of Knowledge I Didn't Want, waiting for the day when my mother would call me back to America and I could forget everything I had learned. One week became two became three. As time dragged on, I thought that maybe I was going the way of the Chin Chin Man, lost to this country, lost to my family.

"Where's my father?" I asked Aunt Joyce one day.

I was already a month into my stay, and I hadn't said a word about him. If Aunt Joyce had been waiting for this moment, she didn't show it. "He lives in town. I've seen him a few times in Kejetia, but he doesn't come to my stall very often anymore. I don't think he even goes to church." She said this last part with her nose scrunched, as though she had smelled something rotten. But the Chin Chin Man's derelict church attendance smelled of roses when compared to the stench of all of his other misdeeds.

"Can I see him?" I asked, and, minutes later, we were climbing into a taxi.

The Chin Chin Man lived in Tanoso, off of Sunyani Road, not far from the Yaa Asantewaa Secondary School. His house was of a modest size, brick red in color, with a tall, imposing steel fence. He must have had at least five dogs, and all of them rushed to the fence in barking menace as Aunt Joyce and I approached. I stood there peering through the cracks, avoiding the gnashing jaws of the dogs, while Aunt Joyce pushed the button at the gate. She pushed twice, three times, and we could hear the high-pitched squeak it made all the way out where we stood.

"Where is he?" my aunt said, pushing again.

Finally, a woman came out to silence the dogs and open the gate. She and Aunt Joyce spent the next minute speaking Twi, too fast for me to understand.

"Gifty, this is your father's wife," Aunt Joyce said.

The woman turned to me and smiled. "Come in, come in," she said, and we all wandered inside the house.

The Chin Chin Man was waiting for us in the living room. He stood as soon as we entered, and stepped toward me, arms open. "Eh, Gifty, look how big you are," he said.

And I couldn't hug him. I couldn't stand to hear his voice, which for most of my life I had only ever heard in disembodied form, through electric currents. Now here it was, coming out of a mouth affixed on a head that rested atop that long, lean, muscular body. Nana's body.

"Did you know I was here?" I asked.

He lowered his arms and his eyes. He cleared his throat to speak, but I wasn't finished.

"She tried to kill herself, did you know that? She almost died and then she made me come here and you knew I was here this whole time, didn't you?"

His wife stepped in, offering drinks and food. Though I had been taught it was rude to refuse Ghanaian hospitality,

I did so anyway, and for an hour, I sat in complete silence, scowling while the Chin Chin Man talked.

In person, he wouldn't shut up. Nervous, loud, bumbling stories about his work, his friends, his life without us. He never said a word about my mother or Nana. He never said sorry, and I was old enough then to know that he never would.

On the car ride home, I asked my aunt if my father had ever asked her about me or my mother on his visits to her stall.

"Oh, Gifty," my aunt said.

"What?"

"Ofere."

"What does that mean?" I asked. I had already reached the limits of my Twi understanding, but Aunt Joyce either could not or refused to speak English for longer than a couple of sentences a day. Whenever I asked her to repeat something in English, she would tell me that I wasn't trying hard enough to understand or she would point out, yet again, all the ways that she thought my mother had done a poor job of parenting me.

"I don't know in English. Your mother should teach you these things," she said.

So, it would be option two.

Later that day I called my mother, something I did once a week. She answered the phone with false cheer in her voice, and I tried to picture which room in our house she might be in. Was she wearing pajamas or proper clothes? Had she gotten her job back?

"She means he's shy. He's ashamed," my mother said.

"Oh," I said. Nana might have cared how the Chin Chin

Man felt, but I didn't. He was as foreign to me as the language, as foreign as every person who passed me by in Kejetia. I'd felt closer to the dreadlocked man.

"When can I come home?" I asked.

"Soon," she said, but that word had lost all meaning. I'd heard it from my father and understood it to be an empty word, a lie that parents told their children to soothe them.

"Anhedonia" is the psychiatric term for the inability to derive pleasure from things that are normally pleasurable. It's the characterizing symptom in major depressive disorder, but it can also be a symptom of substance abuse, schizophrenia, Parkinson's disease. I learned the term in a university lecture hall and immediately felt a shock of recognition. Anhedonia was the feeling of "nothing," the thing that kept my mother in her bed.

Professionally, I am interested in anhedonia because I am interested in reward-seeking behavior, but personally I have never experienced it to the degree of magnitude of the subjects in the cases I study. It is only a symptom, which means, of course, that something else is the cause. I'm interested in the cause as it relates to psychiatric illness, but I research only one piece, one part of the story.

I know what my family looks like on paper. I know what Nana looks like when you take the bird's-eye view: black male immigrant from a single-parent, lower-middle-class household. The stressors of any one of those factors could be enough to influence anhedonia. If Nana were alive, if I entered him into a study, it would be hard to isolate his drug use as the cause of this particular portion of his pain. It would be hard even to isolate the cause of the drug use.

And that's what so many people want to get at: the cause of the drug use, the reason people pick up substances in the first place. Anytime I talk about my work informally, I inevitably encounter someone who wants to know why addicts become addicts. They use words like "will" and "choice," and they end by saying, "Don't you think there's more to it than the brain?" They are skeptical of the rhetoric of addiction as disease, something akin to high blood pressure or diabetes, and I get that. What they're really saying is that they may have partied in high school and college but look at them now. Look how strong-willed they are, how many good choices they've made. They want reassurances. They want to believe that they have been loved enough and have raised their children well enough that the things that I research will never, ever touch their own lives.

I understand this impulse. I, too, have spent years creating my little moat of good deeds in an attempt to protect the castle of myself. I don't want to be dismissed the way that Nana was once dismissed. I know that it's easier to say *Their kind does seem to have a taste for drugs,* easier to write all addicts off as bad and weak-willed people, than it is to look closely at the nature of their suffering. I do it too, sometimes. I judge. I walk around with my chest puffed out, making sure that everyone knows about my Harvard and Stanford degrees, as if those things encapsulate me, and when I do so, I give in to the same facile, lazy thinking that characterizes those who think of addicts as horrible people. It's just that I'm standing on the other side of the moat. What I can say for certain is that there is no case study in the world that could capture the whole animal of my brother, that could show how smart and kind and generous he was, how much he wanted to get better, how much he wanted to live. Forget for a moment what he looked like on paper, and instead see him as he was in all of his glory, in all of his beauty. It's true that for years before he died, I would look at his face and think, *What a pity, what a waste*. But the waste was my own, the waste was what I missed out on whenever I looked at him and saw just his addiction.

43

Dear God,
The Black Mamba had to work today so Buzz made us dinner. He asked me how school was and when I told him that Lauren made fun of me for wearing clothes from Walmart, he said, "Don't worry. She's got a place in Hell with her name on it," and I know it wasn't nice but it made me feel better.

Dear God,
Merry Christmas! We put on a nativity play at church last night and I played the part of a lost lamb. It wasn't a big part or anything. I only had one line: "Behold, the lamb of God." The rest of the time I was just sitting onstage, saying nothing. It wasn't special at all, but when it was time for me to take my bow, Buzz gave me a standing ovation.

44

~

While I was in Ghana, my mother healed at home in Alabama. Her anhedonia was as severe as ever, but her time in
the UAB psych ward seemed to have alleviated some of her
symptoms. She had stopped going to therapy, but she was
at least going to church again. I used to call Pastor John on
Sundays, begging for progress reports, but he could tell me
little beyond how she'd looked that day, what she'd worn.

That summer, I knew that my mother needed healing,
but I didn't understand what she needed healing from. The
only time I heard people talk about depression was when
they were using it as a synonym for sadness, and so I never
thought of it as a disease. "Gifty, I'm sick," my mother had
said, and I knew it was true, but the how of her sickness, the
why of it, I didn't understand.

When I learned about major depression and anhedonia
in college, I started to get a clearer picture of my mother. A
few years after my return from Ghana, I asked her to tell me
about her time at UAB and about the summer she'd spent
alone.

"Why do you want to know about that?" she asked.

"It's for a class," I lied.

She made a noise that sounded like it was halfway between a growl and a sigh. We had been trying something new in our relationship. It involved my mother not evading my questions; it involved telling me the truth. She hated it, but I held more cards than I had in childhood, and so she shared things with me that she never would have back then.

"They wanted me to talk to the doctor, and they gave me some medication to take."

"Did you take it?"

"Yes, I took them while I was in the hospital and then I kept taking them for a while when you were in Ghana, but they didn't help so then I stopped."

"Did you tell them the medicine wasn't helping? You're supposed to tell them when the medication doesn't work so that they can adjust it. The medication doesn't always work in the beginning. It's about finding the right combinations of things in the right doses. Didn't they tell you that?"

"I didn't want to keep talking to them. I didn't want to tell them that it wasn't working because I didn't want them to shock me."

It was my turn to growl-sigh.

"I got better, didn't I?" she said, and I couldn't argue with that, not yet.

Psychiatric care has come a long way since the days of lobotomies. Back then, in the wild, wild west of neurology and psychosurgery, human frontal lobes were excised with little more gravity than one might exhibit when performing an appendectomy. These were the days of lax trial periods, when people experimented directly on human patients, forgoing the many years of repeating the same experiment on mice and rats. When I think about how slow and tedious my research can be, I am sometimes nostalgic for that bygone era. I think, if only I could inject this virus-packaged opsin directly into human patients, I could turn on that blue light, see what this research can really do. But the thing is, you cannot deliver the light without also delivering the virus. And so while the thousands upon thousands of lobotomized patients sometimes improved in ways that related to the symptoms they once exhibited, they also, just as often, became little more than shadows of their former selves, abandoned to the wasteland of bad, hasty science, left sitting in pools of their own drool. Remembering them makes me thankful for my work, how long it takes, how slow it is.

The "shocks" that my mother described have come a long way since they were first used in the 1940s and '50s. We all remember that scene from *One Flew Over the Cuckoo's Nest,* when electroconvulsive therapy was used not as a treatment for mental illness, but as a kind of mind control. Back then, the therapy was performed on anyone from the schizophrenics and depressives who needed mental health care to the homosexuals and "hysterical" women who neither needed nor asked for treatment, who simply lived outside the bounds of what society deemed "normal." It's hard to shake that image of people being forced to correct something that was never wrong. It's hard to forget the primitive beginnings of this therapy, to stand by it. For many, like my mother, the "shock" of this treatment, the way it induces a seizure in order to treat something that is impossible to see, and often difficult to accept, feels like a bridge too far. But the truth is that electroconvulsive therapy can work, does work. It is often presented as a last resort, and it is just as often performed because the patient herself requests it in one final attempt to crawl out of the deep, dark tunnel.

The work that Katherine and those of us who are interested in finding bioengineering and neuroscientific interventions to treat psychiatric illness do is in many ways about moving beyond the last resort, the final attempt. When she returned to her practice, Katherine would become a psychiatrist who only accepted patients who had no other options left, patients for whom everything, even death, had failed. In addition to optogenetics, Katherine's work at Stanford involved improving vagus-nerve stimulation, a treatment for treatment-resistant depression and epilepsy whereby a tiny device is implanted beneath the skin near a patient's collarbone, delivering electrical impulses to the vagus nerve. It is a charger for the depleted battery of a depressed patient's body. The frustrating thing about the technology is that, like with DBS for Parkinson's disease, no one knows exactly why it works, only that it works imperfectly, using electricity that cannot differentiate one cell from another. If we could better understand these treatments, if we could come up with interventions that affected only those specific neurons that are involved in each particular psychiatric illness, then perhaps we could provide something better.

My mother crawled out of her deep, dark tunnel, but perhaps this phrasing is too imprecise, the image of crawling too forceful to encapsulate the relentless but quiet work of fighting depression. Perhaps it is more correct to say that her darkness lifted, the tunnel shallowed, so that it felt as though her problems were on the surface of the Earth again, not down in its molten core.

My aunt took me to church one last time. The pastor didn't like me. He was resentful of my many refusals to get

up on the stage, receive my healing. That day he preached
about how stubbornness is little more than pride in disguise.
He looked right at me when he said that the pride of the
West was in its inability to truly believe.

"Yesterday, I heard about a miracle, a miracle that
reminded me of the miracles we read about in this holy
book. Our sister in America could not rise from her bed, and
she has now risen. Glory to God," he said, and the church
said, "Amen."

"Our sister in America needed the God of miracles and
the God of miracles showed up, amen?"

"Amen!"

"Those in the West might look at her and say that it is
simply a coincidence that she rose from her bed, but we who
believe know the truth, amen?"

"Amen!"

"When God says rise, we rise." He looked around at the
congregation, many of whom were clapping and nodding
and lifting their hands with praise, but our reaction did not
satisfy him.

"I said when God says rise, WE RISE!" He stomped
his foot and the congregation took the hint. All around
me believers rose to their feet, stomping and jumping and
shouting.

I sat in my seat and stared at the pastor, who was watching me in accusation. I couldn't, wouldn't move. Had my
mother really risen? Like Lazarus, like Jesus? I dared not
believe.

The next day, Aunt Joyce and I took a tro-tro to Kotoka.
Several men came up to ask if they might take my bags in for
me. Aunt Joyce chided them all, "Leave us be. Can't you see
we don't want your interruptions?"

When they left, she scooped me up into her arms and lifted me up and down, as if weighing me. She put me down and smiled, satisfied. Her smile was radiant, assured, proud. She was so very different from my mother, but in that moment, her arms around me, holding me as my own mother so rarely did, smiling brightly as my mother rarely smiled, I knew that the woman I had spent the summer with reflected the woman my mother could have been. My mother deserved to be this happy, this at ease in her body and in the world.

"You are a very wonderful child," Aunt Joyce said. "You keep praying for your mother and making all of us proud."

Only weeks before, I hadn't even known of my aunt's existence, and here she was, proud of me.

I boarded the plane and slept most of my first flight away, before transferring half-asleep in New York, then in Atlanta. My mother picked me up in Huntsville. She offered me a smile, and I took it hungrily. I wanted whatever it was she was ready to give.

45

When Mrs. Palmer, the woman my mother had spent years caring for, died after a long illness, I was in the fifth grade. She was ninety-five years old, and I can still remember the sight of her in her open casket. The hundreds of deep wrinkles on her face, her hands, made it look as though countless rivers had once run, crisscrossing and zigzagging, from her forehead to her toes. But the waters had dried up some time before, leaving only these empty basins and beds, rivulets drained of their rivers. I watched my mother pay her respects to Mrs. Palmer's family, a group of people who were a far cry from the acrimonious Thomas family. They hugged my mother close as though she were one of them, and I understood for the first time that, to them, she was.

Who was she then, I wondered, as Mrs. Palmer's children and grandchildren folded my mother into their arms. My mother—who had never hugged us, even when we were little children presenting her with our scrapes and bruises, our wails—accepted the touch of these strangers, who, of course, weren't strange to her. She spent more of her days with Mrs. Palmer than she had ever spent with us. And so

I recognized, for perhaps the first time, that my mother wasn't mine.

Most days I woke up, folded the bed back into the couch, and peeked in on my mother before rushing off to the lab. I had stopped trying to get her up, to make her the meals she might like, make a fuss. But then one day I poked my head into the room and there she was, pulling her pants on.

"Ma?"

"You said you would show me your lab," she said plainly, as though we were living in a world of logic, where time moved in orderly, straightforward ways, instead of here, in the zigzagged upside-down world. I had asked my mom to come to the lab with me a week and a half before only to be greeted with a "maybe," followed by eleven days of utter silence; why now?

I decided to live in her world.

Though the day was overcast, my mother kept squinting and shielding her eyes as we drove to campus. I made a mental note to open the blinds in the bedroom more often even if she objected, adding "not enough vitamin D" to my growing list of worries. The lab was empty, and I felt guilty by how relieved I was to not have to explain my mother, her slightly disheveled appearance, her slow-moving shuffle, to my colleagues. Aside from Katherine and Han, no one even knew that she was staying with me, let alone that she had hardly moved from my bed in weeks. I knew that my reluctancy to tell them went deeper than my natural inclination toward reticence, deeper than the typical embarrassment of introducing family members to friends. It was that I worked in a lab full of people who would see my mother, see her ill-

ness, and understand things about her that the general public never could. I didn't want them to look at her and see a
problem to be solved. I wanted them to see her at her best,
but that meant that I was doing what everyone else did, trying to dress up depression, trying to hide it. For what? For
whom?

Had I known she was coming, I would have adjusted
my schedule so that I'd have something cool to show her,
a surgery or a training session. Instead, I showed her the
behavioral testing chamber, now empty, the tools in my lab,
unused.

"Where are the mice?" she asked.

I pulled out Han's because they were closest to me. They
were sleeping in their box, eyes closed, curled up, cute.

"Can I hold one?"

"They can get kind of jumpy, so you have to be careful,
okay?"

She nodded, and I caught one and handed it to her.

She held the mouse in both hands, brushed her thumb
over its head, and one of its eyes opened, rolled back as if to
find her, before closing again. My mother laughed and my
heart leapt at the sound.

"Do you hurt them?"

I had never fully explained my work to my mother.
Whenever I did tell her about it, I used only the most scientific, most technical of terms. I never used the words "addiction" or "relapse," I said "reward seeking" and "restraint."
I didn't want her to think about Nana, to think about pain.

"We try to be as humane as possible and we don't use
animals if we can do things another way. But sometimes we
do cause them some discomfort."

She nodded and carefully placed the mouse back in its box, and I wondered what she was thinking. The day my mother had come home to find me and Nana tending to the baby bird, she told us that it wouldn't live because we had touched it. She took it up in her hands as the two of us begged her not to hurt it. Finally, she just shrugged and gave it back to us. In Twi, she said, "There is no living thing on God's Earth that doesn't come to know pain sometime."

In the final stage of Mahler's separation-individuation theory of child development, babies begin to become aware of their own selves, and in so doing start to understand their mothers as individuals. My mother walking around my lab, observing things, showing tenderness toward a mouse when she rarely showed tenderness toward any living creature, all while in the depths of her depression, deepened this lesson for me. Of course, my mother is her own person. Of course, she contains multitudes. She reacts in ways that surprise me, in part, simply because she isn't me. I forget this and relearn it anew because it's a lesson that doesn't, that can't, stick. I know her only as she is defined against me, in her role as my mother, so when I see her as herself, like when she gets catcalled on the street, there's dissonance. When she wants for me things that I don't want for myself—Christ, marriage, children—I am angry that she doesn't understand me, doesn't see me as my own, separate person, but that anger stems from the fact that I don't see her that way either. I want her to know what I want the same way I know it, intimately, immediately. I want her to get well because I want her to get well, and isn't that enough? My first thought, the

year my brother died and my mother took to bed, was that
I needed her to be mine again, a mother as I understood it.
And when she didn't get up, when she lay there day in and
day out, wasting away, I was reminded that I didn't know
her, not wholly and completely. I would never know her.

46

And yet sometimes I would look at her and I would see it, that which is alive and shivering in all of us, in everything. She would hold a mouse, hold my hand or my gaze, and I would catch a glimpse of the very essence of her. *Please don't go,* I thought when I drove her home from the lab and she got back into bed. *Don't leave me, not yet.*

I took to working at the desk in the living room, leaving my bedroom door open so that I could hear her if she called for me. She never called for me, and I never worked. I had become a master at thinking about working without actually doing it. *Here's what I would write if I were writing my paper,* I'd think, but then my wandering mind, that old prayer habit, would kick in and before long I'd be thinking about other things—the beach, mostly. I'd never really liked it, that activity of roasting oneself in the sun, turning on an invisible spit. I associated it with white people, and I was a poor swimmer besides.

But my mother's people were from a beach town. I started writing my own fairy tale, wherein my mother, the beauty of Abandze, who grew sleepier and sleepier each

year that she was away until finally she became unrousable,
is carried on her golden bed by four gorgeous, strong men.
She is carried all the way from my apartment in California
to the coast of Ghana, where she is laid on the sand. And as
the tide comes in, licking first the soles of her feet, then her
ankles, to calf, then knee, she slowly starts to wake. By the
time the water swallows the golden bed, stealing her out to
sea, she has come alive again. The sea creatures take bits of
her bed, and with it, they fashion a mermaid's tail. They slip
it onto her. They teach her how to swim with it. They live
with her there forever. The Sleeping Beauty, the Mermaid
of Abandze.

"Inscape," the professor of my Gerard Manley Hopkins class
once said, "is that ineffable thing that makes each person and
object unique. It is the sanctity of a thing. As a Jesuit priest,
Hopkins believed—"

"Do you think it's possible to read Hopkins without bringing up his religion or his sexuality?" a classmate
interrupted.

My professor shook her hair out of her face and trained
her sharp eyes on him. "Do you?"

"I mean, the dude was so repressed by the church that
he burned his poems. It's bizarre to extol his religious ideals
when they so clearly caused him great suffering."

"Church doesn't always have to be repressive," another
classmate said. "I mean, it was a nice way to learn about
morals and how to be a responsible citizen and stuff. That's
really the only reason I would take my kids to church, so
that they could learn about right and wrong."

"Yeah, but it's the way you learn about right and wrong

that's so messed up," the first man said. "I felt so guilty all the time because no one ever actually sits you down and says, 'This task, of being blameless in the eyes of God or whatever, is impossible. You will want to have sex, you will want to lie, you will want to cheat, even when you know it's wrong,' and just that desire to do something bad, for me, was crushing."

Our professor nodded, the curtain of her blond hair that so often hid her eyes parting and closing in time with her movements. I looked at her and wondered if she'd ever heard it, that heart-knocking sound.

We know right from wrong because we learn it, one way or another, we learn it. Sometimes from our parents, who spend most of our early years teaching us how to survive, snatching our hands away from burners and electrical outlets, keeping us away from the bleach. Other times, we have to learn for ourselves, to touch our hands to the burner, to burn, before we know why there are things we can't touch. These lessons that we learn by doing are pivotal to our development, but not everything can be learned that way.

Plenty of people drink without becoming alcoholics, but some people take a single sip and a switch trips and who knows why? The only guaranteed way to avoid addiction is to never try drugs. This sounds simple enough and the politicians and zealots who preach abstinence in all manner of things will have us believe that it is simple enough. Perhaps it would be simple if we weren't human, the only animal in the known world that is willing to try something new, fun, pointless, dangerous, thrilling, stupid, even if we might die in the trying. The fact that I was doing addiction research at a university in the great state of California was the result of the thousands of pioneers who had climbed into their wagons facing disease and injury and starvation and the great, brutal expanse of land that ranged from mountain to river to valley, all for the sake of getting from one side of this enormous country to the other. They knew that there was risk involved, but the potential for triumph, for pleasure, for something just a little bit better, was enough to outweigh the cost. All you have to do is watch a child ride her bike directly into a brick wall or jump from the tallest branch of a sycamore tree to know that we humans are reckless with our bodies, reckless with our lives, for no other reason than that we want to know what would happen, what it might feel like to brush up against death, to run right up to the edge of our lives, which is, in some ways, to live fully.

In my work I am trying to ask questions that anticipate our inevitable recklessness and to find a way out, but to do that I need to use mice. Mice don't seek danger, not the way we do. They, like everything else on this planet, are subject to the whims of humans. My whims involved tests that could greatly advance our understanding of the brain, and my desire to understand the brain superseded every other desire I had. I understood that the same thing that made humans great—our recklessness and creativity and curiosity—was also the thing that hampered the lives of everything around us. Because we were the animal daring enough to take boats out to sea, even when we thought the world was flat and that our boats would fall off the edge, we discovered new land, different people, roundness. The cost of this discovery was the destruction of that new land, those different people. Without us oceans wouldn't be turning to acid, frogs and bats and bees and reefs wouldn't be heading for extinction.

Without me, the limping mouse wouldn't limp; he would never have succumbed to addiction. I grew up being taught that God gave us dominion over the animals, without ever being taught that I myself was an animal.

When the mouse with the limp was finally ready for optogenetics, I pulled him out of the box and anesthetized him. Soon I would shave his head and inject the virus that contained the opsins. Eventually, if all went according to plan, the mouse would never press the lever again, would lose that recklessness I'd trained him to exhibit.

47

Dear God,
Today, Ashley and I were trying to see who could hold
their breath the longest underwater. I took a deep breath
and sat down at the shallow end of Ashley's pool while
she timed me. I held my breath for so long my chest
started to hurt, but I didn't want to lose cuz Ashley wins
everything, but then I got lightheaded and dizzy and I
thought maybe I could just walk into the deep end, just
for a second. I must have passed out because Ashley's
mom pulled me out of the pool and started slapping my
back until water came out of my mouth, and she just kept
saying, "Are you crazy? You could have killed yourself!"
But you wouldn't let me die, would you, God?

48

I have always been slow to recklessness, afraid of danger and of death. I spent years avoiding the red Solo cups and punch bowls at the rare high school parties that I was invited to. It wasn't until my sophomore year at college that I took my first drink. Not out of curiosity, but out of desperation. I was so tired of being lonely. I just wanted to make friends, something I had never been particularly good at. Ashley, my childhood best friend, had become my friend through the sheer force of will and directness that only young children display. She asked, tapping me on the shoulder the day she found me playing in our neighborhood playground by myself, "Will you be my friend?" I said yes. It never happened that easily again.

For Nana, friendships had been different, easier. The sports teams helped, the way they sealed those packs of boys together, giving them names with which to define their togetherness—the Tornadoes, the Grizzlies, the Vipers. A herd of predators, prowling. Our house used to be overrun with basketball players. On those days when my mother worked the night shift, I would sometimes find them dozing off their boozy parties in our living room, a forest of sleeping giants.

Nana had always been well liked, but after he became the best basketball player in the city, his coolness turned boundless. At Publix, where the two of us went to buy groceries for our slapdash dinners, the cashiers would say, "We'll be at the game on Saturday, Nana." It was strange to hear my brother's name come out of the lips of so many Alabamians, their diphthong-heavy accents slowing down the vowels until it sounded like another name entirely. When I heard his name through their mouths, looked at him through their eyes, he didn't feel like my brother at all. This Nana, Naawnaaw the hometown hero, was not the same as the one who lived in my house, the one who heated up his milk before adding cereal to it, the one who was scared of spiders, who had peed the bed until age twelve.

He was quiet but he was good with people, good at parties. I was never old enough to go out with him, and on the nights when he brought the parties to our house I was bribed twenty dollars to stay in my room. I didn't mind. Pious little girl that I was, I would sit on my bed, read my Bible, and pray that God would save their souls from the eternal damnation that seemed inevitable. When I was sure they'd gone to sleep, I would tiptoe through the forest, scared of waking a giant. If Nana was up, sometimes he'd demand his twenty back, but sometimes he would fix me a peanut butter and jelly sandwich before sending me away. He'd shoo everyone out and then spend the rest of the early morning cleaning frantically until our mother returned.

"Nana, what's this?" she would ask, always, always, spotting the bottle cap that had fallen behind the window frame, the beer stain on the dishrag.

"Brent came over," he'd say before sending me a look that said, *Tell her and die.*

I never told her, but there were times I wish I had. Like the time not long after his accident, when his party had included faces I didn't normally see and had lasted longer than these events normally lasted. The OxyContin bottle had started to dwindle, and soon Nana would tell my mother that his pain was worsening instead of getting better. Soon the doctor would refill the prescription and we would watch that bottle, and half of the next one, disappear before cutting him off. My mother would find pills in his light fixture. But that night, before I knew to be afraid, I snuck down to the staircase and watched my brother standing on the coffee table, putting more weight on his bum ankle than he was supposed to, and I watched his friends, circled around him, cheering for something that I couldn't see, and I so desperately wished to have whatever it was that he had that made people want to gather around, that made them want to cheer.

When I had my first drink at that party in the middle of my sophomore year, I thought, *Maybe this is it, maybe I've unlocked the secret.* I spent the rest of that night talking and laughing and dancing, waiting for the cheers. I could see my dormmates looking at me with eyebrows raised, amazed that I had come out, surprised that I was fun. I was surprised too. I was drinking but I hadn't been turned into a pillar of salt.

"You came," Anne said, pulling me into a hug when she got to the party. She glanced down quickly at the cup in my hand but didn't comment.

"I've been here for a while now, actually," I said.

"I can see that."

She had a couple of her friends with her but before long we had lost them. More and more people filed in. The room got darker, danker, the music louder. I had been nursing my drink for an hour or more, and finally, Anne took it out of my hands and set it down.

"Dance with me," she said. And before I could say anything she was on a table, her hand outstretched. She pulled me up, pulled me closer. "Are you having a good time?" she whisper-shouted in my ear.

"This isn't really my thing," I said. "It's too loud; there are too many people."

She nodded. "Okay. Quiet, uncrowded, got it. I'm storing all of this in my 'How to Win Gifty Over' file."

"There's a file?"

"Oh yes. A whole spreadsheet. You'd love it."

I rolled my eyes at her as the song changed to something slower. Anne wrapped her arms around my waist and my breath quickened. On the floor beside us, a group of men dog-whistled.

"Do you like me better when I've been drinking?" I asked Anne, nervous to hear the answer.

"I like you best when you're waxing rhapsodic about Jesus," she said. "I like you best when you're feeling holy. You make me feel holy too."

I threw my head back and laughed.

A week later, the two of us borrowed one of Anne's friends' cars, so that we could drive to Harvard Forest in Petersham. The drive should have only taken an hour and fifteen minutes, but there was an accident on the highway and we'd crawled along in the car for two hours, just waiting for it to clear. When we finally passed by the wreckage, a hunk of metal that hardly even resembled a car anymore, I started having second thoughts about the mushrooms I'd agreed to do.

"The thing about it is, you just have to do it," Anne said. "Like who knows what euphoria actually means until they feel it? It's just a word."

I mumbled noncommittedly.

"It'll be beautiful," Anne said. "Honestly, it's like a religious experience. You'll like it, I promise."

Anne had taken a freshman seminar that spent two weekends exploring the forest, and so she knew it better than most. She guided me off trail until we found a clearing, encircled by trees that seemed to me to be improbably tall. Years later, when I got to California and set my eyes on a redwood for the first time, I thought back to the trees in Harvard Forest, their height a toddling infant compared with the giants that lived on the other side of the country.

But that day, I was impressed. Anne spread out a picnic blanket and lay on top of it for a moment, just staring up. She pulled a crumpled plastic bag from her back pocket and shook the mushrooms into her palm.

"Ready?" she asked, handing me mine. I nodded, popped a gram into my mouth, and waited for it to hit me.

I don't know how long it took. Time stretched out before me so slowly that I felt like an hour was passing between each of my blinks. It was like my entire body was made of thread wound tightly around a spool, and as I sat there, it unspooled, centimeter by centimeter, until I was a puddle on the blanket. Beside me, Anne looked at me with such beautiful benevolence. I took her hand. We were on our backs, looking at each other, looking at the trees, while the trees looked back at us. "Living-man trees," I said, and Anne nodded like she understood, and maybe she did.

When I came down, Anne was already there to meet me. "So?" she asked, watching me expectantly.

"I remembered this story my father used to tell my brother," I said. "I haven't thought about that in years."

"What's the story?" Anne asked, but I just shook my head. I didn't have anything else to give. I didn't want to tell her my stories. I couldn't imagine living the way she lived, free, like an exposed wire ready and willing to touch whatever it touched. I couldn't imagine being willing, and even after those few stolen moments of psychedelic transcendence, nonaddictive, harmless, and, yes, euphoric, I still couldn't imagine being free.

By the end of that semester Anne and I were in the thick of a friendship so intimate it felt romantic; it was romantic. We had kissed and a little more, but I couldn't define it and Anne didn't care to. As her graduation loomed closer, Anne spent most of her time in my room or at the library, hunched over her MCAT practice books, her hair, still awkwardly growing out its old perm, in a disheveled topknot.

Samurai Anne I called her when I wanted to annoy her, or when I just wanted her to look up from her work and pay attention to me.

"Tell me something I don't know about you," she said. She took her hair down and twisted strands of it around her finger.

"Something you don't know?"

"Yes. Please, save me from the boredom of this practice test. I might actually die if I have to do another one. Can you imagine? Death by MCAT as you strive to become a doctor."

"I don't have any good stories," I said.

"So tell me a bad story," she said.

I knew what she was doing. She was trying to get me to tell her about Nana, because while I knew all of Anne's stories, she knew only a handful of mine, and I had always been careful to select the happy ones. She would at times try to get me to talk about him, but never directly, only in these foxy ways that I could always see right through. She would tell me stories about her sister and then look at me expectantly as though I were meant to trade. A sister story for a brother story, but I wouldn't do it. Anne's stories about her sister, about the parties they'd gone to, the people they'd slept with, they didn't feel like an even trade for the stories I had about Nana. My Nana stories didn't have happy endings. His years of partying, of sleeping around, they didn't end with him holding down a job in finance in New York, as Anne's sister's did. And it wasn't fair. That was the thing that was at the heart of my reluctance and my resentment. Some people make it out of their stories unscathed, thriving. Some people don't.

I said, "I painted my brother's nails once while he was sleeping, and when he woke up, he tried to wash the nail polish off in the sink. He didn't know you needed nail polish remover, so he kept scrubbing his hands harder and harder and harder, and I was watching him, laughing. And then he turned around and punched me and I had a black eye for a week. Is that the kind of story you want to hear?"

Anne took her glasses off and put them in her hair. She closed the MCAT book. "I want to hear whatever story you want to tell," she said.

"You're not a doctor. You're not my fucking therapist, Anne," I said.

"Well, maybe you should see a therapist."

I started laughing, a mean laugh, a laugh I'd never heard before. I didn't know where it had come from, and when it escaped my lips, I thought, *What else is inside of me? How dark is this darkness, how deep does it go?*

"He died," I said. "He died. He died. He died. That's it. What more do you want to know?"

49

For a week in high school, I had nightmares that woke me up in a cold sweat. I couldn't remember what happened in them, but every time I woke from one, soaked in my own fear, I would grab a notebook and try to coax the dream out onto the page. When that didn't work, I started avoiding sleep.

I couldn't tell my mother what was happening because I knew that she would worry and hover and pray, and I didn't want any of those things, so instead I would say goodnight to her and head to my bedroom. I would listen for the sound of her shuffling feet to stop, and then, once I was certain that she'd fallen asleep, I would sneak back downstairs and watch television with the volume turned low.

It was hard to fight sleep, and the television, at that volume, did little to help. I'd doze off in the recliner and the nightmare would shoot me upright, awake with panic. I started praying feverishly. I would ask God to stop the dreams, and if he wouldn't stop the dreams, I would ask that he'd at least allow me to remember them. I couldn't stand not knowing what I was afraid of.

After a week of unanswered prayers, I did something I hadn't done in years. I talked to Nana.

"I miss you," I whispered into the dark of my living room, the sound of my mother's snoring the only sound that could be heard.

"It's been hard here," I told him.

I asked him all kinds of things, like "What should we watch on TV tonight?" or "What should I eat?" My only rule for myself was that I could never say his name, because I felt certain that saying his name would make what I was doing real, would make me crazy. I knew it was Nana that I was talking to, but also, I knew that it wasn't him at all, and to acknowledge that, to say his name and not have him appear before me, my fully embodied, fully alive brother, would ruin the spell. And so, I left his name out of it.

One night, my mother found me resting in that recliner. I looked up from the television and she was standing there. It was a wonder to me how sometimes she could move so quietly it was like she was incorporeal.

"What are you doing down here?" she asked.

Nana had been dead four years. It had been three and a half years since my summer in Ghana, a month of bad dreams. In that time, I had promised myself I wouldn't ever burden her, that all she would ever get from me was goodness and peace, calm and respect, but still, I said, "Sometimes I talk to Nana when I can't sleep."

She sat down on the couch, and I watched her face intently, worried that I'd said too much, that I'd broken our little code, my private promise.

"Oh, I talk to Nana too," she said. "All the time. All the time."

I could feel the tears start to well up in my eyes. I asked, "Does he talk back?"

My mother closed her eyes and leaned back into the couch, letting the cushions absorb her. "Yes, I think so."

The night before she was to take the MCAT, I finally told Anne that Nana had died of an overdose.

"Oh God, Gifty," she said. "Oh shit, I'm so sorry. All that shit I said, I'm so sorry."

We spent the rest of the night huddled together in my twin extra-long bed. As the evening grew quiet and dark, I listened to Anne cry. Her body-wracking sobs seemed overly dramatic to me that night, and I waited for her to quiet down and fall asleep. When she finally did, I lay there fuming, wondering, *What does she know? What does she know about pain, the dark and endless tunnel of it?* And I felt my body stiffen, and I felt my heart harden, and I never spoke to her again. She sent me text messages the next day, after she came out of the exam.

"Can I come over and see you? I'll bring a pint of ice cream and we can veg out."

"I'm still so sorry about last night. I shouldn't have made you talk about it before you were ready."

"Hello? Gifty? I get it if you're mad at me, but can we talk?"

The texts came steadily for two weeks, and then silence. Anne graduated, summer came, I went home to Alabama to wait tables so that I could save up some money before I had to go back to school. The next year I started over again, down a friend. I threw myself into my work. I interviewed at labs all across the country. I hadn't prayed in years, but sometimes, before bed, when I missed Anne, I talked to Nana.

50

My mother was awake and sitting up in bed the day after I prepped the limping mouse for optogenetics.

"Hey," I said. "Do you want to go out today? We can get breakfast somewhere. Would you like that?"

She smiled at me a little bit. "Just water," she said, "and a granola bar, if you have it."

"Sure, I have a bunch. Let me see." I rushed over to the kitchen pantry and pulled out a big selection. "Pick one," I said.

She took the peanut-butter-chocolate-chip one and nodded at me. She sipped the water.

"I can stay home with you today, if you'd like. I don't have to go in, really." This was a lie. If I didn't go in I would ruin a week or more of work and have to start all over, but I didn't want to miss my chance. I felt like my mother was my own personal groundhog. Would she see her shadow? Had winter ended?

"You go," she said. "Go."

She slipped back down under the covers, and I closed the

door, rushed out to my car, simultaneously saddened and relieved.

At the lab, there was cause for celebration. Han had gotten his first paper published in *Nature*. He was first author on that paper and I knew that his postdoc would be coming to an end before long. I was already starting to miss him. I bought a cupcake from the shop on campus and brought it to Han at his desk, lighting the single candle in the middle and singing an odd-patchwork version of "Happy Birthday" with the words changed to "Congratulations, Han."

"You didn't have to do this," he said, blowing out the candle. His ears were red again, and I was pleased to see that familiar hue, wistful that it had gone away in the first place. The cost of getting closer to Han had been fewer instances of this strange and delightful trait.

"Are you kidding? I might need you to hire me soon."

"Says the woman with two papers in *Nature* and one in *Cell*. I'm just trying to catch up."

I laughed him off and got to work. I had wanted to be in this lab because of its meticulousness, because of the fact that every result had to be tested and then tested again. But there was a point when confirmation became procrastination, and I knew that I was nearing that point; maybe I had passed it. Han was right. I was good at my work. Good at my work and hungry to be better, to be the best. I wanted my own lab at an elite university. I wanted a profile in *The New Yorker*, invitations to speak at conferences, and money. Though academia wasn't the right route for making loads of money, I still dreamed of it. I wanted to dive into a pile of it every morning like Scrooge from *DuckTales*, the TV show

Nana and I used to watch when we were young and money was scarce. And so, I tested and tested again.

Anne used to call me a control freak. She said it teasingly, lovingly, but I knew that she meant it and I knew it was true. I wanted things just so. I wanted to tell my stories the way I wanted to tell them, in my own time, imposing a kind of order that didn't actually exist in the moment. The last text Anne ever sent to me said, "I love you. You know that right?" and it took everything I had not to respond, but I gave it everything I had. I took pleasure in my restraint, a sick pleasure that felt like a hangover, like surviving an avalanche only to lose your limbs to frostbite. That restraint, that control at any cost, made me horrible at a lot of things, but it made me brilliant at my work.

I returned to my lever-press experiment. I was using both opsins and fluorescent proteins that allowed me to record brain activity so that I could see which specific prefrontal cortex neurons were active during the foot-shocks. The fluorescent proteins were something of a marvel. Whenever I shone blue light on the protein, it would glow green in the neuron that expressed it. The intensity of that green changed based on whether or not the neuron was firing or inactive. I never tired of this process, the holiness of it, of shining light and getting light in return. The first time I ever saw it happen, I wanted to call everyone in the building to gather round. In my lab, this sanctuary, something divine. *Light is sweet and it pleases the eye to see the sun.*

Now I've seen it so many times, my eyes have adjusted. I can't go back to that initial state of wonder, so I work, not to recapture it, but to break through it.

"Hey, Gifty, do you want to get dinner with me sometime? I mean, it was nice to share that Ensure and all, but maybe we can get a real meal this time."

Han had gloves and safety goggles on. He was watching me warmly, hopefully, his ears glowing faintly red.

I wished just then that I had a glow of my own, a bright green fluorescent shimmer under the skin of my wrist that flashed in warning. "I'm horrible at relationships," I said.

"Okay, but how are you at eating dinner?" he asked.

I laughed. "Better," I said, though that wasn't quite true either. I thought about the dinner parties with Raymond five years before, the excuses I'd made to get out of them, the fights we'd had.

"You spend more time with lab mice than you do with people. You know that's not healthy, right?" he said.

I didn't know how to explain to him that spending time in my lab was still a way for me to spend time with people. Not *with* them, exactly, but thinking about them, with them on the level of the mind, which felt as intimate to me as any dinner or night out having drinks had ever felt. It wasn't healthy, but, in the abstract, it was the pursuit of health, and didn't that count for something?

"You hide behind your work. You don't let people in. When am I going to meet your family?"

The cracks in our relationship had begun to show. One crack—that I was bad at dinners. Another—that I worked too much. The biggest—my family.

I had told Raymond that I was an only child. I liked to think of it as a prolonged omission rather than an outright lie. He had asked if I had any siblings and I had said no. I'd continued saying no for months, and then by the time we started having the "When am I going to meet your family?" fight I couldn't figure out a way to say yes again.

"My mom doesn't like to travel," I said.

"We'll go to her. Alabama's not that far away."

"My dad lives in Ghana," I said.

"I've never been to Ghana," he said. "Always wanted to visit the motherland. Let's do it."

It annoyed me when he called Africa "the motherland." It annoyed me that he felt close enough to it to do so. It was my motherland, my mother's land, but the only memories I had of it were unpleasant ones of the heat, the mosquitoes, the packed bodies in Kejetia that summer when all I could think about was the brother I had lost and the mother I was losing.

I didn't lose my mother that summer, but something inside of her left and never returned. I hadn't even told her that I was seeing someone. Our phone calls, infrequent and short, were so terse it was like we spoke in code. "How are you?" I'd ask. "Fine," she'd say, which meant, *I'm alive and isn't that enough?* Was it enough? Raymond came from a big family, three older sisters, a mother and father, too many aunts and uncles and cousins to count. He talked to at least one of them every day. I'd met them all and smiled shyly as they praised my beauty, my intellect, as they called me a keeper.

"Don't mess this up," Raymond's eldest sister had whispered, loudly enough for me to hear, as we left his parents' house one evening.

But Raymond wasn't an idiot. He knew there were things I wasn't saying, and in the beginning, he was content to wait until I was ready to say them, but then, close to six months in, I could feel my grace period winding down.

"I'll try harder, at the dinner parties. I'll try harder," I said one night after a fight had left us both ragged and teetering on the edge of our will to stay together.

He wiped a hand over his brow and closed his eyes. He couldn't look at me. "It's not about the fucking parties, Gifty," he said softly. "Do you even want to be with me? I mean really be with me?"

I nodded. I moved to stand behind him and wrapped my arms around him. "Maybe next summer we can go to Ghana together," I said.

He turned to face me, his eyes filled with suspicion, but also with hope. "Next summer?"

"Yeah," I said. "I'll ask my mom if she wants to come too."

If Raymond knew I was lying, he let me lie.

My mother has never been back to Ghana. It's been more than three decades since she left with baby Nana in tow. After my fight with Raymond, I'd called her and asked if she ever thought about going back. She had money saved; she could live a simpler life there, not have to work all the time.

"Go back for what?" she said. "My life is here." And I knew what she meant. Everything she had built for us and everything she had lost were held in this country. Most of her memories of Nana were in Alabama, in our house on the cul-de-sac at the top of that little hill. Even if there was pain in America, there had also been joy—the markings on the wall off our kitchen that showed how Nana shot up two feet in one year, the basketball hoop, rusted out from rain, disuse. There was me in California, my own separate branch on this family tree, growing slowly, but growing. In Ghana there was only my father, the Chin Chin Man, whom neither of us had spoken to in years.

I don't think this place was everything my mother

hoped for that day when she asked God where she should go to give her son the world. Though she didn't ford a river or hike across mountains, she still did what so many pioneers before her had done, traveled recklessly, curiously, into the unknown in the hopes of finding something just a little bit better. And like them she suffered and she persevered, perhaps in equal measure. Whenever I looked at her, a castaway on the island of my queen-sized bed, it was hard for me to look past the suffering. It was hard for me not to take inventory of all that she had lost—her home country, her husband, her son. The losses just kept piling up. It was hard for me to see her there, hear her ragged breath, and think of how she had persevered, but she had. Just lying there in my bed was a testament to her perseverance, to the fact that she survived, even when she wasn't sure she wanted to. I used to believe that God never gives us more than we can handle, but then my brother died and my mother and I were left with so much more; it crushed us.

It took me many years to realize that it's hard to live in this world. I don't mean the mechanics of living, because for most of us, our hearts will beat, our lungs will take in oxygen, without us doing anything at all to tell them to. For most of us, mechanically, physically, it's harder to die than it is to live. But still we try to die. We drive too fast down winding roads, we have sex with strangers without wearing protection, we drink, we use drugs. We try to squeeze a little more life out of our lives. It's natural to want to do that. But to be alive in the world, every day, as we are given more and more and more, as the nature of "what we can handle" changes and our methods for how we handle it change, too, that's something of a miracle.

51

Katherine had been asking if she could come over.

"You don't have to introduce me or anything. I could just come have a cup of coffee with you and then go. What do you think?"

Whenever she asked, I demurred. I recognized this old pattern in myself, my need to DIY my mother's mental health, as though all it would take for her to get better was me with a glue gun, me with a Ghanaian cookbook and a tall glass of water, me with a slice of shortcake. It hadn't worked then and it wasn't working now. At some point I had to ask for, to accept, help.

I cleaned the house before Katherine came over. It wasn't dirty, but old habits die hard. She came carrying a bouquet of flowers, and a plate of chocolate-chip cookies. I hugged her, invited her to sit at my little dining room table, and put a pot of coffee on.

"I can't believe I haven't been here before," Katherine said, looking around. I had been living there for nearly four years, but you couldn't tell by the look of things. I lived my life like a woman who was accustomed to having to leave at a moment's notice. Raymond had called my apartment "The Witness Protection Pad." No pictures of family, no pictures at all. We'd always gone to his place.

"I don't really have people over very often," I said. I hunted down a couple of mugs and filled them. I sat across from Katherine, cupping my mug, warming my hands.

She was watching me. Waiting for me to talk, waiting for me to take the lead somehow. I wanted to remind her that none of this had been my idea.

"She's in there," I whispered, pointing to my bedroom.

"Okay, we won't bother her," Katherine said. "How are you doing?"

I wanted to cry but I didn't. I'd inherited that skill from my mother. I had become my mother in so many ways that it was hard to think of myself as a person distinct from her, hard to see my shut bedroom door and not imagine that, one day, it would be me on the other side. Me, in bed, except alone, without a child to care for me. Puberty had been such a shock. Before it I'd looked like no one, which is to say I'd looked like myself, but after it, I'd started to look like my mother, my body growing to fill the mold her shape had left. I wanted to cry, but I couldn't, wouldn't cry. Like my mother, I had a locked box where I kept all my tears. My mother had only opened hers the day that Nana died and she had locked it again soon thereafter. A mouse fight had opened mine, but I was trying to close it back up again.

I nodded at Katherine. "Doing okay," I said, and then, to change the subject, "Did I ever tell you that I used to keep a journal when I was young? I've been reading it over since my mother got here and I've been writing again too."

"What kind of things are you writing?"

"Observations mostly. Questions. The story of how we

got here. It's embarrassing, but I used to address my journal to God. I grew up evangelical." I made a kind of jazz-hands motion to accompany the word "evangelical." When I realized what I was doing, I dropped my hands to my lap as though they were on fire, in need of stubbing out.

"I didn't know that."

"Oh yeah. It's embarrassing. I spoke in tongues. The whole thing."

"Why is it embarrassing?" Katherine asked.

I made a kind of sweeping gesture with my hands, as if to say, *Look at all of this,* by which I meant, *Look at my world. Look at the order and the emptiness of this apartment. Look at my work. Isn't it all embarrassing?*

Katherine didn't understand the gesture, or, if she did, she didn't accept it. "I think it's beautiful and important to believe in something, anything at all. I really do."

She said the last part defensively because I was rolling my eyes. I'd always been annoyed by any whiff of the woo-woo, faux spirituality of those who equated believing in God with believing in, say, a strange presence in a room. In college, I'd once left a spoken-word show Anne had dragged me to because the poet kept referring to God as "she," and that need to be provocative and all-encompassing felt too trite, too easy. It also went counter to the very concerns of an orthodoxy and a faith that ask that you submit, that you accept, that you believe, not in a nebulous spirit, not in the kumbaya spirit of the Earth, but in the specific. In God as he was written, and as he was. "Anything at all" didn't mean anything at all. Since I could no longer believe in the specific God, the one whose presence I had felt so keenly when I was a child, then I could never simply "believe in something." I didn't know how to articulate this to Katherine, so I just sat there, watching my bedroom door.

"Do you still write to God?" Katherine asked.

I looked at her, wondering if she was setting some kind of trap. I remembered my jazz hands. I was mocked so much for my religion when I was in college that I had taken to mocking myself first. But Katherine's voice was absent of malice; her eyes were earnest.

"I don't write 'Dear God' anymore, but still, maybe, yes."

When it came to God, I could not give a straight answer. I had not been able to give a straight answer since the day Nana died. God failed me then, so utterly and completely that it had shaken my capacity to believe in him. And yet. How to explain every quiver? How to explain that once sure-footed knowledge of his presence in my heart?

The day Mrs. Pasternack had said, "I think we're made out of stardust, and God made the stars," I'd laughed aloud. I was sitting in the back of the classroom, doodling in my spiral notepad because I was already ahead of the rest of the class. I was taking math courses at the university for college credit, and I was dreaming, dreaming, about getting as far away from home as I possibly could.

"Do you have something you'd like to share with the class, Gifty?" Mrs. Pasternack asked.

I straightened up in my seat. I was unaccustomed to reprimands, to trouble. I'd never gotten detention, and I believed, rightly so it seemed, that my reputation as a bright and good kid would protect me.

"That just seems a bit convenient to me," I said.

"Convenient?"

"Yes."

She gave me a funny look and moved on. I slumped back down in my seat and resumed my doodling, annoyed because I'd wanted a fight. I attended a public school that refused to teach evolution, in a town where many didn't believe in it, and Mrs. Pasternack's words, it had seemed to me then, were a cop-out, a way of saying without saying.

What to make of the time before humans? What to make of the five previous extinctions, including the ones that had wiped out woolly mammoths and dinosaurs? What to make of dinosaurs and of the fact that we share a quarter of our DNA with trees? When did God make the stars and how and why? These were questions that I knew I would never find the answers to in Huntsville, but the truth is, they were questions that I would never find answers to anywhere, not answers that would satisfy me.

"It's good to see you," Katherine said. She drained the rest of her coffee, her third pour since arriving, and got up to go.

I walked her to the door, and the two of us stood in the frame.

Katherine took my hand. "You should keep writing. To God, to whomever. If it makes you feel better, you should keep doing it. There's no reason not to."

I nodded and said thank you. I waved at her as she got in her car and drove off.

52

Never again had come back again. After Katherine left I peeked in on my mother. No change. A few days before, I'd had a meeting with my advisor to discuss the possibility of graduating at the end of the quarter rather than waiting another year or more.

"What are your goals? What do you want?" he asked. I looked at him and thought, *How much time do you have? I want money and a house with a pool and a partner who loves me and my own lab filled with only the most brilliant and strong women. I want a dog and a Nobel Prize and to find a cure to addiction and depression and everything else that ails us. I want everything and I want to want less.*

"I'm not sure," I said.

"I'll tell you what, just finish the paper, submit it, and then reassess. There's no hurry. If you start the postdoc now, if you start it next year, or the next, it really doesn't make a ton of difference."

My lab was frigid. I shivered, grabbed my coat from the back of my chair, and put it on. I rolled up my sleeves and started to clear off my workstation, something I should have done the last time I was there. The last time I was there,

I had finally finished my experiment, answered the question. I had tested the results enough times to be as certain as was possible that we could get an animal, even that limping mouse, to restrain itself from seeking reward by altering its brain activity. When I observed the limping mouse for the final time, fitted as he was with the fiber-optic implant and patch cord, everything had looked the same. There was the lever, the little metal tube, the manna of Ensure. There was that mouse, that limp. I delivered the light and like that, like that, he stopped pressing the lever.

I left my workstation, went to my office, and sat down to write my paper, thinking about all of my mice. I should have been ecstatic to be finished, to be writing, with the hope of a new publication and graduation looming before me, but instead I felt bereft.

The demands of scientific writing are different from the demands of writing in the humanities, different from writing in my journal at night. My papers were dry and direct. They captured the facts of my experiments, but said nothing of what it had felt like to hold a mouse in my hands and feel its entire body thump against my palms as it breathed, as its heart beat. I wanted to say that too. I wanted to say, here it is, the breath of life in it. I wanted to tell someone about the huge wave of relief I felt every time I watched an addicted mouse refuse the lever. That gesture, that refusal, that was the point of the work, the triumph of it, but there was no way to say any of that. Instead, I wrote out the step-by-step process, the order. The reliability, the stability of the work, the impulse to keep plugging, keep trying until I figured a way through, that was the skin of it for me, but the heart of it was that wave of relief, that limping mouse's tiny, alive body, living still, and still.

Pastor John used to say, "Stretch out your hand," before he asked the congregation to pray for a fellow congregant. If you were close enough to the person who needed prayer you would literally touch them, lay your hands on them. You would touch whatever part of their body was accessible to you, a forehead, a shoulder, a back, and that touch, that precious touch, was both the prayer and its conduit. If you were not close enough to reach, if your arm was simply outstretched, brushing air, it was still possible to feel that thing I have often heard called "energy," that thing I used to call the Holy Spirit, moving through the room, through your very fingers, toward the body of the person in need. The night I was saved, I was touched like this. Pastor John's hand was on my forehead, the hands of the saints on my body, the hands of the congregants outstretched. Salvation, redemption, it was as intentional as skin touching skin, as holy as that. And I've never forgotten it.

Being saved, I was taught when I was a child, was a way of saying, Sinner that I am, sinner that I will ever be, I relinquish control of my life to He who knows more than I, He who knows everything. It is not a magical moment of becoming sinless, blameless, but rather it's a way of saying, Walk with me.

When I watched the limping mouse refuse the lever, I was reminded yet again of what it means to be reborn, made new, saved, which is just another way of saying, of needing those outstretched hands of your fellows and the grace of God. That saving grace, amazing grace, is a hand and a touch, a fiber-optic implant and a lever and a refusal, and how sweet, how sweet it is.

53

I finally started writing my paper in earnest. I spent twelve-hour stretches moving from my lab to my office to the coffee shop across the street that served mediocre sandwiches and salads. When I got home at night, I would collapse on the couch, fully dressed, and fall asleep counting the sheep of all the things I needed to get done the next day. The next day, I would do it all over again.

My writing rhythm, when I was in it, involved blaring a mix that Raymond had given me for our six-month anniversary. It was perhaps an act of masochism to play the soundtrack to the final days of a relationship that hadn't lasted very long, but the songs, bluesy and dramatic, made me feel like my work was in conversation with the artists who sang them. I hummed along to the music, typing out my notes or reading the responses from my team, and feeling, for the first time since my mother had come to stay with me, like I was doing something right. I wrote and hummed and avoided anyone who reminded me of the world outside my office. Namely Katherine. She had been trying to get me to go to lunch with her again since the day she'd come over, and I had finally run out of excuses.

We met for sushi on the Friday of my first good week. I ordered a caterpillar roll, and when it arrived I ate its head first, wary of the way it had been staring at me.

"Looks like you've been keeping busy. That's great," Katherine said.

"Yeah, I'm really happy with all the progress I've been making." I watched her break her chopsticks apart and rub them together, tiny splinters of wood shredding off of them.

"And your mother?" Katherine asked.

I shrugged. I tackled the caterpillar's torso and spent the next few minutes trying to steer the conversation toward more solid ground: my work, how important it was, how well I was doing.

Katherine praised me, though not as effusively or as convincingly as I'd hoped. "Are you still writing in your journal as well?" she asked

"Yes," I said. After Nana died, I'd hidden every journal of mine under my mattress and did not take them back out again until the summer before I left for college. That summer, I fished them out, the springs of the mattress creaking and groaning as I lifted it up. I could have taken those groans as a warning, but I didn't. Instead, I started reading my way through every entry I'd ever written, reading my way through what was essentially my entire conscious lifetime. I was so embarrassed by the early entries that I read them all, cringing and squinting my eyes in an attempt to hide from my former self. By the time I got to the years of Nana's addiction, I was undone. I couldn't proceed. I decided then and there that I would build a new Gifty from scratch. She would be the person I took along with me to Cambridge—confident, poised, smart. She would be strong and unafraid. I opened up to a blank page and wrote a new entry that began with these words: *I will figure out a way to be myself, whatever that means, and I won't talk about Nana or my mom all the time. It's too depressing.*

I went off to school and kept writing in my journal, and by the time I got to graduate school it was a regular habit, as vital and unconscious to me as breathing.

I knew that Raymond had been reading my journal for weeks before the truth came out. While I wasn't as clean as my mother, I had inherited her uncanny ability to sense when an item was just a little out of place. The day I found my journal on the left side of my nightstand's drawer instead of the right, I thought, *So, here we are.*

"You want to explain this, Gifty?" Raymond asked. He was waving my journal around in the air.

"Explain what?" I said, and I could hear the schoolgirl in my voice, all the other Giftys whom I had promised to leave behind, who had instead come with me.

Raymond read, " 'I've been letting Raymond think that I'm planning our trip to Ghana, but really, I haven't done a thing. I don't know how to tell him.' "

"Well, now I don't have to tell you," I said, and I watched as his eyes narrowed. I'd written that entry the day I figured out that he'd been reading my journal. It took him two weeks to get to it.

"Why would you do this?" That voice of his, the voice I loved, the voice of a preacher without a pulpit, so low I felt like it came from inside of me, now boomed with rage.

I started laughing, the same mean and terrible laugh that made me afraid of myself. It reminded me of the sound one might make at the very bottom of a cave, piercing, desperate.

The laugh scared Raymond too. He shivered like the baby bird. He shot me a hurt look, and I recognized in that look my window, my opportunity to fix what was broken between us and climb back into his good graces.

I could have groveled, cried, distracted him. Instead I laughed harder. "You really read my journal? What are we, in high school? Did you think I was cheating on you?"

"I don't know what to think. Why don't you tell me what to think? Better yet, tell me what *you're* thinking because I sure as shit can't read your mind. All of this, all of this . . . it's like I don't know anything real about you."

What was I thinking? I was thinking that I had done it again, ruined everything. I was thinking that I could never shake my ghosts, never, never. There they were in every word I wrote, in every lab, in every relationship.

"You're fucked up, you know that?" Raymond said, and I didn't answer. "You're fucking crazy." He threw my journal across the room, and I watched it fly open. I watched Raymond grab his keys and his wallet, his jacket, a heavy, unnecessary thing in that Peninsula sun. He collected every trace of himself and then he left.

"I really appreciate what you're doing, Katherine, but everything's fine. I'm fine and my mom is too."

Katherine was a fast eater. She had cleaned her plate long before I reached the last segments of my roll, and we had spent the last few minutes in silence as I chewed slowly, deliberately.

"Gifty, there's no game here. There's no trick. I'm not

trying to treat you or psychoanalyze you or get you to talk about God or your family or whatever. I'm just here strictly as a friend. One friend taking another friend to lunch. That's it."

I nodded. Under the table, I pinched the skin between my thumb and forefinger. What would it look like, to believe her? What would it take?

54

I left lunch and decided to give myself the rest of the day off. My mother hadn't left the house or the bed since the day she came to visit me in the lab, but still, it made me hopeful that she was making progress. Maybe I could convince her to take a trip to Half Moon Bay with me.

I drove back to my apartment with the radio off and the windows down. My date with Han was coming up that weekend and I was nervous about it, playing over and over again in my head the possible ways it could go. If things went poorly, it might be just the thing I needed to convince me to graduate, leave the lab, if only to avoid seeing him every day. If things went well, well, who knew?

I turned into my complex. Someone had parked in my designated spot, and so I parked in someone else's, becoming a part of the problem.

"Ma," I called as I entered my apartment. "How would you like to see the Pacific Ocean?" I set my bag down in the entryway. I took my shoes off. I didn't expect a response, so I wasn't surprised to be greeted by silence. I poked my head into the bedroom, and she wasn't there.

When I was a child, I had this sense of confidence, this assuredness that the things that I felt were real and important, that the world made sense according to divine logic. I loved God, my brother, and my mother, in that order. When I lost my brother, poof went the other two. God was gone in an instant, but my mother became a mirage, an image formed by refracted light. I moved toward her and toward her, but she never moved toward me. She was never there. The day I came home from school and couldn't find her felt like the thirty-ninth day in the desert, the thirty-ninth day without water. I didn't think I'd be able to survive another.

"Never again," my mother said, but I didn't believe her. Without meaning to or planning to, I'd spent seventeen years waiting for the fortieth day. Here it was.

"Ma?" I yelled. It was a small apartment. From the middle of the living room you could see almost everything there was to see. You could see she wasn't there. I raced to the bathroom, the only room with a closed door, but she wasn't there either.

"Ma?" I ran outside, down the stairwell, across the pristine lawns, the parking lot with all its mis-parked cars, the sidewalks sparkling with silicon carbide. "Ma!"

I stopped short of a fire hydrant and scanned the complex. I didn't even know where to begin looking. I pulled out my phone and called Katherine.

She must have known something was up, because she didn't even say hello, just "Gifty, are you okay?"

"No, I'm not okay," I said, and I wondered when the last time I'd said that was. Had I ever said it, even to God? "I came home and my mom is missing. Can you help me?"

"Hold tight," she said. "I'll be right there."

When she pulled up, I was sitting on the hydrant with

my head between my knees, staring at the striking red, the color somehow a reflection of what I was feeling.

Katherine rested her hand on my shoulder, squeezing it a little, and I got up. "She couldn't have gotten very far on foot," she said.

As Katherine drove us around, first in my little apartment complex, and then out, off onto the main road that led to Safeway, to campus, I pictured every bridge, every body of water.

"Does she know anybody here?" Katherine asked. "Anyone she may have called?"

I shook my head. She didn't have a church here; she didn't have a congregation to hold her up. It was just me. "Maybe we should call the police," I said. "She wouldn't want that, but I don't know what else to do. Do you?"

And then, under a tree, off the side of the road, there she was. She was swimming in her pajamas, no bra, her hair a nest. She used to scold me if I left the house without earrings on, now this.

I didn't even wait for Katherine to pull over all the way. I just jumped out.

"Where did you go?" I shouted, running to her and folding her in my arms. She was as stiff as a board. "Where were you?" I took her shoulders in my hands and shook her forcefully, trying to make her look at me, but she wouldn't.

Katherine drove us back to my apartment. She said a few words to my mother, but other than that the ride was silent. When we got to my place, she asked my mother to wait outside the car. She took my hand in hers. "I can stay if you want," she said, but I shook my head.

She paused, leaned in closer to me, and said, "Gifty, I'll be back first thing in the morning, and I will help you figure this all out, okay? I promise. You call me anytime today. Really, anytime."

"Thanks," I said. I got out of the car and led my mother back to my apartment.

Inside, she looked small and bewildered, innocent. I had been so frightened and angry that I'd forgotten to feel sorry for her, but, now, I pitied her. I pulled her into the bathroom and started running a bath. I pulled her shirt off, checking her wrists. I undid the drawstring on her pajama bottoms, and they slipped down themselves, a silk puddle on the bathroom floor.

"Did you take anything?" I asked, ready to pry her mouth open, but mercifully, she shook her head, quick as a blink. When the bathtub was full, I had her step in. I poured water over her head and watched her eyes close then open, in shock, in pleasure.

"Mama, I beg you," I said in Twi, but I didn't know enough Twi to finish the sentence. I wasn't sure how I would have finished it, anyway: I beg you to stop. I beg you to wake up. I beg you to live.

I washed and combed her hair. I soaped down her body, moving the sponge along every fold of skin. When I got to her hands, she grabbed one of mine. She pulled it to her heart and held it there. *"Ebeyeyie,"* she said. It will be all right. She used to say it to Nana when she washed him. It was true then, until it wasn't.

"Look at me," she said, taking my chin in her hands, jerking my head toward her. "Don't be afraid. God is with me; do you hear me? God is with me wherever I go."

.   .   .

I finally got her into bed. I sat outside her door for an hour, listening to the sound of her snoring. I knew I wouldn't sleep. I knew I should stay there, keep vigil, but then I started to feel like there wasn't enough air in my apartment for the two of us, so I sneaked out, something I'd never done when I was a teen in my mother's house. I got on the 101 and headed north toward San Francisco, driving with the windows down, gulping the air, the wind whipping my face and leaving my lips chapped. I kept licking them.

"That makes it worse," my mother always said.

She was right, but that had never stopped me.

I didn't know where I was going, only that I didn't want to be around mice or humans. I didn't really even want to be around myself, and if I could have figured out a way around that, discovered the switch that could turn my own thoughts and feelings and harsh admonishments off, I would have chosen that instead.

Whether you turn to the right or to the left, your ears will hear a voice behind you, saying, "This is the way; walk in it."

I was waiting for that voice, waiting for the way, driving up and down the narrow streets of a city I had never much liked. I could almost hear my car, huffing through its exhaustion as it climbed those ample hills, and exhaling, relieved, as it flew down them. I found myself in neighborhoods with houses like miniature castles, the lawns vast and vibrant, shimmering green, and I found myself in alleyways where strung-out men and women sat on stoops and convulsed on sidewalks, and I felt saddened by it all.

When we were children, unaccompanied and unsupervised, Nana and I used to sneak into the gated pool a few blocks away from our house at night. Our swimsuits were too tight, several years old. They hadn't kept up with our growth. Nana and I were all too happy to take our dips under the cover of darkness. For years we begged our parents to let us join the pool, but for years they had made up excuses for why we couldn't. Nana figured out that he was tall enough, his arms long enough, to reach up and over the gate, and unlatch it for me. As our mother worked the night shift, we waded in that pool.

"Do you think God knows we're here?" I asked. Neither of us really knew how to swim, and while we were trespassers, we weren't stupid. We knew our mother would kill us if we died. We stayed in the shallows.

"Of course God knows we're here. He knows everything. He knows where every person is at every second of every day."

"So God would probably be mad at us for sneaking into the pool, right? We're sinning."

I already knew the answer to this and Nana knew that I knew. At that time, the two of us had never missed a Sunday at church. Even when I was contagious with pink eye, my mother had fitted me with a pair of sunglasses and marched me into the sanctuary to receive my healing. Nana didn't answer me at first. I assumed he was ignoring me and I was accustomed to being ignored, at school, where I asked too many questions, and at home, where I did the same thing.

"It's not so bad," Nana finally said.

"What?"

"I mean, this is a nice sin, isn't it?"

The moon in gibbous looked off-kilter to me. I was getting cold and tired. "Yeah, it's a nice sin."

I drove past coffee shops and secondhand clothing stores. I saw kids playing in playgrounds, their mothers or nannies watching over them. I drove until it got dark, and then I pulled into the back parking lot of an ice cream parlor and turned the car off.

"My mom's going to get better," I said to the windshield or to the wind or to God, I don't know. "I'm going to finish my paper and graduate and years from now all of this work will have been worth something, will matter to someone out there, and my mother is going to be alive to see all of that, right?"

The lot was empty and dark except for a couple of lazy streetlamps shining their dim light. I turned the car back on and sat there for a minute longer, fantasizing about what my apartment would look like when I returned to it. My mother sitting upright on the couch, a pot of jollof rice warming on the stove.

"Please, please," I said, and I waited a moment longer for some kind of response, some sign, some bit of wonder, something, before pulling out of that spot and starting the long drive home.

From our house in New Jersey, Han and I can hear the church bells ring every Sunday.

"Your people are summoning you," Han sometimes jokes. I roll my eyes at him, but really, I don't mind the jokes, I don't mind the bells.

Once every few months or whenever the mood strikes, I take the long way home from the lab I run at Princeton, just so that I can step into that church. I don't know the first thing about Episcopalianism, but no one seems to mind when they find me sitting in the back pew, staring ahead at the figure of Christ on the cross. Han has been in here with me a couple of times, but he fidgets. He steals glances from Christ to me, in a way that lets me know he's counting down the seconds until I'm ready to go. I've told him many times that he doesn't have to come here, but he wants to. He knows everything there is to know about me, my family, my past. He was with me when my mother finally passed away, in my childhood home, in her own bed, her own caretaker beside her to help us all through to the end. Han understands me, all of my work, my obsessions, as intimately as if they were his own, but he doesn't understand this. He has never heard the knock, and so he'll never know what it means to miss that sound, to listen for it.

Usually, I'm the only one there, except for Bob, the maintenance man who sits in the office, waiting either for the evening service to get started or just to close up.

"Gifty, how are the experiments going?" he always asks with a little wink. He seems to be one of those people who hears "scientist" and thinks "sci-fi," and his winks are to assure me that he won't tell anyone that I've been trying to figure out how to clone an alien. He and Han get along.

I wish I were trying to figure out how to clone an alien, but my work pursuits are much more modest: neurons and proteins and mammals. I'm no longer interested in other worlds or spiritual planes. I've seen enough in a mouse to understand transcendence, holiness, redemption. In people, I've seen even more.

From the back pew, Christ's face is the portrait of ecstasy. I stare at it, and it changes, goes from angry to pained to joyful. Some days, I sit there for hours, some days mere minutes, but I never bow my head. I never pray, never wait to hear God's voice, I just look. I sit in blessed silence, and I remember. I try to make order, make sense, make meaning of the jumble of it all. Always, I light two candles before I go.

Acknowledgments

This novel is, in many ways, a conversation between my work and interests and those of my brilliant friend Christina Kim, a postdoc in the Ting Lab at Stanford University. Gifty's research and thesis project are modeled after Tina's doctoral work in the Deisseroth Lab at Stanford, particularly that which formed the basis of her coauthored paper, "Molecular and Circuit-Dynamical Identification of Top-Down Neural Mechanisms for Restraint of Reward Seeking," published in *Cell* in 2017. The experience of writing this book, which included everything from tours of Tina's lab to rich discussions about questions big and small, is one that I will forever cherish. Thank you, Tina, for the work that you do and for the gift of your friendship.

Thank you to the Ucross Foundation, the American Academy in Berlin, and the University of Würzburg for fellowships that allowed me to devote myself to writing this novel.

Thank you to *Guernica* magazine for giving my short story "Inscape" a home. This novel picks up many of the characters and questions from that short story, reshaping and repurposing them to ask new questions.

Thank you, Eric Simonoff, Tracy Fisher, and everyone at WME for continued faith in my work and career. I'm in the best hands.

Thank you, Jordan Pavlin, editor extraordinaire. What a joy it is to work with you, to know you. Thank you also to everyone at Knopf for making a home for my work. I'm also grateful to Mary Mount at Viking UK, Tiffany Gassouk at Calmann-Lévy, and all of the wonderful editors and publishing houses that have championed my work abroad.

Thank you to Josefine Kals for being the world's best publicist. I'm lucky to have you in my corner.

Thank you to my family and Matt's family and to all of the friends who have held me up these last few years.

Thank you to Christina Gonzalez Ho, trusted reader and beloved friend. I'm so grateful for your time and your care.

Thank you to Clare Jones for your notes on this novel and for our treasured correspondence in general.

Finally, a special thank you to Matt, for reading my work, for all the years of love and faith and bottomless kindness. Life with you has been rich and blessed.